THE SINNER

KELSEY CLAYTON

The Sinner
Kelsey Clayton

Copyright © 2020 by Kelsey Clayton

All rights reserved.

Editing by Kiezha Ferrell at Librum Artis

For my best friend, Ashley.
Thank you for keeping me out of trouble,
and for getting into trouble with me,
and for listening to me even when I
don't make any sense.
You're my better half.
I love you.

P.S - The kitchen floor would have been so lonely without you.

You can take this heart.
   Heal it or break it all apart.
   No, this isn't fair.
   Love me or leave me here.

— Little Mix

1

SAVANNAH

I RUN ACROSS THE BEACH, FEELING THE WIND BLOW THROUGH MY hair. My toes sink into the sand as I scurry away. Just when I think the coast is clear, I'm swept up into my father's arms. An involuntary squeal leaves my mouth, followed by a fit of giggles as he spins us around and tickles my sides. He places me back down and tucks a stray piece of hair behind my ear.

"I love you, my sweet Savi."

The blaring noise of my alarm rips me from my dream and back into reality. My stomach drops as thoughts of the freshly relived memory play in my mind. Of course it wasn't real, not anymore at least. Those days are so far in the past that sometimes I wonder if they actually happened.

I roll out of bed, still feeling half comatose. My feet pad across the floor as I leave my bedroom in search of some water. The small, beaten-down house is in its normal state of post-tornado aftermath. Empty liquor bottles lie across every possible surface, making it hard to get around. If anyone saw this, they'd think a raging party took place last night. *I wish that were the case.*

1

Careful not to make too much noise, I grab some of the glass containers and deposit them into the trash. It doesn't do much, but it's better than nothing. Taking a bottle of water from the fridge, I retreat to the bathroom to get ready for school.

As I climb into the shower and the cold water chills my body, the excitement of senior year adds a little sparkle to my normally grim life. Just one more year and I can get out of this godforsaken place. The moment I graduate is the moment I ditch this lie of a life I'm living.

Once I'm clean, I wrap a towel around my body and quietly slip back into my bedroom. The perfectly dry-cleaned uniforms hang in my closet. I smile as I pull one out and begin to put it on. The gray skirt is disgustingly plain, but provides a sense of safety and security. The maroon shirt isn't much different, except for the school crest in the top corner. It may not be what I would choose to wear on my own, but it makes everything easier in the wardrobe department of my life.

I brush and blow dry my long blonde hair before applying a thin coat of makeup. It's enough to say, "I'm completely put together" yet not enough to look like I just came from a strip club. After a quick once-over in the mirror, I smile at my own appearance and grab my bag.

The house is still just as lifeless—and just as destroyed —as it was when I woke. I lightly tiptoe down the hallway and into the dark bedroom. Blackout curtains covering the windows make it hard to see anything, but I can just make out a body slumped across the bed. As I step further inside, I cover my nose, gagging immediately from the smell.

"Dad?" I whisper-shout, but get nothing in return. "Dad?"

A low grumble comes from the back of his throat. *Well, at the very least, he's alive.* I come closer and see that he's fully dressed and his shirt has what must be dried vomit all over it.

"Dad, come on. Wake up. You're a mess, and we need to get this shirt off you."

I try to pull him up, but he yanks his arm from my grasp. "No."

Usually I'd take a deep breath before trying again, but if I do that now, the contents of my stomach will join his. "You can go back to sleep as soon as I'm done."

Grabbing the hem of the shirt, I start to roll it upwards but I'm pushed away. "Fucking stop, you little bitch."

His words should feel like a punch to the gut, or at the very least cause me to feel sadness, but I've been living this nightmare for so long. There isn't anything he can say that I *haven't* heard. Instead of fighting him further, I pick my bag up off the floor and head out the door. If he wants to stay covered in his own puke, that's his problem.

I'M HALFWAY THROUGH MY walk to school when a familiar SUV pulls up next to me. I pull out one of my earbuds and turn to face the driver. Brady, the closest thing I have to a real friend in this place, gives me a knowing look as he reaches over and opens the door.

"How many times have I told you I would drive you in the mornings?"

"Technically, none. New school year, new rules." I quip as I get in the passenger side.

"Savannah," he deadpans, clearly unamused with my antics. "I'm serious. I don't want you walking through that part of town. Especially not alone."

I scoff. "I'm a big girl, B. I think I can handle a homeless guy or seven."

"I'm sure you can, Rocky, but let's not test that theory."

3

We get to the school in less than half the time it would've taken me to walk. The sidewalks are filled with kids on both sides of the street. On the left is North Haven High, the public school I'd have to attend if it wasn't for Mrs. Laurence —Brady's mom and my incredible dance teacher—paying a hefty sum each year. And on the right is my prestigious private school, Haven Grace Prep. The two institutions across from each other couldn't be more different, and the rivalry between them has run strong for decades. If we aren't battling it out on the football field, we're throwing punches at parties. It's a constant war that shows no signs of ending any time soon.

"Thanks for the ride." I say as I reach over and give Brady a hug before getting out of the car. "I'll see you after?"

He nods. "I'll be here."

As the car pulls away, I take a deep breath and start walking up the steps toward the large doors. Students hanging around outside all say their hellos to me, hoping I'll stop to talk to them, but none are lucky enough to get more than a fake grin sent their way. I go inside and turn right down the hallway, seeing my *posse,* as people like to call them, already surrounding my locker. The urge to roll my eyes is strong, but I guess it comes with the territory of being deemed the most popular girl in school.

The second I'm close enough, I hear Becca ranting about something I can only assume is a rich bitch problem. All eyes turn to me when I reach my locker. My eyebrows raise in a silent command, causing Kinsley and Paige to move out of my way.

"Hey, Savannah," Emma greets.

I smile warmly at her. "Hey, Ems."

Out of the four of them, Emma is the most genuine— though the competition isn't very fierce in that category. I'm not stupid enough to believe their loyalty is any thicker than water. It doesn't take a rocket scientist to know that they would throw me to the wolves if it meant they'd get a little more attention. Hell, I'm pretty sure the only reason they worship the ground I walk on is because they think I'm dating Brady. To them, he's an older college guy with a nice car. To me, he's my dance teacher's very hot, yet *very gay*, son. Still, what they don't know won't hurt them.

"So, what's the issue today, Bec?" I question as I shove my bag into my locker and slip my cellphone into my back pocket.

She runs her fingers through her hair. "I asked for a hot stone massage at the spa, and they gave me a shiatsu."

Yep. I was right—rich bitch problem.

"Ugh, I hate when that happens." The lie comes out of my mouth with a practiced ease and Becca gleams with validation.

It's almost amusing how highly they think of me. If they had any idea how much money I have, or lack thereof, there's no doubt they would treat me like gum under their shoes. Thankfully, with a last name like Montgomery, no one even thinks to question it. There are only a few people who know where I live. One is Brady, and the others are Knox Vaughn and his brigade of goons. Knox lives a couple houses down from me, so it was only a matter of time before they found out. It took a little convincing to get them to keep their mouths shut, but once Brady promised to get them alcohol whenever they want it, they agreed.

The hallway gets louder as the guys from the football team make their way through the school. Carter Trayland is sporting a smile as he winks at a girl passing by. Poor thing almost faints on the spot, yet he'll never give her a second glance. She's too insignificant for him to actually notice her.

Next to Carter is Jace London, the best kicker that Haven Grace has ever seen. The two of them look like Hollister models, with their blonde hair and perfectly muscular physique. Flanking their sides are Hayden Waters and Wyatt

Averson, being every bit as gorgeous but a little less intimidating. Wyatt may be your typical jock, but he's secretly a computer genius. I don't think there's a single thing he can't do in the cyber world. And Hayden, despite being in constant company of the other douchebags, is a total sweetheart. If his crush on Emma wasn't devastatingly obvious, he might even be someone I'd consider dating.

"Well, well, well," Carter says as his eyes land on me. "Hey, gorgeous. Long time no see."

I roll my eyes as I lean against my locker. "I saw you two weeks ago at Jace's end of summer party. You got drunk and used the pool as your own personal urinal."

His grin widens. "Oh, yeah. Good times."

The bell rings and everyone scatters to get to class, except us. We casually make our way to homeroom, knowing there isn't a chance in hell we're getting in trouble. The last time a teacher tried to punish us for something, Carter's father made such a big deal of it she was fired the next day. I guess that's what happens when you're the captain of the football team and your dad is the district attorney.

As we enter the room, everyone stops to stare at us. Some don't mask their irritation at the way Mr. Englewood chooses to say nothing about our tardiness. Just when I'm about to take my seat, my eyes meet a familiar pair in the middle of the room. *Delaney Callahan.* Back in the day, when my life wasn't a sickeningly close resemblance to a bad sitcom, she and I were best friends–but that's just another thing stuck in the past. She gives me a shy smile that I almost return involuntarily, but Kinsley nudges my shoulder to get my attention.

"Who are you looking at?"

I shake my head. "No one important."

With one last glance at Delaney, I notice her smile is gone, and she's averted her eyes. *Good.* The further she stays from me, the better.

I WALK OVER TO the table and place my tray down, taking a seat next to Hayden. Becca, Paige, and Kinsley join us only a couple minutes later. Carter does nothing to conceal the way he's staring directly at Paige's chest. I can't help but laugh as I clear my throat. He reluctantly pulls his eyes away to look at me, knowing he's caught but having no shame.

"You're such a pig," I tell him, only half joking.

He leans forward on his elbows. "Aw, is someone jealous?"

"In your dreams, Trayland."

A devious grin graces his face. "No baby, in my dreams I'm doing a hell of a lot more than checking out your rack."

I chuckle but choose to say nothing. Carter has made his attraction to me known since freshman year, along with every other remotely good-looking girl in this place. Calling him a man whore would be a massive understatement. At eighteen years old, I'm surprised his dick hasn't fallen off from catching something by now. And if I'm being honest, Jace is no better. I prefer to stay in the category of girls they *haven't* fucked.

Emma takes the seat next to me, placing the french fries she bought for lunch down in front of her. Just as she picks one up, Kinsley's voice halt her movements.

"Are you really going to eat that?"

Em hesitates, looking defeated as she stares down at the food. "I guess not."

"Good choice," she answers primly.

"Kinsley," Hayden chastises.

"Aw, I'm sorry. Did I offend your little girlfriend?" she mocks. "I'm just trying to help. Her cheerleading uniform was looking a little tight at practice the other day."

Emma squirms, and I can't listen to this anymore. "That's rich, coming from the girl we needed to move from a flyer to

7

a spotter because she became one of the heavier members of the team." I give her my sweetest *fuck you* smile before turning to Emma. "Don't listen to her, Ems. She's just jealous of your basket toss."

Grabbing a fry from her plate, I grin and bring it to my mouth—giving her the confidence to do the same. Carter's whole body shakes with laughter as Kinsley glares at me from across the table, but she doesn't dare say anything back. For one, what I said was nothing but the truth, and two, she's not ballsy enough to fuck with me.

I'm halfway through my salad when Jace's phone dings on the table. He picks it up and snickers before showing it to Carter. There's the slightest hint of anger on Carter's face before it changes to sheer amusement.

"Yeah, right. Not with our new QB they won't."

My eyebrows furrow. "What's going on?"

"Knox Vaughn is over at North Haven talking shit. Saying they're going to kick our asses on the field this year."

"I swear, all that pot has gone to his head," Wyatt chimes in.

Or it could be the coke I saw him buying the other day. The thought crosses my mind, but I don't dare say it. If I did, they could use it against him, and he'd get kicked off the team. Finding out the info came from me would be detrimental to my reputation. Besides, how do I explain how I saw it? *Oh yeah, I just so happened to be walking through their shitty neighborhood when I came across NH's football captain doing a drug deal?* No thanks, I'll pass.

"Speaking of your new QB, where is he?" Paige questions.

Carter smirks. "He's starting tomorrow. Keep your panties on, Paigey."

"Wait, you have a new quarterback?" I clearly missed something.

"Yes, princess. You'd know this if you showed up to

8

practice the last week and didn't leave their poor souls with Commander Kinsley as acting captain."

I grab a leftover cherry tomato from my salad and throw it at him, only slightly impressed when he catches it in his mouth. "I told you, I was in Bora Bora with my dad."

It's a complete lie, but it sounds so much better than telling them that Brady and I were training to the point where I could barely stand by the end of the week. When Mrs. Laurence told me that she got a scout from Juilliard to come to this year's recital, I knew I had to up my number of practices. Thankfully, Brady has been fully on board. He knows how badly I need not only the admission there but also a full scholarship, to get as far away from here, *and my father*, as possible.

"Well, you'll meet him tomorrow." Carter winks. "Though, don't get any ideas. Seems like your girls here have already staked their claim."

I shouldn't be surprised that Kinsley is already thinking of ways to get in this guy's pants. She's like the female version of Carter, only nastier. At least he has *some* standards. If this new guy knows what's good for him, he'll stay far away from that STD-ridden monster.

2

GRAYSON

I WAKE IN THE MORNING, FEELING WAY TOO OUT OF place in this massive house. One would think that I'd bask in all the memories it holds, being as this was my childhood home—but I don't. Everything in here is tainted with thoughts of a life I'll never get back. A life that was ripped away by the hands of the one person I trusted more than anything. Being back here just fuels my fire, and I'll enjoy getting the revenge I deserve all the more.

"Grayson, breakfast!" My mother shouts up the stairs.

Letting out a groan, I sit up in bed and run my fingers through my silky brown hair. Once I slip on a pair of sweatpants, I ignore the urge to slide down the banister and opt for walking down instead. The smell of pancakes fills the whole lower level, making me instantly suspicious. My mom hasn't made breakfast in years. I didn't expect now to be any different.

"Morning," I say.

She lights up like a fucking Christmas tree, and if I didn't know her better, I'd think she's on drugs. "Good morning, sweetheart. Pancakes?"

"Sure?" If she can sense the hesitation in my tone, she doesn't mention it. "You seem, um, different."

"What? I'm not allowed to be in a good mood?"

I chuckle. "No, you are. I just didn't think you would be."

Her shoulders raise in a shrug. "What can I say? I think you were right. This house, being back here, it helps. It's the closest I've felt to your dad since…"

She doesn't need to finish her sentence for me to know where she was going with it. Still, the topic of my father is not one I like to discuss, so I nod and smile sympathetically. She takes mercy on me and changes the subject.

"So, are you excited for your first day?"

I roll my eyes. "Oh yes, I just love the idea of going to a prep school with a bunch of rich snobs."

She snorts. "Well, I can still get a refund on the tuition check and send you to public school instead."

"No." I shake my head. "I told you, Haven Grace has a better football team."

And my target. I couldn't possibly tell my mother the real reason I wanted to move back here, or why I insisted on her paying a disgusting amount of money for me to go to HGP for my senior year. I'm sure a part of her believes what I told her, that I wanted to be back in my childhood home to feel closer to my dad. Another part of her probably thinks it was just to get away from her most recent scumbag boyfriend. While that part was a major plus, it had nothing to do with my true motivation.

I manage to finish my breakfast while avoiding most small talk, then immediately head up to my room under the pretenses of needing to get ready. As soon as I turn the lock on my door, I grab my pack of cigarettes and go over to the window. Sitting on the roof used to be my favorite place when I needed a second to think. I did it when my parents would fight. When I did something wrong and got in trouble. When my feelings for my best friend started becoming a little less platonic and a little more real. It was the one place where no one would bother me, other than the waterfall. I'm still not sure anyone knows that's there, minus the only person I shared it with.

I take a puff of my cigarette, letting the smoke fill my lungs then exhaling all my stress along with it. Like a bad habit, my eyes instinctively glance over to the house across the street—the one I spent more time in than my own. I can still remember using flashlights with our own personal Morse code at night. If only she used that code to tell me my life was about to get flipped upside down. But of course, she didn't. Not when she was partly to blame.

Putting out the cig on the shingles of the roof, I swallow down the anger burning inside of me and climb back into my bedroom. Today, I kick my plan into action, and I need to be ready. She doesn't know what's coming to her—which is exactly how I want it.

HAVEN GRACE PREP IS everything I imagined it would be. The parking lot is filled with cars that cost more than your average house. Arrogant rich kids roam the halls, their biggest concern being where their next vacation will be. Their naiveté is infuriating. What's worse is knowing that, had my life not been permanently altered by someone else's actions, I'd probably be no different than these trust fund brats.

Despite having the money to live wherever we wanted, my mother leaned on her sister for support—her sister that absolutely refuses to spend more than necessary. They both come from a wealthy family, but none of that matters to Aunt Lauren. She insists that her kids go to public school and earn all the expensive things they want. Following her example, my mother did the same with me, and I'm glad for it. It taught me not to be like these spoiled pricks with their heads stuck up their asses.

"Hey, fucker." *Speaking of pricks.*

I fist bump Carter before nodding at Jace. "What's up?"

"Just another day in hell. How are you liking it so far?"

My shoulders shrug before my eyes land on a girl who has her skirt rolled up high enough to see her ass hanging out. "Can't really complain."

He grins. "That's my man, but maybe not that one. I'm pretty sure J almost caught syphilis from her last year."

Jace punches Carter in the arm. "Fuck off, asshole. I wouldn't let that bitch anywhere near my dick."

"Yeah, yeah, sure. You're a virgin monk." He waves him off. "Who do you have for first period?"

I pull the folded-up schedule out of my pocket and skim over it with my eyes. "Mr. Englewood."

"Sweet. That's where we're all at." He pulls the paper out of my hands. "They must have realized you're on the team. All our classes are the same but one. Come on, your locker is right next to mine."

We walk down the hallway, with Carter and Jace on either side of me. As we approach, four of the girls I recognize from the cheerleading team are standing there with Hayden and Wyatt. Two of them straighten up as soon as they notice me, playing with their hair in a poor attempt to be subtle.

"Hey, Grayson," one greets me, but I can't seem to remember her name. Kasey or Cassy, I think.

Carter snorts. "Easy, Kinsley, your desperate is showing."

"Suck it, Carter."

"Ah-ah, sucking is *your* specialty. I'm more of a licking guy." He sticks his tongue out for emphasis, making Kinsley cringe. Then, as if someone is missing, he looks around. "Where's your captain?"

They all look as clueless as Carter does until one, who I

believe is Emma, looks down at her phone. "I tried texting her but she hasn't answered."

"Why are you so concerned about her anyway?" Kinsley spits.

Carter laughs and doesn't even give her a response. Whoever this girl is, there are clearly some issues between her and little miss spitfire over here.

"All right man, this locker is yours." He knocks on one of them then moves to the one next to it. "This one is mine, and the one next to it is Jace's. Hayden and Wyatt are on the other side of you."

"Cool, thanks." I put in the combination and open it, tossing my bag carelessly inside just before a short tune plays through the speakers. "What the fuck was that?"

Hayden looks slightly uncomfortable. "The bell. We should get going."

Jace chuckles. "Don't listen to him. He just doesn't like bending the rules. We'll get there when we get there."

I nod and follow in step as we all start heading toward another hallway. Kinsley makes sure to slot herself right against my side, all but pushing Wyatt out of the way. I briefly let my eyes rake over her body. Her dark brown hair almost clashes against her pasty white skin, but she's not entirely unappealing. I don't think I'd date her, since I'm entirely noncommittal, but I'd probably let her blow me a time or two.

"Come on. You can sit next to me," she says, wrapping her hands around my biceps. Jace and Carter snicker as I roll my eyes and let her lead the way.

The teacher pauses as we noisily enter the room. He eyes me suspiciously, but I don't have a minute to introduce myself as I'm pulled to a desk toward the back of the room. Kinsley takes the one next to me while Carter and Jace slip in behind us.

"Mr. Hayworth, nice of you to join us," Mr. Englewood greets me. "You *are* my new student, aren't you?"

"Yep, that's me."

He nods. "Well, my rules are simple. Don't cause disruptions in my class and we shouldn't have any issues. Sound good?"

I cover my mouth behind my fist to hide my amusement as the two idiots chuckle behind me. "Mm-hm."

"Great. Now, let's open to..." I don't hear the rest as I discreetly slip earbuds in and turn on some music.

THE CLASS GOES BY rather fast, but that probably has a lot to do with the playlist I had blasting into my ears. I head out the door only to find a familiar face leaning against a locker across the hall.

"Grayson Hayworth," she smirks.

My mood brightens instantly. "Delaney! Is that you?"

In a couple steps, she crosses the hallway and throws herself into my arms. I catch her willingly, spinning us around as she squeals.

"I never thought I'd see you again." She slaps my arm. "Way to go AWOL, jerk."

"I know, I know. I'm sorry. Wasn't really my choice to leave, though."

A frown graces her flawless face. "I heard. I'm really sorry about your dad."

Just as I'm about to answer, someone slips her arm around mine. "Grayson, what are you doing? Why are you talking to *her*?"

My eyes narrow at Kinsley. "*Her name* is Delaney, and because I've known her since I was a kid." I pull my arm from her grasp. "Is that a problem?"

Looking taken back, she pouts before storming away from

us. Delaney grins widely. "Okay, that was amazing. So, does Sa—"

"Who's your friend, Hayworth?" Carter cuts her off, leaning with his hand on the locker right next to us and eyeing her like a piece of meat.

Delaney looks a little intimidated as she moves closer to me. "I've, uh, got to get to my next class. It was good seeing you again. We'll catch up soon."

She scurries away before I even get a chance to say goodbye. Carter's brows furrow as he watches her practically run from him, but then he shakes it off and puts his hand on my shoulder—nodding in the direction of lockers. The two of us walk side by side over to where everyone else is hanging out. I toss my book onto the shelf and then close the door, leaning my back against it.

I'm listening to Jace go over the plans for the party he's throwing this coming weekend when a slim girl with dirty blonde hair makes her way between Paige and Becca. I can't see her face as it's buried in a locker, but there is something oddly familiar about her. I'm waiting for her to turn around when Carter speaks.

"How nice of her royal highness to join us," he quips.

She scoffs. "Don't you have better things to do than focus on my whereabouts, Trayland?"

The second I hear her voice, my blood runs ice cold. I'd recognize that sound anywhere. Hell, I spent enough time listening to it while I was growing up. She turns around slowly, and there's no question about it. As her gaze falls on me, her breath hitches, and I know for sure. She may look older, and a million times hotter, but standing right in front of me is exactly who I came here for. *Savannah fucking Montgomery.*

3

SAVANNAH

THE HOUSE IS ODDLY QUIET WHEN MY ALARM GOES off, and judging by the way there isn't a new set of empty beer bottles on the coffee table, it's safe to assume my father never came home last night. After checking the house, I run my fingers through my hair and walk back to my room to grab my phone. First on my call list is the hospital. I cannot count the amount of times I've found him there, recovering from a drunken injury.

"North Haven Medical. How can I help you?"

I swallow. "Yes, my name is Savannah Montgomery. I'm calling to check if you have a patient there by the name of Craig Montgomery? He's my father."

"Let me check." I hear keys clacking in the background before she answers. "Nope. There is no one here with that last name."

"Okay, thank you for your help." I hang up and immediately call the second place on my list—the police department. I recognize the voice as soon as they answer. "Hey, Barry. It's Savannah. Is my dad there?"

He hums. "Yeah, sweetie, he's here. One of our guys picked him up last night for public intox."

I sigh. "I figured as much when I woke up and realized he hadn't come home last night. Any other charges?"

"Resisting, but just come get him and we'll call it even."

"Thanks, Bar. I'll be there soon."

"Sure thing, Savannah."

Out of the two options, I would've much rather preferred him to be at the hospital. They at least give him fluids, so his hangover isn't as bad and he's a little easier to deal with. I glance down at the time and notice it's already 7:05. *So much for getting to school on time.*

I make quick work of brushing my hair and getting dressed into my uniform. I run out the door, and Brady is already waiting for me at the curb. I smile as I climb into his car.

"Hey, can you do something before you take me to school?"

He eyes me suspiciously before realization sets in and he puts the car in drive. "Do you need bail money, too?"

"Not this time."

At this point, Brady knows better than to try to talk to me about this. The first couple times, he tried to pry information out of me as to when my dad went from father of the year to a worthless drunk. If I'm being honest, I don't even have an answer for that. All I know is that over time he changed, until he became *this*. A mean, ruthless, disappointing mess of a man. Now, it's all I know.

We pull up to the police station, and Brady waits outside while I go in and get my father. I follow the officer back to the cell, watching my dad wince as the sound of his name echoes throughout the room.

"Montgomery! Your ride's here."

Officer Patten unlocks the door, and my father stumbles through it. It's easy to figure out he's still at least partly drunk, but mostly hungover, if the way he shields his eyes from the light is anything to go by.

"What was his BAC when you brought him in?" I ask.

The officer's frown shows his pity at how numb I am to all of this, but I'm not looking for his sympathy. I wait patiently for the answer as he pulls up the report.

"Point 235."

Almost three times the legal limit, lovely. I wish I could say this one takes the record, but it doesn't. The *record* was when he was a .462, and the hospital needed to pump his stomach to avoid liver damage. This is a walk in the park compared to that day.

"All right, Dad. Let's get you home and in bed."

I lead him out to the car, where Brady opens the door and helps me get him in. My father grumbles something inaudible as we child lock the back seat and shut him in. I mumble another thanks to my friend and get in the passenger side.

The ride back to my house is slow, no doubt because Brady doesn't want the back of his car covered in vomit —*again*. It smelled like a dumpster in here for a week before he could get an appointment to have it detailed.

Once we pull up, the two of us drag my dad into the house and to his bedroom. To my relief, he only calls me a piece of shit once before he passes out face down on his bed. I place a bottle of water and a couple Advil on his nightstand for when he wakes up later. Then, I grab my stuff for school and lock the house up.

"Just another day in paradise?" Brady jokes as we get back in the SUV.

"You know it."

INSTEAD OF GOING STRAIGHT to a class I'd inevitably be late for, we decided to grab something for breakfast first— or more like he decided and I had no say in the matter because *"my car my rules."* So, I arrive at Haven Grace Prep just after first period lets out.

After the morning I had, my patience is minimal when I get inside. I push my way through Paige and Becca to get to my locker, not even giving them a chance to move first. Pulling my phone from my purse, I throw the bag inside and grab my book for second period.

"How nice of your royal highness to join us," Carter says with a smirk, but I'm hardly in the mood for it.

I let out a sound of annoyance. "Don't you have better things to do than focus on my whereabouts, Trayland?"

As I turn around, I notice someone new standing between Carter and Jace. My gaze starts at his chest and works its way up. When my eyes meet his, my breath hitches. *No, it can't be.* The dark blue eyes I remember, the same ones I've dreamed about hundreds of times over the last eight years, stare back at me.

The last time I looked into that night sky gaze, I was ten years old, before he and his family completely disappeared. My father said they moved away, but I didn't want to believe it. He would've told me. He would've said goodbye. However, when I ran across the street and into the empty house, I realized he was right. My best friend, my everything, left me without a word.

"Savannah? Hello?" Carter waves his hand in front of my face, snapping me out of it. "Damn, girl. I don't think Brady would be too happy to find out you were checking out the new quarterback."

"Q-quarterback?" I croak. *This* is the new QB?

"Savannah, this is Grayson. Grayson, Savannah. She's the captain of the cheerleading squad." Jace introduces us, completely oblivious to the fact that we already know each other. Hell, at one point we knew each other better than anyone. "You would've met her last week at practice, but her dad took her to Bora Bora."

I'm about to open my mouth when Grayson cuts me off. "I've got to get to class." He snarls, walking away before anyone gets a chance to say anything.

My eyes can't seem to look away from his retreating body as he disappears into the crowd. The last thing I ever expected was for Grayson Hayworth to be the new quarterback. I've spent countless hours trying to find him, never with any success. No social media. No listed phone number. No address in the phone book. Even Brady's boyfriend, Jacob, the son of a private investigator, couldn't find anything on him. Still, that hasn't stopped me from trying every now and then.

"What's stuck up his ass?" Becca asks.

Carter smiles. "I saw him talking to one of the Callahan twins a few minutes ago. She ran off when I asked who she is. He's probably pissed I fucked up his game."

Kinsley shakes her head. "No, he said he's known her since he was a kid. I didn't think Grayson knew anyone from here."

"Before this morning, all you knew was his name," Paige sasses.

She scoffs. "Whatever. I'm going to go make sure he's okay."

Just as she goes to walk away, I grab her by the wrist—a little tighter than necessary. "Leave him alone and go to class."

The thought of Kinsley going anywhere near Grayson has me seeing red. If she knows what's good for her, she will stay away from him. Otherwise, I'll do whatever it takes to ruin her life, and I won't even bat an eye as she begs me to stop.

"Ooh," Jace coos. "Has someone other than Brady Laurence finally gotten Savannah's attention?"

"Please." I wave him off dismissively. "I'm just trying to save the poor guy from being hounded on his first day. The last thing your shitty team needs is for your new star player to run off because Kinsley is breathing down his neck."

Carter scowls. "Aye! Who are you calling our star player?"

Laughing, I reach up and pat his cheek. "Aw, don't get butthurt, Carter. You're still my favorite."

"Damn right, I am."

The bell rings, and we all start heading separate ways. It's the one period we aren't all in the same class. When I get to mine, Miss Layton gives me a look, but it softens when I smile shyly. It's when I'm about to reach my seat that I stop. Sitting in the normally empty seat next to mine is Grayson, and he looks anything but thrilled at my presence.

"Fifty-eight, fifty-nine, sixty! Ready or not, here I come!"

I start looking around for my friends. If I know Tessa as well as I think I do, she ditched this game as soon as I started counting and went inside for a snack. As for Delaney, she's probably somewhere stupid like behind a tree or in a bush.

"Laney," I singsong as I walk around the backyard. "Come out, come out, wherever you are." A giggle from behind one of the bushes gives her away. "Ah-ha! Got you!" I jump out in front of her.

She screeches and falls back onto her butt, totally caught off guard. "Savannah!" she whines. "Do you really have to scare me every time?! Stop it!"

"What's the fun in that?" I offer her my hand and pull her up off the ground. "I think Tessa went inside. Go find her while I go find Grayson."

Looking around my yard and hers, I know he's not here. There's only one other place I can think to look. I run across the street and into Grayson's backyard, quietly closing the gate behind me. I get to the treehouse and climb up. If he isn't up here, it'll at least give me a good vantage point to look from.

The second I open the hatch, Grayson pops out with a "Boo!" My foot misses the step and I scream, nearly falling out of the tree. He grabs my hand at the last second and holds onto me while I find my footing again, then he falls over—laughing hysterically.

"It's not funny, Gray! I could have gotten really hurt!" I sit in the corner and cross my arms, pouting.

He looks over at me and smiles. My heart rate quickens at the sight of it, something that's been happening more and more often lately. Just like that, I can't possibly be angry at him anymore. Not when he's smiling at me like I'm his favorite person. Still, I do my best to act upset.

"Oh, come on. I had to after the way you scared Delaney. I could hear her squeal from here." He gets up and comes over to sit next to me, poking me in the cheek when I refuse to look at him. "Savi." Poke. "Savi." Poke. "Savi."

This time when he goes to poke me, I slap his hand away. "Stop. I'm mad at you."

He sighs and wraps his arms around me, pulling me into him. I try my best to control my breathing, but with him this close, I don't stand a chance. Instead, I lean my head against him, and the tension leaves my body.

"I'm sorry," he whispers.

"You're still a jerk."

I can feel him relax, realizing he's already forgiven. "I know."

But that's the thing about being best friends; we can never stay mad at each other for long.

EACH CLASS PASSES, AND I'm yet to get a second glance from Grayson, let alone get to talk to him. I can't figure out whether he doesn't remember me, or he doesn't *want* to remember me. Even when we're all in a group conversation, he keeps to himself and messes with his phone, not even looking up when someone says his name. If I didn't recognize him, I'd think he just coincidentally has the same name as the boy who stole my heart all those years ago.

At the end of the day, I'm packing up my stuff when Carter and the others saunter off down the hall. I say goodbye, still distracted by making sure I have everything I need. The second day of school means homework starts, and I don't have the luxury of slacking, unlike some of the people here. Just as I close my locker, I turn around to see Grayson leaning against his. His eyes bore into mine, but not in the way I imagined so many times over the years.

It's clear he has no intention of saying anything to me, so I start to walk away. However, at the last second, I realize that I can't let this fester. I need to know what's going on. I stop and twist back.

"Do you really not remember me?" All the strength in the world wouldn't be enough to mask the pain in my voice.

He shoves his phone into his pocket and steps toward me. "Oh, I remember you, *Sweet Savi*." The nickname is spit from his mouth like venom, making my insides churn.

"Y-you do?"

"Of course I do. I remember *every last thing* about you." He invades my space, pushing his body up against mine and placing his lips next to my ear. "But trust me when I say you're going to wish I didn't."

4

GRAYSON

I PUSH PAST SAVANNAH, MENTALLY PLEADING FOR her not to come after me. Seeing her again has threatened to knock me off my axis. She's just as gorgeous as I remember, and that could be nothing but detrimental to my plans.

A part of me had hoped that she was just as unhappy as I have been. That her life was irrevocably changed by her actions, the way mine was. It may not have made up for the pain she caused, but it would have helped. However, when I heard Jace say that she wasn't at practice last week because her father took her on vacation to Bora Bora, I could hardly contain the anger inside of me.

"Yo, Hayworth!" Carter shouts as I step outside.

I pull the pack of cigarettes from my pocket and put one in my mouth, lighting it as soon as I sit on the ledge. Kinsley scowls, making her distaste for my choices obvious.

"Smoking is bad for you, Grayson."

I snort and blow the smoke right into her face. "Do I look like I give a fuck?"

Carter pats my shoulder as Jace laughs. "As long as you can play like you have been, I don't give a shit what you do."

A few minutes later, the door opens, and Savannah comes

walking through it. She doesn't even acknowledge us, or me for that matter, as she walks down the stairs and straight to a black Cadillac Escalade.

"Who's that?" I question, nodding toward the car.

Kinsley turns around to see what I'm referring to and then rolls her eyes. "That's Brady."

Brady. I heard Carter say the name earlier, but I was too furious to even process the importance. It sounds familiar, but I can't quite put my finger on it. Even with all the research I've done on Savannah, I don't remember anything about him.

"Is he her boyfriend or something?"

Jace raises his eyebrows. "Why? You interested?"

An involuntary grunt leaves my mouth. "Nah. Stuck-up bitches aren't really my thing."

I level Kinsley with a look, hoping she gets the message. Emma narrows her eyes at me while Paige and Becca can't seem to contain their amusement.

"Yeah, it's her boyfriend," Paige finally tells me. "She doesn't really talk about him though. She's protective of their relationship."

I mull that over. There was a time where she was protective of *our* relationship too, before she went and fucked me over like it was the easiest thing in the world. I breathe in the nicotine, hoping for it to calm me down before I take my anger out on some undeserving fool. It's important I save my wrath for the only one who truly deserves it. I want her to rue the day she turned her back on me.

I WALK IN THE front door, hearing the sound of my mom giggling in the kitchen. As soon as I enter the room, every bit of patience I built up on the drive home vanishes.

"What the fuck is *he* doing here?" I growl, referring to my mother's shithead ex-boyfriend.

My mom frowns. "Grayson, be nice. Justin drove all the way from Campton to see us. The least you could do is be respectful."

"Yeah, *Grayson*," Justin taunts. "Show a little respect."

I take a step forward, clenching my fist tightly. "Shut the fuck up, prick. You don't get to speak to me after what you did to her."

"Grayson Matthew!"

Turning my murderous stare from Justin to my mother, I shove my finger in his direction. "*He* doesn't belong here. I want him gone, and you should, too."

I don't give her a second to answer before I storm out of the room and up the stairs. How dare she let him come here after the night I had to pry him off of her. He had been staying with us for a bit—which essentially was the PG way of telling your son that your boyfriend is moving in—when he came home wasted off his ass one night. My mom started yelling at him, pissed that he smelled like some other bitch's perfume.

I had gone into my room until I heard a bang over my headphones—making the whole wall vibrate. I ran out to find him on top of her, with his hands around her neck as she was clawing at his arms. In a split-second decision, I charged at him full force. It knocked him over and freed my mom from his grasp, but that didn't stop me. I pummeled my fist into his face so many times I lost track of when he went unconscious.

The cops came and arrested him that night, and my mother was granted a restraining order. He was sentenced to a year in prison, but judging by the fact that it's only nine months later and he's out, I'm assuming he's on parole. The fucker is lucky I didn't kill him that night. Had my mom not screamed at me to stop, I probably would have.

I slam the door shut behind me with a force that causes it to echo through the entire house. He has a lot of fucking nerve coming here. I grab the closest thing to me, a picture frame from my dresser, and throw it across the room. It shatters into a million pieces as soon as it hits the wall and only then do I realize what I just threw. I watch the photo fall gently to the floor before going and plucking it up out of the scattered pieces of glass.

I'm only a kid in the picture, standing in front of both my parents with a broad grin across my face. My father has a protective arm around my mother's waist, holding her close to him, while my mother beams happily. It's exactly what I envision when I remember the happier times of my childhood, but like the frame the photo was in, those times are just a memory.

I walk over to the window and look out at the house across the street. The blue shudders and beige siding look the same as they always have, but something about it feels different. A part of me wonders if she and her father still live there.

"Grayson?" My father calls from downstairs. I'm up in my room playing with the new dinosaur toys I got for Christmas. "Come down here. There's someone I'd like you to meet."

I groan quietly as I get up and leave my toys behind. When I reach the top of the steps, I can see my parents standing with another man and a little girl by the front door. She looks shy, with her blonde hair in a ponytail as she keeps a tight hold on the bear in her arms. I slide down the banister, laughing the whole way until my father catches me.

"Honey, what did I say about sliding down that?" my mom scolds.

I drop my head toward the floor. "That I'm going to get hurt one day."

My dad drops down onto one knee in front of me. "Your mother just wants to keep you safe, Gray. She's not trying to ruin your fun."

"Your name is Gray? Like the color?" the little girl asks.

I look up at her, and the first thing I notice is her light blue eyes. They remind me of the sky right before sunset. I smile, and it widens when she smiles back.

"Grayson, but my dad calls me Gray." A slight look of disappointment graces her face before I continue. "But you can call me Gray, too."

That makes her happy. "Okay! I'm Savannah, but my dad calls me Savi."

"Savi." I test the name on my tongue. "I like it."

"Why don't you take Savannah to see your new toys?" my mom suggests.

I nod, grinning widely, and wave for Savi to follow me. We go into the den where the Christmas tree is, my presents still scattered underneath it from after I unwrapped them all. She instantly starts playing with the remote-controlled car—one of my favorite presents this year.

"So, did you just move here? I've never seen you before."

She nods, still shy. "Yeah. We moved in across the street. My dad said that he's been friends with your parents since he was in college. Whatever that is."

"Did you want to move here?"

I can tell it's a touchy subject by the way she won't look at me. I almost tell her she doesn't have to answer when she sighs. "No, but when my mommy went to heaven, Daddy said we should move."

My eyes water at the thought of losing one of my parents. "I'm sorry."

She wipes a stray tear from her cheek. "Me too."

We spend the afternoon playing with every toy I have, and when we get bored of them, we move on to playing hide and seek. She's not a very good seeker, but I'm also the best at hiding. By the time her dad announces that it's time for them to go, we are both exhausted. I walk her to the door and give her a hug goodbye.

31

"I'm really glad you moved across the street," I tell her.

She smiles. "Me too. Bye, Gray."

"Bye, Savi."

***

PULLING UP TO SCHOOL the next day, I'm not entirely prepared to see Savannah again. In my plan to ruin her life, I never considered that she might be the most popular girl in school. It's one thing to torment and torture someone who only has a couple of friends. It's another to get away with doing it to the captain of the cheerleading squad. Still, I'm determined to get my revenge. I just need to be more careful and calculated about it.

I park my car and get out, walking up to the front steps. I decide to have one last cigarette before going inside. Just as I start to light it, that same familiar Escalade pulls up out front. I can see through the mirror as Savannah reaches over and gives the driver a hug before getting out. She starts to walk toward the doors when she stops. As if she can sense my presence, she turns to look at me. Her eyes start at my face and move down my body. When she reaches my hand, she frowns—clearly spotting the lit cigarette.

A decade ago, I wouldn't have dreamed of doing anything that causes her even the slightest bit of upset. If she told me I shouldn't do something, I'd drop it in a heartbeat. But now? I bring the cigarette up to my mouth and take a long pull. She stares intently as I exhale. It's nothing more than a silent *fuck you*, and she knows it.

Her shoulders fall and she turns away, continuing her walk inside. However, when the sun hits her just right, I notice the light reflecting off a chain around her neck. For a brief second, I wonder if it's the same necklace I got her for her tenth birthday, but I quickly brush that thought off. She destroyed my entire life while still acting like my best friend.

32

If she did keep the gift, it's probably tossed in one of her many jewelry boxes somewhere.

I finish my cigarette and walk inside, deciding to skip my locker and head straight to class. I wave hello to Delaney as I take the desk I sat in yesterday. She and I really need to get together and catch up. We haven't talked since the day before my mom and I left town. I'd be lying if I said I didn't miss her and her crazy-ass sister.

A couple minutes after the bell rings, the door opens, and in walks Carter and the rest of the gang—including Savannah. She's laughing at something Jace said, and I grip the edge of the desk to keep my cool. It's not that I'm jealous. I just don't believe she deserves anything good in life. If Jace wants to fuck her, then....yeah, no. Over my dead body.

I fist bump Carter as he walks by and takes the desk behind me. Kinsley smiles flirtatiously and slips into her seat. Then, I spot Savannah. She stops short as she sees me, and something unfamiliar flickers in her eyes. She looks like she's fighting an intense mental battle before she runs her fingers through her hair.

"You're in my seat." She tells me, and well, I may not be able to do much until I figure out the social dynamic in this place, but this is one thing I *can* do.

I chuckle and raise my brows at her. "I'm not moving."

Looking around, she spots the only other available seat—next to Delaney. I half expect for her to smile triumphantly, since it should hardly be an inconvenience to sit next to her best friend, but instead, she frowns.

"Grayson, just go sit over there."

"No, thanks. I'm good." I cross my arms over my chest.

The teacher clears his throat behind us. "Miss Montgomery, is there a problem?"

She rolls her eyes before she focuses them on me, glaring. "Nope."

Kinsley snickers next to me as Savannah makes her way to the seat across the room. However, she shuts up as soon as Sav turns around and glowers at her. I make a mental note to pay attention to the relationship between the two of them, but first I want to see what's up with her and Delaney.

Throughout class, I subtly glance their way, only to find them completely refusing to look at each other. It's strange to see them like this. Hell, there were times I was sure Savannah liked Delaney more than me—something she always denied, but it still made me wonder. Now, it's like they were never friends at all.

THE BELL RINGS AND the entire class gets up. Savannah is out the door like she's in some kind of hurry, but it's probably just to get away from me. *Good, I make her nervous.* I mouth for Delaney to wait for me, and thankfully she listens. After telling Carter and Jace that I'll meet them at the lockers, I head out the door.

"Okay, so what was that?" Laney asks as soon as I'm close enough.

I tilt my head to the side. "What was what?"

"That." She points toward the classroom. "In there. I don't think I've ever seen you and Savannah act that way toward each other."

"Yeah, well." I shrug. "We're not the same kids we used to be. Speaking of which, what's up with *you* and Savannah? You two hardly acknowledged each other."

Delaney looks down at her sweatshirt sleeve and plays with it, almost like a distraction or a nervous habit. "I wish I knew. After you moved away, things were different. Her dad sold their house a year after you left, and I didn't see or talk to Savannah for a while. Tessa either. It was like she fell off the face of the earth."

My brows furrow. "But you two go to school together."

"We didn't." She shakes her head. "No one had seen or heard from her until freshman year, when she showed up here, looking like *that*. I tried to talk to her a few times, but it's never gone well. She's not the same girl she used to be."

"Apparently not." I shrug. "Well, you've always got me."

She smiles. "Thanks, Grayson. I've got to meet Tess before class, but I'll talk to you later."

I give her a hug and the two of us go our separate ways. Just before I get to my locker, I can see everyone watching intently as Savannah says something to Kinsley, her body unnecessarily close. Her eyes catch sight of me, and while it looks like she wants to soften, she doesn't. She shoves herself past her so-called friend then pushes her shoulder into me as well. Only difference between me and Kinsley is that I won't lie down and take it.

Grabbing her wrist, I ignore the feel of her soft skin under my fingertips as she spins around. She looks at my hand and then up to my face. It's then that I see it—the white gold plate with her name engraved on the front hanging from her neck. Unless she got a new one, which I doubt, it's the same necklace that has "Love, Grayson" etched into the back of it. The sight of her wearing it has me ready to explode all on its own.

This bitch is the reason my father is fucking dead, and now here she is—wearing something bought with his money like a fucking trophy. I release her arm with force and wipe my hand on my jeans.

"Don't *ever* fucking shove me again."

She swallows harshly before composing herself and continuing her escape. I watch as she disappears, not looking away until she's out of sight. Once she's gone, I walk up to Kinsley and place my hand on her cheek, rubbing my thumb across it.

"Are you all right?" I ask her.

"Y-yeah."

It may be cruel to use her as a pawn in my sick and twisted game, but I've never been more determined than I am right now. Savannah is going to wish that lie never left her pretty little mouth.

5

SAVANNAH

"And five, six, seven, eight!"

I count in the team as they practice their scorpions at extension. Emma nails it as usual, while Becca's could really use some work. Kinsley stands back, watching, with a scowl on her face. She really needs to get her damn attitude in check before I kick her ass off the team. The only reason I haven't is because she's the only person, besides myself, who can do a back aerial—a trick I find useful to impress the judges during competition season.

"Bec, you need to work on getting that leg straighter," I tell her.

She cradles out of the stunt and goes over to Liam, knowing no one can help her stretch better than him. The sight of the football team in the distance has my stomach churning. I watch as Grayson throws the ball across the field, looking like a fucking god when his muscles contract with the movement.

After the little spat in the hallway, I threw myself into brainstorming ideas for cheer and the winter dance recital. It was the best way I could think to avoid him. Between the feeling I get seeing him again, and the way he looks at me, like I repulse him, I can't seem to get a grip on how I feel about him being back here. My heart wants me to run as fast as possible into his arms, while the logical part of me is screaming to stay away. There was a point in time where he knew me better than I knew myself. If anyone can figure out my whole reputation is a lie, it's him.

"Okay, now onto basket tosses. Em, let's see what you've got."

After counting her in, she's tossed in the air and does the stunt flawlessly. Without hesitation, if someone asked me who my favorite girl on the team is, it would be her. She's always willing to try something new, and if I tell her to fix something, she does it. The other girls are good, but she's exactly what we need on this team.

"Heads!" Carter yells as the ball comes flying toward us.

I manage to catch it and throw it back. "Tell your QB to watch where he throws that thing. We're practicing stunts and if one of my girls gets hurt because he can't aim a ball, we'll have some problems."

"Tell him yourself." Grayson says, standing closer than I had thought.

My heart starts to race as I swallow down the lump in my throat. Turning around, he's no more than ten feet away from me, staring me down like he's daring me to go against him. The T-shirt clings to his body in all the right places, showing off his toned muscles. His shorts rest low on his hips. It's everything that could render me completely defenseless, but if I show weakness now, I'll never recover.

Placing one hand on my hip, I channel all the confidence I have into my words. "I would, but that'd mean giving you a second thought—and I don't waste my time on the insignificant."

His head falls back as laughter bellows from his mouth. "That's rich coming from a spineless little bitch like you.

Don't fuck with me, Montgomery. You'll only end up burned."

"I love it when people insult me. It means I don't have to play nice anymore."

"All right," Carter intervenes. "Let's not kill each other on the damn field. It'll take weeks for the blood to wash out of the turf." He comes over and places his hands on my shoulders. "You okay, Sav?"

I watch as Grayson goes over to Kinsley and whispers something in her ear. She giggles happily, and within seconds, she's practically salivating at the mouth. The sight alone is enough to send me into a jealousy fueled rage.

"I'm fine." I spit, ripping myself from Carter's grasp. "Kinsley, get back to practice! Or would you rather give your uniform to someone that'll actually add something to this team?"

She rolls her eyes but backs away from Grayson. I notice the smirk on the asshole's face, as if he knows his actions are getting to me, but how could they not be? This is the same boy I was sure I was going to marry one day. We promised we'd always end up together, and now here is he, hating my guts and flirting with Kinsley right in front of me.

As she goes to walk by, I step directly in her way. "Roll your eyes at me again, and I'll ruin you." She swallows hard as I back up. "Now go work on your form. Spreading your legs for every guy who looks at you doesn't count as stretching."

PRACTICE FINISHES A COUPLE hours later, without a single word from Kinsley. She may have had a sour look on her face the whole time, but she kept her mouth shut and that's all that matters. Grayson, however, has been staring me down almost constantly — glaring at me like I'm the worst person in existence.

"Savannah." Emma gets my attention then nods to look behind me.

I turn around and light up when I see Brady leaning against the bleachers. "Hey, you."

He smiles and comes toward me, then wraps me tightly in his arms. The hug is everything I needed after the day I had. Suddenly though, Brady tenses.

"Uh, should I be concerned by the football player murdering me with his eyes right now?"

I don't need to look to know that it's Grayson. "Do me a favor? Play it up."

He chuckles. "Let's do this."

Pulling away from the hug, he keeps one hand on my back. His lips meet mine as he dips me. To anyone else, we probably look like a loved-up couple. Even some of the guys whistle playfully. Then he breaks the kiss and wraps his arm around my shoulder. With one last wink at Grayson, Brady leads me off the field and toward his car.

"Have I mentioned lately how much I love you?" I ask when we're safely inside the vehicle.

He grins widely as he puts it in reverse to back out of the space. "I'm glad, because that's the first time I've kissed a girl since playing spin the bottle freshman year."

"Think Jake will be mad?"

"Eh. Special circumstances, and it's you. I don't think he'll mind."

I laugh softly and fix my ponytail. "Well, I appreciate it."

Glancing between me and the road, he narrows his eyes. "Are you going to tell me what the deal is with that guy, or am I just a pretty pawn to you?"

Even if I wanted to, how could I even begin to explain Grayson Hayworth? Since he showed up the other day — looking every bit like the boy I had a crush on from when I was eight years old, yet acting like someone who would run me over without even tapping the breaks—it's almost like my brain has been turned to mush. I don't understand what changed in him, or why he's treating me the way he has. The whole thing is just one big mind-fuck, and I'm tired of the headache.

"I'd say you're more of a pretty knight than a pawn," I quip.

Thankfully, he takes the hint and drops the subject —for now.

THE SOUND OF SHAWN Mendes and Camilla Cabello blasts through the speakers as Brady and I move rhythmically to the beat. It's not a complete reenactment from the music video, but the routine is sexual enough to look like one. The concept, paired with tune of *Señorita*, is perfect for a showcased duet in the winter recital.

I spin four times before he catches me and practically uses my body as a human prop, flinging me around him and making it so I end up on his shoulder. If I wasn't as petite as I am, the move would be impossible, but our size difference makes it work.

Still, no matter how much I'm into this dance, there is no denying my head isn't in the game today. I've messed up more steps than normal and even managed to step on Brady's foot. By the third time I fall out of my turns, he stops me.

"What the hell is up with you today?" he asks as soon as he hits pause on the music.

"What do you mean?"

The knowing look on his face tells me I'm busted. "You're all over the place. Wrong steps, sloppy moves, off beat—it's not like you."

41

I groan, grabbing my bottle of water and taking a longer sip than necessary. "I'm just having an off day, that's all."

"Mm-hm, right." He sits on the floor and leans on his elbows. "Now, let's try that again, but this time, actually try to sound believable."

Smirking, I can't help but laugh. That's the thing about Brady. He's known me long enough to gauge when he can push on a topic and when to just let it go. And right now, with this, me being unfocused could mean not performing my best at the recital. If I don't get the scholarship to Juilliard, I'll be stuck here for God knows how long. *That* would be my worst nightmare come to life.

I sigh and sit down next to him, trying to figure out how to explain the last couple days. "The football player is Grayson."

"Grayson? Is that name supposed to mean something to me?" He looks confused before it all becomes clear. Then he reaches forward and plucks at the pendant hanging against my chest. "Necklace Grayson?"

"That's the one."

Letting out a long breath, he uses a towel to wipe the sweat away from his forehead. "Well, that's probably the last thing I expected. When's the last time you saw him? You were a kid when he moved away, right?"

I nod. "I was ten. I went to visit my grandmother for a weekend, and when I came back he was just gone. His house was empty, and he was nowhere to be found. He didn't even say goodbye."

"Yeah, I remember. You came to dance looking like someone broke your favorite toy for weeks."

"There are a few things in life that break you. Change who you are as a person. Him leaving was one of those for me. I feel like that was the start of everything falling apart."

After Grayson's family moved away, my dad started drinking more. He ended up getting fired from his job for showing up intoxicated one too many times. Instead of using his savings to pay the bills and finding another job, he ended up going further downhill. Then, the drugs started. Within a year, he sold our beautiful house and moved us into the shack I have the misfortune of calling home.

If it wasn't for Mrs. Laurence allowing me to keep taking dance here free of charge, I don't know where I would've ended up. Her generosity, along with her tendency to be a role model for me and taking me under her wing, kept me motivated to strive for a better life than what mine had become. So, when she offered to pay my tuition at Haven Grace Prep, I thanked her profusely and promised to make her proud. Brady's older sister taught me how to do my makeup and even gave me some designer clothes she grew out of. By the time freshman year started, I showed up determined to be something more than the poor girl from the wrong side of town.

One of the downfalls to my newfound popularity, however, was having to see Delaney and Tessa in the hallways and act like they were nothing to me. It was a necessary evil, because if anyone could expose me for the fraud I am, it would be Delaney. Still, that didn't make it any easier to see her look at me the same way she always has—no matter how cruel I am for ignoring her existence. Tessa never seemed to care. From what I've heard, she's become quite the rebel lately. But Delaney? She's exactly the way I remember.

"Okay, so wait." Brady snaps me out of my thoughts. "Why is Grayson being back a bad thing?"

I lie down on the floor and stare at the ceiling. "Because he hates me."

"How could anyone hate you? Especially someone you used to be so close with. Are you sure you're not just misreading the situation? Maybe he's just shy."

Snorting, I shake my head. "No, B. He's anything but shy. He literally hates me. If looks could kill, I'd be six feet under

43

with him pissing on my grave by now—and he's only been back a couple days. I just don't get it. I don't know what I did."

He sighs. "I don't know, babes. If I know you as well as I think I do though, I'm sure you'll find out. You're Savannah Montgomery. Since when do you take shit from anyone?"

"Grayson's different. He's like the definition of every good childhood memory I have. My own personal kryptonite. He has the ability to ruin me, and he knows it. It's dangerous."

Brady looks down at me and smiles. "Well then it's a good thing danger stopped scaring you years ago." He gets up and offers me his hand. "Now, come on. We've got a routine to nail."

LATER THAT EVENING, BRADY drives me home. As we pull up in front of the house, I notice all the bikes and crappy cars parked outside—Dad has "friends" over. I cringe, knowing how drunk he gets when he has people drinking with him. Last time he had them here, I damn near broke a guy's fingers for trying to slip his hand up my uniform skirt.

"Do you want to sleep at my place? Jake won't mind," he offers, but I shake my head.

"Thank you, but no. I have an essay to write, so I'm going to lock myself in my bedroom and focus on that."

He nods in understanding. "Okay, well, remember the self-defense moves I taught you, and call me if you need anything. I can get here in ten minutes if I ignore all traffic laws."

I smile. "And that's why I love you." Reaching over, I give him a tight hug. "Bye, B."

"Later, Rocky." Just as I'm climbing out of the car, he stops me. "And Sav? I'm sure everything with Grayson will work itself out in time."

"Thanks. I hope so."

As soon as I open the front door, the smell of alcohol and cigarette smoke is so strong I nearly choke on it. My father and a bunch of his scumbag friends fill the living room. They're watching some stupid show on TV that's meant to be funny, but isn't. Bottles of booze are already covering the coffee table.

The second I walk in, all eyes turn toward me. I'm thankful I wore yoga pants over my leotard today instead of the booty shorts I'm usually in. My father perks up at the sight of me, then instantly starts digging in his pocket.

"Savannah! Good you're home." He takes $40 out of his wallet. "Be a good girl and run down to the liquor store for me. I need more vodka."

I roll my eyes. "Dad, I'm seventeen."

"Oh." His face drops, then he waves me off and shoves the cash in my hand anyway. "Well, go anyway. You look old enough to drink. Show a little skin if you have to."

Instead of arguing, I slip my hands into my sweatshirt pocket and head out the door. I go a couple doors down, to a house I really don't like coming to unless absolutely necessary, and knock. A few seconds later, Knox comes to the door. He's completely shirtless, with all his tattoos full on display. I notice the hickeys on his neck and chuckle as a girl slips past us to leave.

"Classy," I say with an eye roll.

He shrugs. "What can I say? I'm a man of many talents."

"I'm sure you are." I smirk and slip inside. "I need a couple empty bottles of vodka. You got some?"

He looks confused, but goes over to his recycling bin and pulls out two. I take them from him and head to the sink, filling each one to the brim with water. My father is too drunk to know the difference anyway, and maybe it'll hydrate him some. Knox watches my actions with amusement.

45

"You don't think he's going to notice that's not really alcohol?"

"Nope. I could convince him sugar is cocaine right now. He's too drunk to tell."

He nods. "Sounds like a party."

Not wanting to stay and make small talk, I make my way back toward the front door. "Thanks for the bottles, shithead."

"No problem, Princess."

It only takes a couple minutes to get back and as soon as I walk in, my father grabs the bottles from my hands. "See? You *are* good for something."

One of his friends looks me up and down. "I'm sure she'd be good for something else, too."

My dad laughs, despite the fact that this creep is hitting on his *underage* daughter. I ignore them completely and go straight to my room, locking the door behind me and barricading it with a chair against the knob, just in case those perverts get any sick ideas while I'm sleeping.

I take the money out of my pocket and slip it in the envelope labeled "bills." Then, I put headphones on and drown them out with the beautiful sound of Ed Sheeran. Placing my school-issued laptop on my bed, I place my fingers on the keys and get to work on my essay.

THE NEXT MORNING, I'M already in a bad mood. My father and his idiotic friends managed to break a window last night, and there were two major altercations where bottles were shattered. Needless to say, I got practically no sleep at all.

I'm quiet as Brady drives me to school, drifting in and out of sleep in the passenger seat. He tells me to have a good day, like a caring big brother, and I make my way into the building. When I get to my locker, Carter looks me up and down.

"Late night with the boy toy?" he inquires, only half joking, but I don't give him an answer. If they want to think *that's* why I'm so exhausted, so be it. It's better than the truth.

The bell rings, but as I go to walk to class, Grayson steps in front of me, blocking my way. Some of our friends stop to wait, but he gives them a look that makes them all walk away. *So much for loyalty.*

I watch him expectantly, too tired to argue, but he doesn't say anything. Once the hallways are empty, he spins us and pins me to the lockers. My back slams against the cold, hard metal as his hand wraps around my neck.

"Does your boyfriend know what a fucking *liar* you are?" he spits. The anger seeping out of him is evident as I pull at his wrist.

"I'm not a liar, and I haven't done anything to you. Get off me!"

A low growl emits from the back of his throat. "*Sweet Savi,* always playing the victim."

"Don't call me that." I try to maintain my composure, but everything coming out of his mouth has the potential to break me. "If you don't like me, fine. Just leave me alone."

He laughs darkly. "That's the thing, I don't just not like you. I *despise* you, and I'm going to make sure you know just how much."

Putting a little more pressure on my neck, he pushes himself away from me and walks toward the classroom, leaving me panting, and for the first time in my life, wondering if Grayson Hayworth has the potential to literally kill me.

6

GRAYSON

I CAN FEEL SAVANNAH'S EYES ON ME AS I LEAVE HER standing there, scared and alone. To be honest, I may have gotten slightly carried away with the way I practically choked her before letting go, but I couldn't help it. I thought she would at least have the decency to own what she did. Instead, she played innocent and pretended she had no idea what my problem is with her. It infuriated me.

With more force than necessary, I pull the door open and step inside the classroom. Mr. Englewood's eyebrows raise at my expression.

"Nice of you to join us, Mr. Hayworth." He gestures forward. "Take your seat so I can continue teaching."

I don't bother answering him as I move to my desk and slip into it. Carter and Jace are watching me curiously, probably wondering where Savannah is, but Kinsley gives me a bright smile—one I return as best I can. If she wasn't so fake all the time, and didn't sleep with half the damn town, she would probably make a pretty good distraction from everything. Unfortunately for her, STDs aren't on my wish list.

A few minutes later, the door opens again and Sav walks

in. She doesn't dare look at me, let alone ask me to sit somewhere else. Instead, she walks straight up to Kinsley and stands in front of her desk.

"Move," Savannah demands.

Her eyes widen. "What? Why?"

"Because I said so. Go sit somewhere else or don't show up for practice today."

She rolls her eyes but ultimately gets up. Savannah takes her seat with a smug look on her face, fist bumping Carter as he fails at controlling his laughter. I'm almost impressed with the way she's managing to stay strong. I half expected her to cower to me, but maybe I underestimated her. She is definitely not the same shy girl I left behind. Then again, perhaps I never knew her at all.

My mom and I pull up to the large gate, rolling down the window to speak to the guard.

"Hello," she says. "We're here to see my husband."

"Inmate or corrections officer, ma'am?"

She swallows. "Inmate."

He types a couple things into his computer before giving us directions and opening the gate. No matter how many times we come here, it never gets any less intimidating. As we walk into the building, we have to go through metal detectors, and they even search my mom's purse. I can't wait for the day my dad gets out of this place. Then he'll be back home with us where he belongs.

Sitting at the table, we wait until two guards bring my dad into the room. His wrists and ankles are shackled, connected to a belt around his waist. The orange jumpsuit is such a contrast to the suits he usually wears. I don't think I'll ever get used to seeing him in here.

"Hi guys!" He greets us excitedly. All I want to do is hug him, but we're not allowed to touch. "I've missed you so much."

My mom gives him a sad smile. It's hard to see how much this has broken her down. My parents have always been inseparable. To see them torn apart like this even makes my heart hurt. Still, I try to make it a point to enjoy these visits. They're the only ones I get.

"I missed you too, Dad! I've been playing with Tyson a lot lately."

He grins. "That's great, bud. You and your cousin should be close. You're family."

I nod. "I miss Savi though. Mommy said maybe next month she'll take me to see her!"

His happy expression drops right off his face, and his eyes narrow on my mother. "You said what?" His voice is a whisper, but you can hear the anger in his tone. "Grayson, there is something I need to tell you."

"Landon," my mom warns. "He's just a child. Don't concern him with this."

"No," he demands. "He needs to know." His attention turns entirely to me. "Gray, buddy, you have to stay away from Savi and her dad."

My brows furrow in confusion. "What? Why? S-she's my best friend."

"Because they're not who you think they are. They're dangerous. I don't want you to get caught up in something that could get you in trouble." It's not nearly the explanation I was looking for, but his face shows his desperation. "You have to promise me you'll stay away from them. I need you to promise."

My stomach churns with the thought of never seeing her again. For the past five years, Savannah has been everything. She's the one I tell all my secrets to. The one who can cheer me up when I'm having a bad day. The one who gets my heart racing just by smiling at me. But as I'm sitting here, seeing the sheer terror in his eyes at the idea of me being anywhere near her, I can't help but agree.

"Okay, I promise."

The fact that I'm breaking the last promise I made to my dad weighs heavily on me. However, after finding what I did only a few months ago, I knew I had to come back. To let her get away with ruining my entire life is not something I'm willing to do. If it takes breaking a promise in order for Savannah to get what's coming to her, then so be it.

THE CAFETERIA IS CROWDED with students trying to get their lunch fast enough to be able to eat it. By the time I walk in, Savannah is already at the table with Carter, Jace, and Emma. I spot the seat next to her royal bitchness and smirk, making my way over and plopping my ass right next to her. The way her whole body tenses at my presence does not go unnoticed. *Perfect. I want her to fear me.*

"Grayson, just the man I wanted to see." Carter slaps my back. "Practice was moved from tomorrow to this afternoon. So, make sure you're there."

"You got it."

Kinsley sits down across from me, looking at me like a heart-eyed emoji. Savannah follows her gaze to me then drops the pen she was holding onto the table.

"Kins, be a doll and go get me a blackberry Snapple."

She gives her a disbelieving look. "I just sat down."

Savannah leans her elbows on the table and levels her with a look. "You'll be *sitting down* plenty at practice if you don't go get me a blackberry Snapple." Kinsley sighs but gets up to do it anyway. "And don't come back without one."

As soon as she walks away, Jace smirks. "Do they even sell that here?"

"Nope," she replies, popping the P for emphasis. "I had to get rid of that chick. She's been getting on my last nerve lately."

He chuckles. "Not everyone can be flawlessly gorgeous with a killer personality, Sav."

"Flawlessly gorgeous, huh?"

"Oh, come on. Don't act like you don't know it." His fingers run through his hair, messing it up intentionally. "Whenever you decide to ditch that Brady fucker, just say the word, babe, and I'll pick you up."

She laughs. "I may just take you up on that."

Unable to listen to their blatant flirting any longer, I subtly sneak my hand under the table and grip onto her thigh. She lets out a squeal as she jumps, and then smacks my wrist. Everyone looks confused, but I play it off perfectly. The conversation between Savannah and Jace is effectively ended, and if the way she lets my hand stay on her leg is any indication, that's exactly how she wants it.

The thought of Savannah being with any guy puts an uneasy feeling in my stomach. There was a point in time where she belonged to me, and swore it would stay that way. Now, she's anything but mine.

I know I shouldn't want her. It's bad enough that I'm here. To even be friends with her again would be a completely betrayal to my dad and *not* something I'm interested in. So, I force away the feelings that come alive when she's near and chalk them up to teenage hormones and nostalgia.

THE COACH HAS US running drills and practicing our throws. Personally, I liked practice better when Carter was in charge. All he did was had us scrimmage for a couple hours and run some plays out of the book. Today, however, we're under different authority—which means drills.

Running back and forth across the field is annoying, but nothing is worse than seeing the entire team basically undress Savannah with their eyes. A few of them don't even try to hide it, whistling at her as she bends over to stretch. I clench my fist when I hear it, and it takes every ounce of restraint I have to keep from pounding their faces into the ground.

"All right. Shirts versus skins," Coach announces. "We're going to run plays for the next half hour."

He calls out names to be on the skins' team, including myself, Jace, and Wyatt—so we pull our shirts off and toss them onto the sidelines. We call tails on the coin toss, getting the ball first. As I listen to Coach tell me the play, I'm having trouble focusing. Savannah is on the sidelines, wearing her booty shorts and a tight-fitting tank top. It leaves practically nothing to the imagination, and I'm drowning in the thoughts of her skin and curves.

"Hayworth!" Coach yells in my face. "Get your damn head in the game!"

I roll my eyes as I jog over to the guys. After I repeat the play, we get into formation. I receive the ball from Wyatt and throw it down the field to Peyton. No part of me cares to watch how it plays out. I'm too focused on Savannah.

It's as if I can still feel the softness of her skin. The way her body fit against mine as I had her pressed up against the locker. If she was able to feel my heart racing in that moment, it would have given everything away—but God, she felt so damn good against me.

It isn't until Wyatt steps up beside me that I even acknowledge there are other people around.

"Don't even think about it, man. You're wasting your time," he tells me.

I don't turn away. "No idea what you're talking about."

"Savannah. I see the way you're looking at her, but trust me. You don't have a chance. She only dates college guys. Specifically, ones named Brady Laurence."

I chuckle and shake my head. "You've got me all wrong, man. I don't *want* a chance with her."

"Dude, do you see her? She's the hottest girl in school,"

he deadpans, letting his eyes drift over to Sav. "Everyone wants one."

A mumbled groan of obscenities leaves my mouth as I walk away from him and down the field. It's hard enough to deal with the fact that I'm feeling things for her I shouldn't. Hell, every part of me should hate her with a burning passion, and most of me does. But there is still part of me that wants to throw myself at her feet and give her everything she's ever wanted. I need to get this shit under control before it ruins me—before *she* ruins me. Again.

I PULL UP TO my house, wanting nothing more than to go inside, take a shower, and climb into my bed. However, fate must have other plans for me, because just as I'm about to get out of my car, Justin walks out the front door. Every bit of frustration that has built up over the past few days boils inside of me. Slamming my car door shut, I storm up to him until I'm right up in his face.

"The fuck are you doing here? Didn't I tell your ass to stay away from her?" I don't budge as he tries to push me back a little.

"Your mother is a big girl. She can make her own choices."

I growl, ready to hit the prick. "Like hell she can. She proved that shit wrong when I had to knock your ass out as you tried to strangle her to death."

The smirk that graces his face tells me he would do it again if given the chance. "Yeah, well, clearly she doesn't quite mind a little breath play. Your mom is quite the freak."

Without letting him get another word out, I swing my fist right into the side of his face, immediately knocking him off balance. "Don't ever fucking talk to me about her like that again! Do you hear me?"

"Watch it, Grayson." He stretches out his jaw. "You're eighteen now. There is nothing to keep me from kicking your ass."

I step toward him, once again leaving him with no personal space. "I'd *love* to see you try."

The door opens and my mother stands there, wide eyed and panicked. "What the hell is going on out here?"

My hand pushes Justin down onto the lower step. "I'm just telling this prick to stay the fuck away from places he doesn't belong."

"Grayson!" She hisses.

"What? You know what—I'll make this real fucking easy for you. It's him or me, because I'm not just going to sit here and play happy family with him until he decides to try his hand at attempted murder again."

My mom glances between him and me, not saying a word. When I realize she isn't going to answer, I shake my head.

"Un-fucking-believable."

Ignoring the calls of my name, I get back into my car. My tires squeal against the pavement as I peel out of the driveway. That answer should be one of the simplest decisions of her life. What kind of mother would hesitate when needing to choose between her son or the man who almost took her life? All I know for sure, is that my father would be disgusted with who she's become.

I'M DRIVING AROUND, TRYING to kill time and calm down before I go back home. Since we moved back, I haven't really gotten a chance to look around this place. So much has changed from what I remember. The restaurants have all either closed down or been renovated. The stores I remember going to have all been replaced, except for the big department stores. Even the playground I used to love has been torn down. It's just another harsh reminder that nothing in my life will ever be the same as it was.

As I pull down Main Street, a familiar Cadillac catches my eye. The same Haven Grace Prep sticker sits in the back window, making me sure it's his car. *Savannah's boyfriend.* Even thinking about him enrages me. She was supposed to be *mine*. She and I stood there in that stupid treehouse and promised that when we were old enough, we would get married. We may have only been nine at the time, but I've never meant something more in my life. And then she went and ruined it.

I park my car and get out. It only takes a second before my eyes land on her. She's moving gracefully across a dance studio floor. I lean against the hood and watch her through the large window. The way she throws herself into every movement, telling a story using only her body—it's mesmerizing. She lifts her leg as she spins, completing so many rotations I'm getting dizzy just watching her, but she doesn't seem to falter at all. She continues to move in ways that make me imagine myself pressed against her as her ass grinds into me, touching all the right places.

Like the universe is playing some kind of sick joke on me, she's suddenly not alone. Brady joins her and runs his hands over her shoulders. They move together in synchrony, but it's clear everything he's doing is meant to showcase her.

I glance up at the name of the studio and it all comes flooding back to me. An eight-year-old Savi, sitting in my room and telling me about the boy she met at dance. Her teacher's son. I didn't like him then, and I sure as shit don't like him now. *Brady Laurence just became another one of my targets.*

7

SAVANNAH

I'M GETTING READY FOR SCHOOL IN THE MORNING when the doorbell rings. I freeze. The last time someone came here this early, it was a big guy ready to wring my dad's neck for owing him money. Still, after the second time, I head to the door.

"Savannah Montgomery?" a guy asks, looking down at his clipboard then back up at me.

"Yes?"

He smiles. "We're here to install a new window. Mind showing me where it's going?"

"Uh, sure." I answer hesitantly and lead him into the house.

I'm not stupid enough to believe my father used his precious drug and alcohol money on a new window. The night it broke, he sat in a drunken stupor and watched as I cut my hand on the broken glass and then covered the gaping hole with a large piece of cardboard. No, this has to be the work of someone else.

"It's this one." Pointing to the window, I back away. "I have to go to school. My dad is asleep in his room, I think. So just lock the door behind you when you leave."

He nods and then gets to work, starting to remove the makeshift cover.

I grab my bag from my room and head out to where Brady is already waiting. It's unusually chilly for a September morning in California, so when I climb into the car, I welcome the warmth. He looks over at me and grins as he puts the car in drive.

"New window?"

"Yeah." I sigh. "Thank you."

He chuckles at how I already know who's responsible. "Don't mention it."

We pull up to the school a short while later, only to find Kinsley hanging out with Grayson, *alone*. She's laughing at something he said as he smokes his cancer stick. A sickening feeling settles in the pit of my stomach at the sight.

"What the hell is Grayson doing with *her*?" Brady asks.

I roll my eyes and sink into the seat. "I'm pretty sure he's using her to make me jealous. Though, I don't think *she* knows that."

The bad blood between Kinsley and me goes back for years, which is why no one gets involved or tries to defend her when I treat her like shit. When we were freshman, she saw me as a threat, and in a horrible attempt to ruin me, she told police that I tried to rape her little brother. It was as sick and twisted as she is. Thankfully, her brother denied all allegations, and her parents got her to admit that she made the whole thing up.

After that, I kept to the age-old saying: *keep your friends close, and your enemies closer.* As messed up as she is, it makes more sense to keep her on my side. Otherwise, she'd spend all her time thinking of new psychotic ways to mess with me, and I don't need her finding out my secret. However, all this shit she's pulling with Grayson is really pissing me off. She may already think I'm a bitch, but if she keeps this up, she's going to find out just how ruthless I can be.

THE MORNING IS SO slow that I almost consider trying to leave early. It's only second period, and I'm doing by best to ignore the unfortunate blast from my past beside me. If he's trying to be subtle with the looks he's shooting my way, he's failing miserably. A part of me wants to snap at him, but I have a feeling it would do no good.

Halfway through the class, I stand from my desk and walk up to Miss Layton. She eyes me curiously, leaning back in her chair.

"How can I help you, Savannah?"

I fake a smile. "Can I have a hall pass? I need to use the ladies room."

It's obvious she wants to protest, but she pulls the pad from her desk and signs it anyway. *Smart woman.* I take the paper and thank her as I leave the room. It's not that my need to pee is dire, but my need to get some space from Grayson is. When I have people around to distract me, it's easier to ignore him, but when it's just the two of us, my focus stays solely on him.

Maybe I could get Brady to pick me up. It wouldn't be the first time he's signed me out of school. His mom is on my emergency contact list, and he just acts like he's picking me up for her. He and I could go back to the studio to rehearse some more. Dancing is exactly what I need right now—to throw my body into the music and forget the world around me.

I finish my business and flush the toilet with my foot, because there's no way in hell would I ever touch that thing with my hand. As I'm standing at the sink, the door opens, and Grayson walks in. *Fucking fantastic.* I throw away the paper towel and turn to face him.

"You know, you might be lacking in male genitalia, but the guys' bathroom is across the hall."

He narrows his eyes on me, and I think I even see the corner of his mouth twitch—but that could be my mind playing tricks on me. "Funny, because the Savi I knew would turn bright red at the slightest mention of a dick."

I cross my arms and lean back against the cool ceramic. "That girl is long gone."

"So I've noticed." He crosses the distance between us and reaches his hand out to brush the hair out of my face. "It's a shame. She was my favorite."

He's so close that his scent overtakes my senses. The smell of smoke masked over by cologne, yet still him. I don't dare to move as he brings his hand to the back of my neck and presses his forehead against mine. Even after all these years, he's makes my whole body come alive. Every nerve ending concentrates on his touch. He remains still, his lips only millimeters from mine.

"Gray." I whisper, but regret the nickname as soon as it comes out of my mouth.

He tenses instantly, and the energy in the room changes. His grip tightens as he pulls back, and the fire in his dark blue eyes sends fear straight through me.

"Don't call me that," he growls. "*You* don't get to fucking call me that."

My brows furrow. "What happened to you?"

The dark chuckle that comes from his mouth echoes around the small room. "Isn't it obvious, Savannah?" My name is like poison on his tongue. "*You* happened to me. There isn't a single thing in my life that you haven't ruined. Broken everything that ever meant anything to me. Now, I won't stop until *I break you.*"

His hand clenches around my necklace, and with one harsh pull, he snaps it right off my neck. The one thing I held onto all these years—the only thing that reassured me my life wasn't always a fucking disaster—is in the hand of the one who gave it to me. As he storms out, I can't control it as I break down. The tears pour from my eyes as my hand searches for the piece of jewelry I know is no longer there. Somehow, it doesn't feel like he just took back a gift that meant the world to me. It's like he's taking back our entire past together, and I don't know how to handle that.

I TRIED TO GET Brady to pick me up, but unfortunately, he was visiting Jake at work. He offered to leave, but the last thing I want is for my best friend's boyfriend to feel like I'm stealing even more of his time than I already do. So, I told him I'd stick it out and see him at the end of the day. Thank God it's Friday, because I don't know how much more of this I can take.

It would be one thing if I knew why Grayson hates me so much. I've spent more time than I'd like to admit racking my brain for anything I've done wrong, but nothing comes to mind. He's the one who left without saying goodbye. He's the one who vanished from my life and broke my heart in the process. Every promise we ever made, every dream we ever had, was gone along with him. I've never felt as alone as I did that day.

The cafeteria is crowded as I walk over to our table and sit down. Jace and Carter are already there, as usual. They must see how defeated I feel because they share a concerned look before Carter reaches over and places his hand on mine.

"Are you all right?"

I shrug. "I'm fine. Just over this week."

He nods slowly and then smirks. "This wouldn't have anything to do with a certain moody quarterback, would it?"

"Don't mention Grayson to me," I snap. "Seriously, don't."

He raises his hands in surrender. "Okay, okay. No need to bite my head off."

I'm about to apologize when the rest of the table fills, including my two least favorite people. I hadn't seen Grayson since he walked out of the bathroom with my favorite belonging. No part of me wanted to go back to second period, so I told the nurse I didn't feel well and wanted to lie down. She sent someone to get my things, and I spent the rest of class there. With him being in all four of my classes, I've never considered changing my schedule so much in my life.

He takes the seat next to Kinsley, making me roll my eyes and focus on my phone. How am I supposed to have an appetite when I have *that* sitting in front of me? She giggles at something he says and slides her tray over to share with him. It's sickening, and almost makes me feel bad for her. *Almost.* Anyone with eyes can see that he's not actually interested. For some reason, he's got this undying need to torment me, and he's using her to do it.

A tap on my shoulder pulls my attention away. Lennon, a junior here and someone I know from dance, stands behind me. Her blonde hair and bright red lipstick are only a small part of what makes her gorgeous. She's a little spitfire, both on and off the dance floor. She's the only other person besides Brady who I'll do a duet with. No one else can keep up.

"Hey, Lennon. What's up?"

She smiles sweetly. "My dad is stuck in some business meeting today, and the chauffeur is sick. Do you think I could catch a ride with you and Brady to dance?"

I nod. "Of course, babes. Just meet me out front after school."

"Thank you."

"No problem."

She's about to walk away when a familiar voice stops her. "And who might *you* be, beautiful?"

Her eyes land on Grayson and widen. However, before she has a chance to answer, I put my hand up.

"Don't answer him, Len. He's a pig." To my relief, she laughs and walks away—taking my advice. I focus my attention solely on Grayson. "Leave her alone. She's too good for you."

He scoffs. "Whatever." He turns to Kinsley. "Babe, let's get out of here."

I don't miss the evil glint in her eye as she stands and walks away with his arm draped over her shoulders. If I had eaten anything at all, it would have come back up after seeing that. I'd rather him be with anyone but her, and the problem is, I think he knows that.

"He's got balls, hitting on Lennon Bradwell like that," Jace remarks. "Her dad would have his head on a silver platter by nightfall."

Carter snickers. "I don't think he knows anything about her. Might have been fun to watch if jealous Judy over here didn't ruin it for us."

I groan. "I'm not jealous. She just has the recital to focus on. It needs to be perfect. No distractions."

"Sure. We'll go with that," he quips then turns to Jace. "I wonder if he was this much a player in Campton."

In a single second, all the air gets sucked out of my lungs. "Campton?" I croak. "As in, an hour away, Campton?"

Jace nods. "Do you know of any others?"

Red lights go off in my head as I get up from the table and march out of the cafeteria. I know chasing them down is a bad idea, but I can't help it. Thankfully, I find them in the hallway, not far from Grayson's locker. I go directly up to them and narrow my eyes on Kinsley.

"Leave."

She crosses her arms. "No."

Grayson must know something is up because he presses a kiss to her forehead and then pushes her away. "Go, babe. I'll find you after."

Kinsley glares at me as she walks away. Once she is gone, all my anger is aimed directly on Grayson.

"Campton?" I shout. "All this time, you were in *fucking Campton?*" He closes his locker and leans against it but doesn't say anything. "Do you know how hard I tried to find you? How many times I looked for you and came up empty? You left me! I came back from my grandmother's house, and you were fucking *gone*! And now I find out you were only an hour away?" I press my hands against his chest. "I couldn't fucking find you!"

He grabs my wrists and shoves me off him. "I didn't want to be found, especially not by you. Ever think of that?"

It's like a punch directly to the gut, because no, I hadn't thought of that. Why would I? He was my best friend. The two of us were inseparable. No part of me considered the fact that he wouldn't want anything to do with me.

Before I give him the satisfaction of seeing me cry, I shake my head and take a step back. "Fuck you, Grayson."

"In your dreams."

I don't justify him with an answer as I walk away, knowing I can only hold back my emotions for so long. The part of me that was once hard as stone is breaking in his presence. I need to learn how to control myself before I let him destroy everything I worked so hard to attain.

THE MUSIC FILLS THE studio as I throw myself into every move. All the anger, the sadness, the pent-up frustrations—I let it all out in the best way I know how. Losing myself in the song, I hardly notice anyone around me. The dance everything I need right now, and as the beat fades away, I collapse to the floor, breathing heavily but feeling less like a glass squeezed to the breaking point.

"If I ever become half the dancer you are, I'll be so happy," Lennon says with a sigh.

I sit up and chuckle. "Shut up. You're amazing. Don't even."

"Maybe so, but you're something else. The way you tell a story with your body, it's everything a dancer aspires to be."

"She's right," Brady says as he helps me off the floor. "Though I know you well enough to know that had more to do with personal issues and less to do with the choreography."

We walk over and sit down next to Lennon. Everyone else has since gone home, but Brady is Lennon's ride, so she stayed to hang out.

"And I take it this is when you interrogate me?" I joke. He does a quick side glance at Lennon, mentally asking if he shouldn't say anything, but I shake my head. "It's fine."

"Grayson again?" he guesses.

I give him a sad smile. "Nothing gets by you, does it?"

"Is that the new guy? The one you told me to ignore at lunch?" Lennon questions.

I nod. "That's the one."

"He's like, crazy hot," she says, but then backtracks as she sees Brady wince. "I'm sorry. Was that wrong of me to say?"

"No, it's fine," I reassure her. "He and I just have a history."

Brady snorts. "If that's what you want to call it." He turns to Lennon. "They were married."

"What?" she shrieks.

"Oh my God, don't listen to him. We were eight."

I spend twenty minutes getting a confused Lennon up to speed on everything, and then another ten telling her and Brady everything that happened today. By the time I'm done, I realized I've been absentmindedly rubbing my hand against where my necklace used to be. I feel completely naked without it.

"Ew, what a dick." Lennon makes a face of disgust. "And Kinsley, too. Isn't she supposed to be your friend? Hasn't she ever heard of girl code?"

I can't help but smile at how angry she is *for* me. "Kinsley has never been my friend. It's just easier to keep tabs on her crazy ass when she's close by."

"Ah, okay. That makes more sense."

"Well, there's only one thing left that you can do," Brady says with a frown. "Act like he doesn't exist."

I scoff. "Easier said than done, B."

He shakes his head. "No, listen. He clearly has some kind of vendetta against you, and he's out for blood. The best way to beat that is to completely ignore him. Fight fire with fire, and you risk getting burned. But, if you leave the fire to starve, it'll eventually burn out."

I ponder his words as Lennon hums. "He's got a point."

Brady smiles. "Take the weekend to get it all out of your system. Then, starting Monday, you act like you don't even know who he is—because let's face it, you don't. Not anymore."

8

GRAYSON

I LOOK AROUND BEFORE CROSSING THE STREET AND slipping behind North Haven High—the hood on my sweatshirt pulled over my head. The last thing I need is someone at Haven Grace seeing me over here. I'd not only get the third degree from Carter, but someone may catch onto my plans. I don't need any of that happening.

"Grayson Hayworth," Knox greets me, though I wasn't aware he knew my name. "You're on the wrong side of the street, aren't you?"

His friends surround him, eyeing me like I'm the devil just for stepping foot on their territory. He's not the kind of person you would expect to be the captain of the football team. His tattoo-covered body and his obvious tendency for drug use would lead me to think he'd be more partial to being lazy and partying all the time. Still, he's the best one for the job I'm looking for.

"I need something from you."

A dry laugh leaves his mouth. "Do I look like your fucking slave, pretty boy?" I take the wad of cash out of my pocket and toss it to him. His eyes widen at the large sum of money, and he gestures his friend toward me. "Hook him up."

I shake my head when I see the guy digging in his pocket. "I'm not looking for drugs."

"Then what is it you want? Don't tell me Haven Grace's new quarterback is gay. This is a lot of money, but I won't drop to my knees for anyone."

The thought alone is repulsive and I cringe. "What's wrong with you, man? I just need you to follow someone for me." He raises one eyebrow, looking for me to elaborate. "Brady Laurence."

"Ah," he says with a nod. "Princess's boyfriend."

"I need to know when he's alone. In the middle of the cash is a piece of paper with my number on it. Call me when no one is with him, especially Savannah."

I spent almost the entire weekend lurking outside of the studio. I watched her as she danced for hours on end, somehow looking even more breathtakingly beautiful than she usually does. Every part of me wanted to go in there and claim what has been mine from the start, and it took all the restraint I had not to.

On Friday, when we were alone in that bathroom, I was seconds away from giving in. Had she not called me by the nickname that no longer belongs to her, I may have. Hearing that name slip from her lips brought me back to reality. A reality where she and I can never be what we once were. But damn did I want to go right back to that, which is exactly why I'm here.

If I've learned anything over the last week, it's that the first thing I need to do is separate her from those keeping her strong—in particular, Brady. Seeing the way that she is with him doesn't just make my blood boil—it shows their comfort level together. I want to take that from her, along with everything else good in her life.

"Consider it done," Knox tells me. "You'll hear from me soon."

With that I leave, anticipating his call and the next part of my plan.

DAYS PASS, AND I'M starting to get impatient. Not only have I heard nothing from Knox, but something is different about Savannah. She hasn't so much as looked at me this week. The glares I send her have decreased down to glances and still go completely unnoticed. I can't tell if she genuinely just doesn't care, or she's doing it to piss me off. If it's the latter, it's fucking working.

Even as I flirt with Kinsley right in front of her, she doesn't acknowledge it. Judging by the way Carter keeps looking at her, waiting to see what she does, he's thinking the same thing. All I know is that Knox better do the damn job I paid him for, or I'll take my anger out on him instead.

I'm sitting next to Savannah at lunch, trying to make her uncomfortable but having no luck. She's focused on her notebook, writing down what looks like either cheerleading stunts or dance moves.

"Grayson," Kinsley whines to get my attention. "Come sit next to me. I'm cold."

It's a somewhat tempting offer, and if Sav had the slightest reaction to it, I'd probably do it. However, the less she cares about me flaunting her so-called *friend* in her face, the less appeal it has.

"Kins, stop pissing off Savannah. You're going get kicked off the team," Becca hisses.

Kinsley is about to defend herself when Sav looks up. "No, it's fine Bec. If Grayson wants to get chlamydia, that's on him." For the first time all week, her eyes land on me. "Though I can't imagine you'd be a very good quarterback with your junk on fire."

A bright, involuntary smile spreads across my face. I bite my lip to contain it but it's pointless. It's been days since her attention was on me, and no matter how much I try to push it down, I can't fight the feeling that courses through me at having it again. She seems caught off guard, and her breath hitches for a second, but the moment is quickly interrupted.

"Are you seriously going to let her talk about me like that?" Kinsley shrieks.

Everyone at the table, sans me and Savannah, are struggling to hold in their laughter—making it very hard to keep my composure. Still, I turn my attention to her.

"You really want a knight in shining armor to come to your defense? I thought you were stronger than that."

Savannah chuckles and levels her with a look. "She wouldn't dare."

Kinsley opens and closes her mouth before getting up and flouncing out of the room. The second she's gone, the whole table breaks out in hysterics. Carter looks like he's about to piss himself, and Wyatt's face is bright red as he clutches his stomach and tries to breathe. In complete curiosity, I focus on Savannah.

"What do you have on her, anyway?"

She's back to writing in her notebook, but she mumbles a response. "What do you mean?"

"There has to be some reason she's afraid of you, or at least a reason you hate her so much."

Shrugging, she packs up her things and gets up from the table. "Psychotic bitches just aren't my forte."

Leaving that as her explanation, she leaves the cafeteria. My eyes stay glued to her until she's out of sight, and I'd be lying if I said a part of me didn't want to go with her.

"Bro, you're so fucked," Jace comments.

"Huh?"

He shakes his head. "She has a boyfriend, and even if she didn't, you don't have a chance in hell."

I roll my eyes. "Like I've told you before, stuck-up bitches aren't my thing."

"And yet you flirt with Kinsley."

Little do they know, every single thing I've done since I got to this place was to get a reaction out of Savannah. Still, I don't know where their loyalties lie. I may be their teammate, but they've known her for years.

A devious smirk appears as I chuckle. "What can I say? A mouth is a mouth."

I SIT ON THE window sill, smoking a cigarette and watching as the rain pours down outside. I should be at practice right now, but it was canceled on account of the weather. The house has been empty since I got here. God only knows where my mother is—probably out with Justin. I have half a mind to just kill him and claim self-defense. With his record, I'm sure I'd get away with it, and then I wouldn't have to worry about him showing up here anymore.

A car pulls into the driveway of the house across the street—Savannah's old house—and for the first time, I get a glance at the person who lives there now. She's a young woman, probably early thirties. Judging by the stickers on the back of her car, she has a husband, two young kids, and a dog. I wonder if she knows the things that have happened in that house. The kind of secrets it holds.

I knock on the door, anxious to show Savi the new walkie-talkies my dad bought me. After a couple seconds, I get impatient and go to knock again when it opens. Savannah's dad smiles down at me.

"Hey, Grayson."

"Hi, Mr. Montgomery. Is Savi here?"

He nods and opens the door wider to let me in. "She's in her room. Go on up, and I'll make you two a snack."

I run up the stairs and into Savannah's bedroom, only to find her sitting on the bed with tears in her eyes. Dropping the walkie-talkies to the ground, I climb up and sit beside her. I tuck my hand into my sweatshirt sleeve and use it to wipe the tears from her face.

"What happened?"

She sniffles. "A boy in school called me ugly."

I don't know who this boy is, or why he had the nerve to call the most beautiful girl I've ever seen ugly, but I already want to punch him in the face. This is why I wanted us to be in the same class, so I could be there to protect her from things like this. But our parents insisted we have at least some distance from each other. Stupid parents.

"He doesn't know what he's talking about."

A small smile graces her face. "My dad said boys who pick on you do it because they like you."

If I wasn't mad before, I am now. The idea of Savi spending time with any boy but me makes me want to lock her in my treehouse and never let her out. Catching me off guard, she looks up at me through watery eyes.

"Do you make fun of any girls in your class?"

I shake my head and watch as relief washes over her. She looks away and rests her head on my shoulder. "Good."

"Yeah...good."

I knew then that there was something more to her than just my best friend, and I made it a point to find out who made her cry. He wasn't hard to find on the playground. It was fun to watch him go and apologize to Savannah. Even at eight years old, I was so protective of her.

How do you fight feelings that are basically wired into your brain? That girl has more control over me than I've ever been willing to give anyone, and it's only a matter of time before she figures that out. From the desire to have her attention on me at all times, to the way I've almost given in to temptation—if I don't get a grip, I'm screwed.

I've already let my guard down around Savannah once. There's no way I can do that again. I damn near didn't make it through the first time she wreaked havoc on my life. She'll never get the opportunity to hurt me like that a second time. I won't allow it.

Taking out my phone, I scroll down to the one contact I need to stop myself from continuing down memory lane. It only rings twice before a giggly voice comes through.

"Hey, you," Kinsley greets.

"What are you up to right now?"

I can practically hear her grin. "Oh, you know. Just hanging out in my room—alone."

"Good," I murmur, putting my shoes on. "Send me the address. I'll be right over."

KINSLEY STANDS IN FRONT of me, wearing nothing but a T-shirt and panties. I growl as I push into the house and kick the door shut behind me. Within seconds, she's all over me. My lips press into her neck, trying to ignore the fact that her skin just isn't as soft as Savannah's. That she doesn't smell like Savannah. That she doesn't turn me on just by existing. *No, this is to forget her.*

Grabbing my hand, she leads me up and into her bedroom. The pink walls and white decor remind me of an innocent little girl. Do her parents know she's hardly the princess this room seems to describe? I wonder how many other guys have bent her over that bed.

"You have no idea how bad I've wanted this," she tells me as she steps further into the room.

"Oh yeah? Why don't you show me?"

She comes closer, grabbing onto my waistband and

75

undoing the button and zipper. Her hand slips into my boxers and wraps around my cock. I kiss her roughly, letting my tongue tangle with hers in order to get myself to harden, but it's no use. She's not...

At the mere thought of Savannah, my dick comes to life. The thought of her doing this to me, being able to touch her like this—within seconds, I'm rock hard. I keep my eyes closed as Kinsley pulls my pants and boxers down to free me. She drops to her knees and takes me into her mouth. This may have started out as a way to forget, but instead, all I can picture is *her*.

I lace my fingers into Kinsley's hair, imagining it being blonde, and thrust myself into the back of her throat. She doesn't protest. Instead, she places her hands on the back of my legs and encourages me. As she takes me deeper and deeper, she gags around my length. I moan, mentally picturing Savannah with tears in her eyes as she chokes on my cock.

It doesn't take long before I'm exploding into her mouth with a silent plea of the wrong name. We're both panting as she swallows everything I've given her and rises to her feet. She rests her arms on my shoulders and goes to kiss me, but I turn my head just in time.

"Do I look like I want to taste my own damn cum?"

She smirks. "Fine, you can just taste mine then."

Pulling me toward the bed, Savannah's words replay in my mind. *If Grayson wants to get chlamydia, that's on him.* I'm sure it was just a vicious dig, but I don't think that's something I'm willing to risk. I detach her hand from my wrist and pull my pants up.

"Sorry babe, maybe another time."

Her outrage is evident. "Are you kidding me?"

Just as I'm about to answer, my phone rings. I pull it out and practically jump at the sight of Knox's name on the screen. Holding one finger up at Kinsley, I answer the call.

"What's up?"

"I've got a location for you, but you better come quick. Can't guarantee he'll stay here long."

I grin, knowing I'm finally going to get him alone. "Text it to me. I'll be right there."

Hanging up the phone, I find Kinsley glaring at me still. "Are you seriously leaving? What about me?"

My eyes land on her nightstand, and I go over to it. I open the drawer and, sure enough, there is a bright pink vibrator. I take it out and toss it onto her bed. "Use that."

I race down the stairs and into my car, putting the address Knox sent me into my GPS.

WHEN I SPOT BRADY, he's leaning up against the wall of some bar. It looks like he's waiting for someone, so I know I need to make this fast. The last thing I want is for Savannah to show up in the middle of what I'm about to do.

I climb out of my car and walk up to him. When his gaze lands on me, his eyes widen, and he looks around before focusing on me again.

"Grayson, right?" He asks. "What can I do for you?"

I stick my hands in my pockets. "For starters, you can stay the fuck away from Savannah."

"Excuse me?"

"You heard me. If you know what's good for you, you'll break up with her."

He chuckles, amused by all of this. "And if I don't?"

I smile, looking like I'm going to leave, before turning back around and swinging a right hook into the side of his head. It feels good to do that, being as I've wanted to for years—even as a kid. His eyes narrow on me as he grips his jaw.

"The fuck, man?"

I get into his face. "I told you, break up with Savannah and stay the fuck away."

"Why, so you can have your way with her? Not a fucking chance."

Another punch lands straight to his nose and I feel the bone snap against my fist. This time, he reacts, coming at me swinging. He lands one hit to my head before I knock him to the ground with a kick to the stomach. I climb on top of him, pummeling my fists into his face repeatedly. One for taking her attention from me when we were younger. One for having it all the time I've been gone. One for standing in the way of my plan. One for getting everything that was always meant to be mine.

"Get off him!" a guy screams.

Before I know it, two bouncers from the bar are pulling me away. My hands are covered in blood, and I grin evilly as I watch some guy help a dazed Brady get up. Judging by the look in his eyes, I know I got my point across.

I'm ushered into a small office-like room with two men that I don't think it would be smart to try and fight. One of them pulls out a phone and calls the police, telling them they've got someone who needs to be picked up. I roll my eyes, thinking about my mom having to bail me out. It won't be the first time, but it's still something I'd like to avoid.

"How much do you want to pretend like you didn't see anything tonight?"

They share a look before shaking their heads. "We don't take bribes from arrogant pricks like you who think money solves everything."

If only they knew me. "Let me explain. That guy tried to rape my girlfriend. I was only protecting her."

One of them starts laughing, like it's the most absurd thing he's ever heard, and the other smiles in amusement. Still, there's no way they're budging. *Guess I'm spending my night in a jail cell.*

I'M STARING UP AT the ceiling, counting the tiles, when my name is called. I stand up to find a familiar face, Travis Kennedy. He's a lieutenant here, and used to be good friends with my father before his arrest. I smile as he looks me up and down and shakes his head.

"Grayson," he greets. "What are you doing locked up? Like father, like son?"

I give him a hug, being as it's been years since I've seen him. "Why can I say? I had something I needed to take care of."

He leads us away from the cells and to the front. "I never took you for a homophobe. You're lucky Mr. Laurence doesn't want to press charges. His boyfriend has been screaming 'hate crime' for hours."

"Hate crime?" I ask, confused, until the other words sink in. "Wait, boyfriend? Brady is gay?"

Looking at me like I've grown an extra head, he nods. "Wasn't that why you beat the shit out of him?"

Suddenly, it all makes sense. Why she doesn't talk about her relationship with him. Why he dances with her at the studio. Who that guy was who was helping him up after I pummeled his face in. He isn't *Savannah's* boyfriend. He has a boyfriend of his own.

If she's pretending to be dating a gay guy, there must be a reason for it—and I'm determined to find out what that is.

"Hey, Travis, do you happen to have Savannah Montgomery's new address? I've been trying to find her since I got back to town, but she doesn't live across the street anymore."

He looks hesitant at first, but ultimately types the name into the computer. I may have found what I need after all.

9

SAVANNAH

I WAKE IN THE MORNING, FEELING MORE ALONE than I usually do. As I go into the kitchen, I notice the house is still clean. Yesterday, when cheer practice was canceled, I danced for an hour before Brady had to get ready for his date with Jacob. So, having nothing better to do, I cleaned the house. However, usually that doesn't stop my father from messing it up.

Walking down the small hallway, I find his bedroom empty. *Of course.* I grab my phone and make the usual phone calls, finding him at the hospital this time. Well, at least there's that. They tell me he had a drunken accident at a friend's house and managed to step on a nail that went right through his foot. I cringe at the thought, but it serves him right. Maybe if he was sober, it wouldn't have happened.

I make quick work of taking a shower and getting ready for school, being able to enjoy the clean house for a change. Once I'm done, I hear Brady pull up and head out the door.

"Hey. I need you to take me to the hospital first, my dad will be getting discharged s—" My words are cut off as I take in my best friend, who looks like he got hit by a truck. "What the fuck happened to you?"

He has a cut above his eyebrow, his lip is split open, his nose is clearly broken, and he's covered in bruises. I reach over to run my hand across his cheekbone but pull away when he winces.

"It's nothing."

My eyes narrow. "It sure as shit isn't nothing. Who the fuck did this to you?"

He shakes his head. "Don't worry about it, Rocky. I'm fine."

"No," I stop him, hand in the air. "What the fuck happened, Brady?"

Looking down at the steering wheel, he finally sighs. "Grayson came to find me last night, and we got into it."

"Grayson did this?!" The outrage coursing through my veins is enough to take down an entire army. "I'm going to kill him."

"Don't. I'm telling you, I'll be fine. So, hospital? What did your idiot dad get himself into this time?"

I glare at him. "Stop trying to change the subject. Take me to school."

"But what about your dad?"

"He's a grown man, in a hospital with a ton of doctors and an excuse for pain meds. I'm sure he's perfectly fine. School, *now*."

Not trying to fight me on it anymore, he puts the car in drive and heads toward Haven Grace Prep.

BY THE TIME WE pull up to our destination, I'm so mad that I'm shaking. I go to hop out of the car when Brady grabs my wrist.

"Don't get yourself hurt, Sav."

I give him a reassuring smile. "Oh, trust me, I won't be the one hurting today."

Turning around, I march up the steps and into the school. The second I turn down the hallway, I see Grayson standing with the rest of the guys and Kinsley. The girl is like a bad infection that won't fucking go away, but she's not my problem right now.

"I need to talk to you, right *fucking* now," I tell him, not taking no for an answer.

Carter's eyes widen as he looks at Grayson. "Damn. What the fuck did you do?"

Pulling him to the nearest empty class room, I shut the door behind us. As soon as I turn around, my fist goes flying and punches him right in the mouth. He recoils slightly, clearly surprised that I hit him, and covers the lip I've now split to match Brady's.

"You wanted my attention. Well, congratulations—now you fucking have it," I all but shout. "Who the fuck do you think you are, attacking Brady like that?"

He laughs in a way that sends a chill down my spine. "Who do I think *I* am? That's a good question coming from a *fake* like you." My heart stops, and I can tell by the look in his eyes, he knows. "That's right. I figured out your little secret." He steps closer. "Is there *anything* about you that's real? Because all I've found is fake. Fake boyfriend. Fake wealth. Fake life." His thumb pulls my bottom lip out from between my teeth. "Just *fake*."

"You should talk, being as your relationship with Kinsley is *so real*. I may not like the little slut, but even I think she deserves better than being your pawn in some sick attempt to get to me."

He stands before me like a king who holds all the power. "You know, it's funny how you still act like you're in control. *You're done.* I've been looking for the one thing I could use to tear you down, and now, I've found it." Coming even closer, he whispers into my ear. "And I'm going to love to watch you crumble."

I can't hear any more of this. I'm already on the verge of a panic attack as I go to leave, but Grayson grabs my wrist and pulls me back into him.

"Don't fucking walk away from me."

Without a second thought, I lift my knee quickly and slam it as hard as I can into his groin. He releases his hold immediately and bends over, trying to catch his breath.

"You bitch!" he screams, but I'm already out the door and running down the hallway.

There are a lot of things I can handle. My mother dying at five years old. My father turning into a raging alcoholic. Even losing my best friend, only for him to come back hating me eight years later. But having my most harmful secret in the hands of someone whose only mission in life is to destroy me? That's not one of them.

I make my way to the janitor's closet and shut the door behind me, sliding my back against it until I'm sitting on the floor. My breathing becomes shallow and rapid as tears pour from my eyes. How did everything get like this? What have I done to make him hate me so much? How the hell did he even find out?

Taking my phone out, I send a text to Brady.

Savannah: What happened after you and Grayson fought?

Thankfully, he responds almost instantly.

Brady: He was arrested. Jake wanted to press charges but I declined. Why? Are you okay?

I don't need to ask to know that Brady didn't tell him. He must have somehow gotten one of the officers at the precinct to give him information on me. I try to get a handle on my breathing, but it's pointless.

Savannah: Not even a little.

TODAY IS DEFINITELY ONE I could have gone my whole life without living. I keep to myself, not in the mood to partake in the usual obnoxious conversations Carter starts. Brady had offered to come back and pick me up, but that's only giving Grayson a silent message that he wins—that I'm running away scared. I may be a lot of things, liar included, but I'm not a coward.

Throughout the day, he watches me with a smug look on his face, as if mentally telling me he could ruin my life with the snap of his fingers. I do my best to ignore it, but I can't. My reputation is the only good thing in my life other than dance, and it rests in the palm of his hands. I can only imagine what the kids in this school would do to me if they knew the truth.

"So, remember. Party tonight. My place. Starts around ten," Jace reminds everyone, then looks at me. "Sav, you coming?"

I want to say no, not really in the mood to party with a bunch of people who are bound to hate me soon, but for some reason my eyes drift over to Grayson. He raises his eyebrows, as if challenging me to say yes. I know if I back down now, I don't stand a chance in hell.

"Yeah, I'll be there."

Jace smiles triumphantly. "Sweet. You can bring your boyfriend with you if you want."

Grayson snorts, but quickly covers it with a cough. I glare at him before answering. "W-we broke up."

"Damn, really?!" Carter looks shocked. "You two have been together since freshman year."

I shrug. "Nothing lasts forever."

Emma places a supportive hand on my back, and I smile sweetly at her before my attention is pulled back to Jace.

"Well, remember what I said," he winks. "Just say the word and I'll pick you up."

I can't help but laugh, though the smile falls of my face as I notice Grayson's murderous eyes on him. I don't know what the fuck his deal is, but he doesn't get to torment me and get jealous over me, too. He laid his cards on the table and chose where we stand. He can't take that back now.

THE LOUD MUSIC IS practically deafening as Brady pulls up to the house. It's not the first time I've been to one of Jace's parties, but they only seem to get bigger. People fill both the inside of the house and the backyard. It's a known rule that every room is free game except Jace's. I wonder what his parents would think about the number of people who have had sex in their bed.

"Are you sure you're going to be all right?" Brady asks.

I nod. "I'll be fine. I just need to be here to prove a point."

"And that is?"

"That I'm not backing down. If Grayson wants to ruin my life, he's doesn't get to do it without a fight. He doesn't get to break me that easily."

Brady smiles. "That's my Rocky. I can stay if you want."

"No." I shake my head. "I already told them today that we broke up. There's no way I'm giving him a reason to come after you again. And besides, it's one less thing he can hold over my head."

He looks hesitant, but knows there isn't much he can do about this. I've made my decision, and that's all there is to it.

"Well, be careful. Call me if you need a ride home."

"I will."

Giving him a hug goodbye, I climb out of the car and go

inside. It's so loud inside that I can barely hear myself think. The house is packed, and there are already drinks spilled on the floor. *Typical Jace London party.*

I make my way into the kitchen and find Carter, Jace, Wyatt, and, to my utmost misfortune, Grayson. Carter immediately smiles, wrapping his arms around me.

"If it isn't my favorite little dancer," he quips, but Jace pulls me from his hold.

"Don't hog her. She's single now. It's the first time I'm allowed anywhere near her without worrying about Brady coming after me."

I chuckle slightly, but after a quick hug, I back away. I've already seen what Grayson did to Brady when he thought we were dating. I don't need him going after Jace too, or worse, exposing my secret in a pissed-off rage.

"Where's everyone else?" I ask.

"Well, Kinsley can't come," Carter tells me and I practically gleam with excitement. "Apparently, she had to go out of town with her parents, but Paige and Becca are on their way."

"No Ems?"

He shakes his head. "I think she and Hayden are on a date, but neither of them will tell us."

I can't help but smile. "About damn time."

"You're telling me." He turns around and looks for the keg. "Let me get you a drink."

As he goes over to pour me a beer, he realizes the keg is empty. Calling over to Jace, he and Wyatt leave to help retrieve a new one from the garage, leaving me alone with Grayson. It's everything I didn't want, but walking away now would make me seem weak. So, I hold my ground and turn to face him.

"I didn't think you'd show," he tells me.

"Well, I did."

"I see that."

I roll my eyes and step closer, pulling myself up to sit on the table next to him. "I'm not afraid of you, Grayson."

He grunts and takes a sip of his beer before answering. "Maybe not yet, but you will be."

AN HOUR INTO THE party, everything is going better than I thought it would. Grayson has yet to bring up exposing me, and without Kinsley here pissing me off, I'm free to have fun with my friends. Becca hangs on me like she needs my stability to keep herself upright, while Paige laughs and takes pictures. It isn't until a familiar face catches my eye that I freeze.

"Grayson? Is that you?" Tessa Callahan comes up, giving Grayson a big hug and getting one in return. "Shit. Delaney said you were back."

"I am. How've you been? You look good."

Tessa is Delaney's twin sister, and while they're fraternal twins, both are gorgeous. Tessa's hair is a lighter brown than Laney's, and her eyes are brown instead of green—something she spent her whole childhood sulking about. Their personalities, however, are night and day. Delaney is the golden child. I don't think she's ever done a single thing wrong in her life. Meanwhile, Tess has always been someone to see how far she can bend the rules without completely breaking them. Laney used to get stressed out when thinking about her sister's behavior, but I guess after years, she got used to it.

She smiles. "Been all right, can't really complain. And me? Look at you!" Reaching forward she squeezes his biceps. "Bench press has been good to you, hasn't it?"

"I guess so."

Watching them together, I get a tight feeling in my chest. This is the kind of reunion we should have had. No, scratch

88

that. We should have had better. Fireworks going off as I ran and jumped into his arms. A kiss so hot it could melt the arctic tundra. I would have taken him to bed and given him everything I've kept to myself for all these years—no hesitation. Instead, what I got was a Grayson that's eight years older and the total opposite of the sweet boy I remember.

"Sav." Paige tugs my sleeve gets my attention. "You were staring."

I'm about to make an excuse to leave when Tessa's attention lands on me. "Savannah. Of course. Shouldn't be surprised you two would gravitate to each other again."

Grayson won't look at me, but everyone else seems confused.

"Wait. You two knew each other, too?" Carter questions.

"Knew each other?" Tess laughs. "They were practically married. Actually, if I remember correctly, there was even a little fake wedding."

"Tess." Grayson stops her and shakes his head.

She gives him an odd look and starts to back away. "Okay, weirdo. I'll see you later."

Everyone is quiet, until realization crosses over Becca's face.

"That's where I know you from! I knew you looked familiar!" she slurs to Grayson.

"Huh?"

"Bec!" I try to interrupt, but she's like a freight train and can't be stopped.

"You're the little boy in the picture! The one in Savannah's locker!"

I'm not sure if I want to run and hide, or play it off as if she's just drunk and doesn't know what she's talking about. However, as soon as Paige chimes in, telling Becca she's right, I know the second option is off the table.

"Damn." Carter shakes his head. "With how much you

two hate each other, I figured there had to be some kind of history."

Jace looks dumbfounded yet intrigued. "So, what the hell happened then?"

"Nothing," the two of us answer in unison, but while mine sounds sincere—his is forced.

Our eyes meet the second the word leaves our mouths. There's something unspoken about the look he's giving me, something sinister. It's as if he would set me on fire if given the chance. I shiver as I look away, until his next words slide into my chest like a knife.

"We lived across the street from each other as kids. That's it. Nothing special," he explains. "She was just as annoying and fake then as she is now."

I glare at him, knowing I shouldn't poke the bear but not able to hold back. "Fuck you. Why don't you go crawl back into the hole you came out of?"

His eyebrows raise. "Speaking of holes, should we talk about yours?"

Everyone thinks it's some sexual dig, but I know the underlying meaning. He's holding my secret over me like a guillotine. One wrong word and the rope will snap, cutting off my head in the process. My breath hitches as I prepare for impact, but he remains quiet.

"I'm all out," he acknowledges, looking down at his cup. "Anyone want another drink?"

Everyone shakes their heads, and he walks over toward the keg. Carter brings the conversation back to something neutral, like I can always trust him to do. As soon as their attention is off me, I slip away and to the hall I saw Grayson go down.

"You didn't tell them," I say as I see him leaning against the wall.

He takes a sip of his drink. "Nope."

"Why?"

The storm brewing in his eyes is intense and dangerous as he stares me down. I swallow hard, wondering how I wasn't aware that the boy I used to call my best friend was capable of such hatred.

"Because this is more fun." He takes a step closer. "When they find out—and they will—I want to make sure you feel it. I want it to hurt."

GRAYSON

To be in possession of the exact thing that could cause Savannah's downfall feels like glorious retribution. Not only could I turn all her friends against her and strip her of the people who make her strong, I can make her anticipate and fear the moment her world comes crashing down. While I had the perfect opportunity to break her tonight, my plan is to play her like a fiddle.

When Travis wrote down the address, I thought there must have been a mistake—until he told me what a piece of shit her father has become. Originally, I was going to come after him once I was done with taking down his daughter, but it appears that won't be necessary. At the rate he's going, he'll drink himself to death before Savannah graduates high school.

In all actuality, he's probably getting drunk and high to block out the guilt of what he did to his best friend. My father was hurt, being forced away from his family like that, but nothing was quite as painful as the betrayal of the man who helped frame him for the crime. I don't believe he ever got over that before the riot that took his life just six months later.

I watch as Savannah sways from side to side, too intoxicated to realize she's dancing alone. At some point after our little conversation in the hallway, she switched from beer to something stronger. I don't know what exactly is in the drinks Carter keeps passing her way, but I can only assume his motives are less pure than I'm willing to allow.

She may be a liar—a deceitful little bitch—but she's mine and mine alone.

"So, you know a little more about Montgomery than I thought, huh?" Jace appears next to me.

I shrug. "You could say that, I guess."

"What the hell happened between you two?"

Knowing better than to think I can trust him, I take a sip of my beer as I ponder my answer. "Nothing really. Sorry to disappoint."

He snorts. "Well, it must have been something if it got to her like this." Nodding toward Savannah, I spot her now dancing on top of a table, drawing a crowd. "I've never seen her so drunk."

I try to keep my composure, and my distance for that matter, but the second a guy reaches up and gropes her ass, I see red. I'm up in seconds, pushing through the group of people who have all gathered around to watch Haven Grace's favorite cheer captain put on a not-so-flattering show. Just as I get to the front, she slips and falls back—landing directly in my arms.

"You caught me," she slurs and wraps her arms around my neck. "My hero."

The close proximity we're in, paired with the fact that she could have gotten really hurt, has my need to protect her on overdrive. I don't question the decision for a second as I walk her right out the front door. Carter spots us from where he stands in the front yard and jogs over.

"Whoa, what happened to her?" he questions, following me to my car.

"Whatever you were putting in those drinks you made her." I manage to pull my keys from my pocket and unlock the doors. "Do you mind?"

He opens it and helps me place her in the passenger seat, then steps back as I shut her in. "You taking her home or *taking her home*?" He raises his eyebrows at me in a suggestive manner.

I roll my eyes. "The first one. Passed-out drunk isn't exactly a turn on." I glance inside to see her holding her head. "All right, let me go before she vomits in my car."

"Good luck."

I walk around and get into the driver's side. As I pull out of the driveway, I can feel Savannah's eyes on me—burning into the side of my head. I steal a glance at her, just to be sure, and she smiles.

"What?"

She shakes her head. "Nothing. You're just pretty."

I snort. "Pretty?"

"Yeah." She reaches across and runs her fingertips down the side of my face. "Like a manly kind of pretty."

Taking her wrist, I place her hand back on her lap. "Let's keep our hands to ourselves, shall we?"

"No fun." She hiccups and turns to look out the window.

By the time I get across town and pull up to her house, I can't believe what I'm looking at. This place looks like something that should have been condemned years ago. The porch is missing some planks, the railings are rotted and the roof is sagging. Judging by how dark it is, I can only assume no one is home.

I look over at Savannah to find her sleeping soundly. I know what I *should* do. I should bring her inside, put her in her bed, and leave—but I can't. She's too drunk, too vulnerable, if someone breaks in. I may despise her, but no one gets to cause her pain but me.

Putting the car back in drive, I pull away from her four walls of hell and head toward my own.

THE LIGHTS IN MY house are on, telling me that even though it's close to midnight, my mother is awake. *This should be interesting.* I go and open the front door before coming back to my car and lifting Savannah out of it. By the time I get inside, my mom is standing by the stairs, concern etched across her face.

"What's going on?" she asks, her eyes widening when she sees who is in my arms. "Oh my God, is that Savannah?!"

I shake my head. "Everything's fine, mom. She just had a little too much to drink."

Carrying her up the stairs, she stirs awake and nuzzles her face into my chest. "Mmm. You smell good."

Her drunken honesty is comical to me. "You're just full of compliments tonight, aren't you?"

"Maybe." As I slip into the guest room, she sighs. "Is this when you have your way with me?"

My steps stutter, and my lungs forget how to breathe. *Am I hearing things? Did she really just ask that?* "No, Savannah. This is when you go to sleep."

"Oh." She sounds almost disappointed before nodding. "Well, that's good, 'cause I'm a virgin, and it would probably hurt."

It's clear she doesn't know what she's saying, and if she did, she'd probably smack herself for giving me yet another piece of leverage. However, hearing her say those words is like heaven to my ears. I had my assumptions, being as she pretended to date Brady for almost all of high school, but to have them confirmed is something else entirely. No one has taken what should have been mine, and for as long as I'm around, that's how it's going to stay.

I place Savannah down on the bed, thinking she's asleep, but as I turn to walk away, her delicate fingers wrap around my wrist.

"Wait," she mumbles. "Lay with me."

I shake my head. "I shouldn't."

"Please? Just for a minute."

Everything in me is screaming to leave. Hell, I shouldn't have brought her back here in the first place, let alone get in bed with her, but there's something about the way she's asking—like she's damaged and needs someone to hold her for a moment.

Against my better judgment, I kick off my shoes and slip in the other side. As soon as I'm lying next to her, she slots herself against me, with her head on my chest. All I can do is hope she's too drunk to notice the way my heart is pounding. If she's not, she'll realize the effect she has on me.

"My Gray," she murmurs, just before her breathing evens out.

I take a deep breath, letting myself get high on the smell of her hair. She's sound asleep, and I could leave at this point, but I don't. With everything the two of us have been through, it feels good to be here. To forget everything and just allow myself to pretend like this is okay. This is right.

"Gray! Wait up!" Savi calls, not able to ride her bike as fast as I can.

"Come on, slowpoke!"

I know I should slow down and wait for her, but I can't help it. After finding this place over the weekend while she was at her grandmother's, I've been itching to show her. I pedal faster, going past the playground and into the woods. We follow the small dirt trail until the point where I know to turn and go off track.

"Where are we going?"

"You'll see!"

Like I knew she would, she follows me through all the overgrown foliage until we finally get to the clearing. I stop my bike before it and climb off, wanting to see her reaction. She pulls up behind me and looks around.

"You're not taking me out here to kill me, are you?"

"Don't be stupid." We walk over to the last bush that's still blocking our view, but you can hear the splashing of water. "Are you ready?"

She nods, and I pull the bush back to let her walk through, then follow. The waterfall is gorgeous, with rocks around it. It's probably twenty feet high, and the water falls into a small pond-like part of the river before flowing further downstream.

"Whoa." Her gaze searches around the area, taking it all in. "How did you find this place?"

I shrug. "I was exploring."

She doesn't need to know that I was bored without her and couldn't sit around my house because it just made me miss her more. Or that I was in these woods looking for pretty flowers to make into a bouquet and ended up finding something much better.

"It's so pretty," she whispers.

I take a deep breath and turn to face her. "You're prettier."

Her cheeks turn a light shade of pink as she smiles at me, and I don't think I've ever seen her look at me that way before. I bravely brush my hand against hers, feeling relief as she laces her fingers with mine. We stand there together, holding hands and admiring this waterfall—and I couldn't be happier.

I jolt awake, realizing I fell asleep in bed with Savannah. Thankfully, I look out the window to find it's still dark outside. With as much control as I can manage, I slip out from under her slowly and leave the room. The last thing I need is for her, or my mother, to find me holding her.

THE NEXT MORNING, I wake to the sound of laughter. My brows furrow, and the first thing I think is that Justin is here again. However, as I get to the door of my room, a familiar voice reminds me of last night. *Savannah.*

"I'm so glad you and Grayson reunited!" I hear my mom tell her as I walk down the stairs and toward the kitchen. "You two were always the best of friends, and it makes me happy to see you've gotten back to that."

"We haven't," I interrupt and both their heads turn toward me. My attention focuses solely on Savannah. "I called you an Uber. It'll be here in three minutes."

My mom shakes her head. "Don't be silly. At least let me make you two breakfast first."

"No. Savannah was just leaving. Weren't you, *Savi?*"

"Y-yeah. I, um, I have stuff I need to do today anyway." She stands and moves toward the door. "It was nice seeing you again, Mrs. Hayworth."

"You too, dear. Don't be a stranger, okay?"

She nods. I glare at my mother as I back out of the room. I'll deal with her later.

With one hand on her back, I lead Savannah out the front door. She shivers from the chilly morning air.

"You know, you really shouldn't drink that much. Someone may take advantage of you."

Her brows furrow while she looks down at the ground. "So, we didn't—"

I shake my head before she even finishes the question. "No."

A part of me considers telling her what she revealed last night, but I don't think I could stand to listen to her lie and try to tell me something different. She looks up at me, and for once, I see the vulnerability in her eyes.

Real.

Honest.

Exposed.

It almost knocks the wind out of me, and I grip the door handle to keep from doing something I'll regret.

Thankfully, the car pulls up, and she walks down the steps to get in it. I don't wait for it to drive away before I turn around and go back inside. When I reach the kitchen, my mom glances from where she's standing at the stove, her disapproval obvious.

"What?"

She shakes her head. "Nothing."

I sit at the counter and rest my elbows on it. "You've got something on your mind, so spit it out."

Sighing, she drops the dish towel onto the counter. "I just think you should be a little nicer to Savannah, that's all."

My jaw drops, and I can't believe what she's saying. After everything that girl has done to my family, she thinks I should be *nicer*? That bitch should be grateful I didn't leave her at that party and let her enjoy the consequences of her choices.

"I don't get it," I say in utter shock. "I know you've seen the tape. The one that helped convict dad of a crime he didn't commit. For God's sake, it was practically the final nail in the coffin. Why the fuck would you be so forgiving of her?"

"She was a child, Grayson. She didn't know what she was saying."

"Oh, like hell she didn't!" I shout. "She was old enough to tell me she wanted to marry me one day. Old enough to sneak out of her house to meet me in the middle of the night. Don't try to tell me that bullshit. She knew *exactly* how wrong it was when it came out of her mouth."

Not wanting to hear another word of this nonsense, I get up and storm out of the room. There isn't a damn thing anyone can say to change my mind. She deserves to pay for the things she's done.

SAVANNAH

THE SUN SHINES IN THROUGH THE WINDOW, pulling me from what was such a good dream. My head is pounding, but something feels different. This bed is more comfortable than I remember mine being, and none of the windows in my room face the sunrise.

I peek my eyes open, and my breath hitches. I'd recognize this room anywhere. I spent so much time here when I was younger, it was practically my second home. *Grayson's guest room.* Whenever our dads would have to go away on business, Grayson's mom would watch us both. I always loved this room, because of how close it was to his.

How did I get here?

Getting out of bed, I realize I'm still in the same clothes I wore to the party last night. Thank God. At least they're still on. I slip out the door, trying to be as quiet as possible as I make my way down the stairs. Just as I get to the bottom and think I'm home free, a voice startles me.

"Hey, stranger."

Mrs. Hayworth stands in the doorway to the kitchen, smiling brightly.

"Oh my God, hi."

To my relief, she walks toward me with open arms. The moment she embraces me the way she always used to, I get hit with an overwhelming wave of emotions. This woman was like a mom to me after mine had passed away, and I was so afraid she was going to hate me like her son does.

"How have you been? Look at you. You've become so grown up!"

I run my fingers through my hair. "Yeah, I'm turning eighteen in a few weeks."

"That's crazy. I feel like just yesterday you were this big." She holds her hand near her hip. "Come on, let's go in the kitchen and talk."

I should turn down the offer, but to be honest, this is the closest I've felt to my old self in years—before everything went horribly wrong. Taking a seat at the table, she pours us each a cup of tea and sits across from me.

"So, how are things? What's been new?"

Where do I even begin? With my father turning his bloodstream into straight alcohol? With the fact that I live in what can only be considered a death trap, not a home? On second thought, I shouldn't bore her with all the gory details of what my life has become.

"Just going to school and dance."

"You're still dancing? That's wonderful. You were always so talented."

I blush. "Yeah. I'm trying to go to Juilliard for college. That's the dream, anyway."

"Well." She reaches across the table and grabs my hand. "I'm sure you'll get there. They'd be crazy not to take you."

"Thank you. And if I don't, then clown college always has its perks."

A good-hearted laugh bellows out of her. "Oh, I've missed you." She takes a sip of her tea. "I'm so glad you and Grayson reunited. You two were always the best of friends, and it makes me happy to see you've gotten back to that."

I bite my lip, trying to keep from telling her that what we are now is the furthest thing from what we were, but suddenly I don't need to.

"We haven't." Grayson's voice booms into the room and his eyes land on me, a clear indication that I should have left by now. "I called you an Uber. It'll be here in three minutes."

Mrs. Hayworth stands. "Don't be silly. At least let me make you two breakfast first."

"No. Savannah was just leaving. Weren't you *Savi?*" The way he snarls my nickname reminds me just how different things are now.

"Y-yeah." I stutter. "I, um, I have stuff I need to do today anyway." I get up. "It was nice seeing you again, Mrs. Hayworth."

"You too, dear." She answers sweetly. "Don't be a stranger, okay?"

I nod, but with no intentions of ever actually coming back. Clearly, Grayson would rather I be anywhere else, though he had to be the one to bring me here in the first place. I walk toward the door, trying to ignore the feeling of Grayson's hand on my back, all but pushing me out. Once we step outside, I mentally curse myself for not grabbing a jacket last night.

"You know, you really shouldn't drink that much. Someone could have taken advantage of you."

I stare down at my shoes, finding them very interesting and a much better view than his hateful glares. "So, we didn't—"

"No," he confirms, and I can't deny the slight disappointment I feel.

I look up at him, knowing he holds all the cards—not just with my reputation, but with my heart. Let's be real, I don't think there was ever a time where he didn't. No matter how much he may hurt me now, he's always been my weak spot. His expression changes slightly, and I notice the way his knuckles turn pale from the grip he has on the door handle.

Interrupting the moment with perfect timing, the Uber pulls up. With one last look at Grayson, I turn around and go to get in the car. By the time I close the door behind me, he's already gone.

I SIT ON THE FLOOR and spread my legs, stretching as much as I can. Brady mimics my movements, but the confused look remains on his face. I try to ignore it, though it's obvious he won't let me.

"Wait, so he brought you back to his house and put you to bed?"

I roll my eyes. "I guess? All I know is that I woke up in his guest room. The last thing I remember is drinking at Jace's party."

"And you're sure you two didn't have sex?"

"Wouldn't I be sore after that? You know I've never…"

He groans and throws his head back. "You can say it, Savannah. *Had sex.*"

I reach over and slap his arm as best I can from my spot on the floor. "Shut up. I'm not afraid to say it." He gives me a teasing look, challenging me. "Ugh, fine. Sex. Happy? Sex. Sex. Sex."

"Wow," Mrs. Laurence says, capturing both our attention. "I'm not sure exactly what I walked into, but just ignore me."

My face turns beet red as Brady falls onto his back from laughing so hard. She grabs her clipboard from counter and winks at me before leaving the room. Once she's gone, I kick Brady in the leg.

"Shut up. It's not funny."

"It is." He chuckles again. "It really, really is."

After we finish stretching, he starts the music, and I get

104

lost in the dance. Thoughts of Grayson pop up at times, like when hearing certain lyrics, but I do my best to push them down. He's already planning on ruining my whole life and taking everything from me. I can't give him the satisfaction of taking Juilliard, too.

———

BRADY DROPS ME OFF after the two of us have lunch. I'm just about to step inside when someone whistle behind me. Turning around, I see Knox walking toward me. *Just what I need.*

"What do you want, Vaughn?"

He holds his hands up in surrender. "I'm just surprised, that's all. You really seem to get around lately."

I cross my arms over my chest. "What the hell are you talking about?"

"Last night with Grayson, and today you're with Brady. I mean, hey—I'm no one to judge you for sleeping around."

"Wait." I hold up a hand. "You saw me with Grayson last night?"

He nods. "Yeah, he pulled up in front of your house. I thought he was dropping you off but you never got out of the car before he drove away." *Why would he...* "I'm just curious as to why he hired me to follow your little boyfriend when he could've just had you do it. Pretty fucked up of you to let your boyfriend get his ass kicked, though."

"Grayson had you follow Brady?"

"Oh, he didn't tell you?" He grins. "Yeah. Pretty boy gave me five grand to call him when Brady was alone."

And just like that, it all becomes clear. That's how Grayson knew to find Brady outside of the *gay bar* in the next town over.

I place my hands against his chest and shove him back.

"Are you out of your fucking mind? You could have gotten Brady killed!"

He laughs, as if there is something comical about all this. "Chill, Princess. A few cuts and bruises will do the man some good. Besides, I'm sure his *boyfriend* took great care of him afterward."

My stomach drops. "You knew."

"Of course I knew. It wasn't hard to figure out why he never came inside. You can't play like you're dating someone who acts like your brother."

Taking a deep breath, I try to keep my cool. "What do you want?"

He licks his lips and looks me up and down, but before I lose my shit on him, he shakes his head. "I know you saw that deal a couple weeks ago. I just want to make sure you know to keep your pretty little mouth shut about it."

"Haven't said anything yet, have I?"

"Nope, and let's keep it that way."

"Whatever." I open the door and slip inside, locking it behind me.

The sight of an empty bottle of Jack on the counter tells me my father's been home since I left yesterday evening, but God only knows where he is now. Probably taking too many of the pills the doctor prescribed for his foot.

I make my way into my room and throw myself down onto my bed. Everything from the last couple days is really starting to mess with my head. First, Grayson has the one piece of information that could destroy my reputation, and instead of using it, he's taunting me with it. However, that isn't nearly as surprising as finding out that he brought me here last night before bringing me to his house. Why didn't he just drop me off? Judging by the look on his face this morning, seeing me was the last thing he wanted. It's all just really confusing and starting to give me a headache.

FOR THE FIRST TIME in years, I skip dance on Sunday morning. Between rehearsing for the winter recital, cheer practice, and dealing with all the mind games of Grayson Hayworth, I'm exhausted. All I want is to stay cooped up in my room, eat Ben and Jerry's, and binge watch Netflix.

Halfway through an episode of *Friends*, my dad comes stumbling into the room. The smell of booze radiates from his body, and it looks like he hasn't showered in weeks. I hit pause before sitting up.

"Everything okay?" I ask hesitantly.

He looks around the room, slurring his words and mumbling something about his pills. Then, he stops and turns to me. "I need you to go to the liquor store."

I could argue, but it would be useless. So instead, I climb off my bed and take the money from his hand. Just as I go to slip past him, he grips my arm and slams me against the doorway—knocking the wind out of me.

"And don't even think about trying to trick me with water again, you little shit."

Afraid to move, I stay completely still until he releases me and walks back into his room. Once he's gone, I all but run from the house. I pull my phone from my pocket and call Brady. Thankfully, he agrees to meet me at the liquor store down the street. I zip up my sweatshirt and start to walk down the sidewalk.

"Well, damn." A kid I don't recognize says to me as he saunters up close. "Who might you be, pretty thing?"

I try to go around him, but he moves directly in my way. *Seriously, I am not in the mood for this shit.*

He looks like one of Knox's friends, only younger. His black hair is spiked up, as if no one told him that style went out with the 90s. His shirt sleeves have been torn off, and his jeans are cut into shorts. It's like he came straight out of a bad independent film.

"Where you going, beautiful? I just want to talk."

I take a step back to gain some personal space. "No, thanks. I'll pass."

"Aw, come on. At least let me get your name."

"Is there a problem here, Trey?" Knox appears out of nowhere.

Judging by the way he freezes at hearing Knox's voice, I'm guessing they're not friends. Good. That's something I can use to my advantage.

"No, not at all," he says, demeanor changing. "I was just trying to get my new neighbor's name."

New neighbor?! Fuck my life.

Knox comes up next to me and places his hand on my shoulder, leading me around Trey so he doesn't stop me again. "Well, it doesn't look to me like she wants to give it to you."

As pissed off as I am at him, and think he should reevaluate his life choices, I've never been so glad for his stalking tendencies. I swear, the guy manages to see and hear everything around here. Nothing happens that he doesn't know about. It's why, despite wanting to punch him in the face sometimes, I try to stay on his good side.

Giving Knox a thankful smile, I continue my trek to the liquor store, because what better way to spend my Sunday than getting more vodka for the alcoholic?

MONDAY MORNING, I'M ALREADY over the day when I get to school. While walking to first period, I realize Grayson isn't with us. Strange, because I saw his car in the parking lot when Brady dropped me off. When I walk into the classroom, however, I see why. He's already here, but he's no longer occupying the seat he's taken just to irritate me. Instead, he's sitting next to Delaney. They're laughing about something when her eyes meet mine.

To see them together makes the usual feelings of nostalgia so much worse. If things hadn't changed—if Grayson hadn't moved away and my life hadn't gone from blessed to broken —we'd probably all be sitting together. Gray and I would be a power couple, and Delaney would still be my best friend.

"Why is he sitting with her?" Kinsley asks, as if we're close.

I roll my eyes. "I'm sorry, last time I checked, I wasn't his minder."

We take our seats, and I do my best to ignore them, but it's easier said than done.

THE OBJECTIVE IS SIMPLE—create a graphic using at least five different Photoshop effects. It couldn't be any more straightforward, and it would be easy, if I was allowed to focus on it. For the third time, Grayson drops his stylus on the ground. I glance at it but continue to do my work.

"Savannah," he whispers, but I don't answer. "Savannah. Psst. Savi."

"What?" I snap.

"Get that for me."

"No. Get it yourself. I've already picked it up the past two times you dropped it."

He leans forward on the desk, looking at me with an evil glint in his eyes. "Are you sure you want to tell me no?"

Of course, he's going to play this game. "Is this really how you're doing this? Making me your personal bitch? I thought you were more creative than that."

"I think you need to a little taste of humility." He smirks. "And nothing would make me happier than having Miss Queen B at my beck and call."

Not wanting to piss him off, I bend down and grab the stylus before slamming it on his desk. "You really are a dick, you know that?"

He grins smugly. "Yup."

FOR THE REST OF the week, he continues to test my limits. Having me get him a drink during lunch, carrying his books to class, and even making me tie his shoe in the middle of the hallway. Everyone looks confused as I obey his every word, and I'm about to snap. I may be a lot of things, but I'm no one's slave.

"I'm starving," Grayson moans at lunch, looking over at Carter's plate. "That looks good. What is that?"

"Get your own, douchebag. I don't share food."

Gray smiles, looking over at me, and I already know what he's going to say before he opens his mouth. "*Oh, Savi…*"

"No."

His eyebrows raise in surprise. "No?"

"You heard me. *No.* Go get your own damn lunch."

Jace exhales in relief. "It's about time. Damn, Sav. I was starting to wonder where your backbone went."

"Yeah, well, I can only try to be nice for so long before people need to know their place."

It's probably stupid to provoke him, and there is such a huge chance of this backfiring in my face, but I get the feeling he isn't ready to show his cards just yet. He still wants control. He wants to make me suffer, and he can't do that without dragging this out. So, I'm calling his bluff.

"Know my place, huh?"

He wraps one arm around Kinsley. She beams up at him, like she always does when he shows her any kind of attention. It's almost sad to watch. She's so wrapped up in him that she can't see how bad he's playing her.

"Is that supposed to intimidate me? You've fucked the school slut. Congratulations! So has the rest of the zip code."

Carter chokes on his drink while Kinsley's face turns an angry shade of red.

"I'm starting to think you're so obsessed with my sex life because you don't have one of your own. What are you, a virgin?" she retorts.

I chuckle, playing it off with ease. "No, sweetie. I may not sleep with half the town, but I'm definitely no virgin."

"Prove it," Jace quips flirtatiously.

Grayson's jaw ticks at the offer. I bite my lip and look Jace up and down. "Let's go."

"Don't you fucking dare." Gray's voice is so low, it's almost demonic—the look in his eyes challenging me to push his restraints.

Carter throws his head back, laughing. "There are definitely two people here who need to fuck some shit out of their systems, but *Jace* isn't one of them. Sorry, bud."

Every part of me wants to throw caution to the wind and screw Jace just for the sake of pissing Grayson off. He's been rubbing Kinsley in my face for weeks, and the thought of being able to make him feel even an ounce of that jealousy is so tempting. However, the last thing I want is give up that part of myself so I can inflict pain on someone else.

"Fuck this. It isn't worth my time." I stand from the table, grabbing my things and heading for the door.

The hallways are a ghost town as I make my way through them. *Who the fuck does he think he is?* He's done nothing but made a fool out of me the last few days, used Kinsley to make me jealous for weeks, and now he thinks he can tell me what I can and can't do? Not a chance in hell.

I open my locker and spot the familiar picture taped to the door. Gray and I were only six when it was taken, right after his dad finished building the treehouse in the backyard. We look so happy as we smile from the windows. What happened to the boy in that photo? Hell, what happened to the *girl* in that photo?

"I should've known then what a liar you are."

I spin around to find Grayson standing there, staring at the picture like he wants to burn it with his eyes. As he goes to reach for it, I swing my locker shut. I already lost my necklace. He doesn't get to take another damn thing from me.

"Open it," he demands.

"No."

Stepping closer, he invades my space. "You're getting a little too comfortable with that word."

"What made you so cold?" I question in complete disbelief. This can't be the same boy I used to share milkshakes with.

"Letting myself believe you were a good person. That I could trust you." He sneers. "Everything that has happened to you, and everything that will—you deserve it." The corner of his mouth raises, like he knows the next words will sting. "Even having a drunken addict for a father."

My hand flies up to slap him in the face, but it's already something he anticipated. He catches my wrist in midair and that irritating smirk deepens.

"You want to try that again?"

I swing with my other hand, only for him to catch that, too. In one swift move, he has me pinned against the cold metal with my arms trapped above my head. Our eyes lock, both furious and determined, until his lips crash into my own.

1 2

GRAYSON

OUR MOUTHS MOLD TOGETHER LIKE THEY WERE meant only for this. Like everything was intended to come to this very moment. Like all my life, this was where we belonged. I release her wrists and wrap my arms around her tiny waist. Her hands move to the back of my head, pulling me closer while she breathes me in.

My tongue finds hers, and she releases a breathy moan. It's everything I've dreamed of for years—heated, intense, and passionate as sin. I want nothing more than to pick her up and take that sweet little cherry of hers right here, without giving a damn who might see.

Sliding my hands down her back, I grab onto her hips and lift. She immediately wraps her legs around me, and my cock hardens painfully inside my pants. I grind against her as she laces her dainty fingers into my hair. I take her bottom lip between my teeth, sucking and nibbling on it in a way that's driving her crazy.

"Gray," she pants, and it's like being doused with a bucket of ice water.

What the fuck am I doing? I release her in an instant, letting her slide down until her feet are resting on the ground. I walk away and leave her standing there—alone and confused.

THE AIR IS COOL and breezy as I run. My lungs burn with every breath, but instead of stopping, I pick up the pace. I deserve all the pain in the world after betraying the one man who always wanted what's best for me. Kissing Savannah was never part of the plan, but she's an irresistible fucking vixen. Once I had her in my hold, completely defenseless, I couldn't help myself. All the self-control in the world wouldn't have stopped me.

After I walked away from her, I left school entirely. There was no way I could sit there for the rest of the day, with her sky-blue eyes desperate for clarity and puffy lips that felt perfect against mine. No, I needed to go. To remind myself of the reason I'm here. It's certainly not to make out with the girl who helped ruin my life and take my father from me.

I get back to my house, finding it's still as empty as it was when I left. Wherever my mother is, I just hope it's not with Jackass. She just doesn't learn. When someone shows you who they really are, believe them—something I should remember.

I open the fridge to grab a beer and sit at the island. The cold feels good as it runs down my throat. Turning on my laptop, I click on the folder labeled DAD and press play on the first video. A little girl appears on the screen. It's the same Savannah, only eight years younger.

"And when you went down to get a drink, what did you see?" a man off-camera asks her.

She swallows, looking at something before answering. "I saw Mr. Hayworth putting money under the floorboard in the den."

"Did you look in there after he was gone?"

She shakes her head. "I just saw there was a lot of money in there."

———

Savi looks shy as she hands me a folded-up piece of paper. A part of me wonders if I should take it. She doesn't look so sure.

"What's this?"

She shrugs and looks away. "Just something I drew today."

I carefully unfold it before looking at the picture. It's the two of us, holding hands at the waterfall. Our names are written at the top with a heart in between them. A bright smile spreads across my face as butterflies flutter in my stomach.

"Do you like it?" Her voice is timid—not at all like the girl I know.

I nod. "I love it."

Reaching for her, I wrap her in my arms and give her a tight hug. She lets out a breath, like she was holding it in this whole time. Did she really think I wouldn't like it? Like her? She's perfect.

"Just don't let your parents see it."

We both laugh. "Yeah, that would be embarrassing. I know just where to put it. Come on."

The two of us go downstairs and into the den, checking to see if the coast is clear before I move the rug and pull up a loose floorboard. Savi's eyes widen when she notices my secret hiding spot.

"That's so cool! How'd you find that?"

"I was jumping around when it sounded different here. I keep all my best secret stuff in here."

There are only a few items inside. A picture of Savi and me. The ticket stub from a baseball game I went to with my dad. The Hot Wheels car my mom wanted to throw away because it's missing a wheel. And now, Savi's drawing.

I put the floorboard back and lay the rug over it again. No one knows this secret spot but Savi and I—and that's exactly how I want it to stay.

Fury boils inside of me as I watch the girl who was supposed to be my best friend, *more* than my best friend, blatantly lie and help throw an innocent man in prison. Unable to control my anger, I throw the half-empty beer bottle across the room, seeing amber glass and liquid fly as it shatters against the fridge.

"Last time I checked, the recycling bin is in the garage." My mom's voice catches me off guard.

I turn around to find her standing in the doorway, holding a bag of groceries and looking at the mess I just made. "I'm sorry. I'll clean it up."

She shakes her head. "Don't. I've got it. I don't want you to cut yourself."

Carefully crossing the room, I grab the bag from her and set it on the counter. "Where were you?"

"I had a job interview." She gets the broom and dustpan from the closet. "And then I went to the store to get stuff for dinner."

I nod, looking down at my hands. Since when did I start thinking the worst in people—my mom, especially? "I thought you were with Justin."

She sighs, clearly upset by the mention of him. "He won't be coming here again."

"Why?" The level of concern grows rapidly inside me. "He didn't hurt you again, did he? I swear to God, if he laid a hand on you—"

"No, no." She calms me with a single look. "He didn't touch me. You didn't want him here, and you were right."

"You got rid of him for me?"

"You're my son, Grayson. I may have made some mistakes since we lost your father, but there isn't anything I wouldn't do for you."

AFTER CHOOSING TO SKIP school on Friday, I spend the weekend with my mom in Campton, visiting my aunt and cousins. It may only be about an hour away, but I haven't been back since we moved. Tyson and I play football in the backyard during the day, and Saturday night, we end up at a party.

"Grayson?" Alexa looks surprised to see me. "I thought you moved."

I give her a one-armed hug. "I did. I'm just visiting for the weekend."

"Shame. I've missed you around here."

The flirtatious glint in her eyes is clear, and who am I to deny her? I finish off my drink and place the empty cup down on the counter.

"Well, I'm here now."

She takes my hand and leads me to an empty room. The second the door closes behind us, my back is against it, and her lips are on mine. It's not the first time I've hooked up with her, or even the fifth, but something feels different. Her lips aren't as soft as the last ones I kissed. Her body doesn't fit against mine like we were made from the same mold. She doesn't taste like strawberries and summer. *She's not Savannah.*

Frustrated, I push away from the door and turn her, so she's pinned to the wall. Running my hand up her shirt, I roll her nipple between my fingers. She mewls at the feeling, but still—nothing in me is reacting to her.

She's. Not. Savannah. My subconscious reminds me for the second time, and for fuck's sake, it's right. The little bitch has dug her talons in me. Maybe that kiss had more of an effect that I realized, and that can only mean one thing.

I'm so fucked.

GETTING TO SCHOOL MONDAY morning, I can already feel the tension. It's as if I'm hyperaware of her location at all times. When she pulls up in Brady's car while I'm smoking my morning cigarette. When we're sitting in class and she keeps glancing over at me. When she walks into the cafeteria that's swarming with people. I can sense her presence before I see her, and that makes me nervous. I've already seen what can happen if I get too close, and I *can't* have a repeat of that. What I must to do is clear, but won't be easy.

I need to ignore her until I have more control over my feelings.

A WEEK AND A HALF passes, and while it's been difficult, I've successfully managed to ignore Savannah completely. It's taken a little more effort than I thought it would though— actively avoiding her in the hall, and making a conscious effort to not look at her during practice. I'd hoped it would have worked by now, and it has, to a degree, but I still need more time. It's worth the wait to make sure the revenge I have planned is executed perfectly.

"Yo, Hayworth. Wait up," Carter calls as he jogs down the hallway.

I give him a look, wondering what's so important. "Everything okay?"

"Yeah, I just wanted to see if you plan on coming Friday night."

My brows furrow. "Coming where?"

"Savannah's birthday. Weren't you paying attention?"

"No," I admit. "I've been distracted lately."

It's a lie. I've been purposely ignoring everything the

118

second someone mentions her name, but I can't exactly tell him that. He'll grill me about it for hours.

He nods in understanding. "Well, you should come. We're going to Hypnotic."

"Isn't that a twenty-one and over club?"

Giving me a knowing look, he chuckles. "Yes, Mormon Grayson. That's what fake IDs are for." He takes out his phone and sends me a text. "Meet me at that address after school. We'll get you a good one."

Well, fuck. I guess I'm going to Savannah's birthday party.

IT'S PROBABLY IDIOTIC TO go to a club when you're *this* sexually frustrated—not that I could do anything about it if I tried. After the incident with Alexa, I haven't even attempted to hook up with Kinsley. The last thing I need is for her to go around telling people I can't get it up. Still, not going tonight could potentially make Savannah think she has the upper hand. Can't have that, now can I?

As soon as the bouncer hands me back my fake ID, I slip past the rope and inside. The place is nice, filled with different colored lighting and loud music. I instantly spot the guys at a VIP table. *Of course.*

"Aye!" Carter says excitedly when he sees me. "I didn't know if you were going to make it."

"What can I say? You talked me into it." The level of sarcasm in my voice is obvious, but he's too drunk already to notice.

I say hello to everyone else before my eyes land on Savannah. *Fuck. Me.* She's wearing a white dress with lace across the top and bottom. The view of her legs is incredible, as the dress only goes down to mid-thigh. Her hair cascades down and lays gently against her chest. The gloss she has on

119

her lips reflects in the light and draws my attention, making me crave kissing her again.

Clearing my throat, I try to ignore her surprise at my being here. "Happy Birthday."

"Thank you."

It's the first thing we've said to each other in two weeks, since I made the colossal mistake of giving myself a small taste of her. Not only did that kiss show me what I'm denying myself, but it confirmed what I assumed all along— she wants me, too. It's a shame she ruined everything before we even had a chance to get started. We could have been explosive.

FOR MOST OF THE night, I manage to stay in check. Keeping drinks to a minimum so my judgment isn't clouded, and focusing more on talking to the guys than admiring how Savannah looks tonight. However, not a damn thing in the world could have prepared me for seeing the way she moves on the dance floor.

Her hips sway to the beat, displaying her expertise so well that people around start to watch. She spins around as she smiles brightly and laughs with Emma. Anyone in this room can tell she's a professional. Confidence radiates off of her. One thing is clear— she's at her best when she's dancing.

"She's something else, isn't she?" Hayden says, and my hand tightens around the rail, making him chuckle. "Don't worry, my eyes are on Em."

I relax slightly. "Sorry, I'm just so tired of people trying to talk to me about Savannah."

"I get that." He takes a sip of my drink. "Jace said you two already knew each other?"

"What do you fuckers do, sit around and discuss other people's lives?"

He laughs. "The easiest way to make sure everyone finds something out is to tell Jace or Carter."

"I've noticed."

Whatever Hayden says next goes completely unnoticed as I watch a guy walk up to Sav and put his hands on her hips. She startles for a second, but then grins and keeps dancing—grinding her ass into him. My blood runs hot, and I bite down on my lip so hard it bleeds. *She's mine.*

Hayden watches me carefully. "Should I be concerned you're about to kill someone? Cause you have that look in your eyes."

Fuck it. I throw caution to the wind and hand Hayden my beer before making my way down there. Emma sees me coming, but Savannah has no idea. In one fluid motion, my fingers wrap around her wrist, pulling her from his grasp and into my own. She catches herself with one hand against my chest, and when her gaze meets mine, her breath hitches.

"The fuck, man?!" the douchebag protests.

"Tell him to leave," I order, keeping my sights on her.

She turns and gives him a sympathetic smile. He rolls his eyes but walks away, probably to find someone else to make a move on. Meanwhile, Sav focuses her attention back on me.

"Are you happy now?"

I smirk and glance down at her lips for only a second before spinning her around and gripping her waist, covering his touch with my own. "Show me what you've got, tiny dancer."

13

SAVANNAH

THE BUZZING IN MY EARS DOESN'T EVEN BEGIN TO compare to how my body feels, pressed against Grayson's. After he's completely ignored my existence for the past couple weeks, the last thing I expected was for him to come tonight, let alone be dancing with me. It's wrong, screwed up beyond belief, and I should hate him. His tendency to play hot and cold is a proverbial mind-fuck. Yet, as his chest is pressed against my back, I couldn't care less. This is what I want—what I've always wanted—and I'm not about to deny myself of it—especially on my birthday.

I reach back and place my hand on the back of his neck, pulling him closer. The glaring looks I'm getting from Kinsley are only motivating me further. With one particular circle of my hips, a low groan emits from the back of Grayson's throat. His lips move to the shell of my ear.

"Keep doing that, and I can promise you the whole club will find out just how easily that dress can be torn off."

A shiver runs down my spine. My nerve endings come alive, and all I want is for him to make good on that promise. Repeating my actions, his grip tightens hard enough to bruise.

"Savannah Jade," he warns, and hearing him say my middle name reminds me that this isn't just some guy.

This is Grayson.

This is Gray.

My Gray.

IT'S ONE O'CLOCK IN the morning by the time we're all leaving the club. After spending hours on the dance floor, I've never been so exhausted—and so turned on—in my life. The second we finished dancing, he went right back to the quiet, brooding guy I've come to see him as, but his eyes stayed on me.

As we get to the parking lot, Jace pulls up in his Mercedes. Carter walks toward the passenger side, and Jace motions to the backseat.

"Come on. I'll give you a ride home."

I hesitate, but as soon as I open my mouth to answer, Grayson comes out of nowhere.

"I've got it."

Carter beams like a proud parent while Jace snickers. "About damn time. Come on, Kinsley. Get in."

"B-but…"

Standing up through the sunroof, Carter points at her and then the car. "Let's go, or we're leaving you here to walk home."

She sulks like a child as she gets in the back and closes the door behind her. I give her a fake smile and wave as Jace drives away.

"Come on."

Grayson and I walk to his car in total silence. He unlocks the door, and we both climb in. There are so many things I want to say to him, but judging by the look on his face, he doesn't want to hear it. Gone is the hot and fiery

124

guy whose jealousy took over tonight. Instead, he's stone cold.

Halfway through the ride home, I can't take the silence anymore. I reach to put the radio on, but he immediately turns it right back off. Rolling my eyes, I turn to look at him.

"Thank you for giving me a ride home. I wasn't sure what to tell Jace back there."

Nothing. Not a smile, or a hum. He's just blank. I focus on staring out the window, watching the lights go by as we drive out of the city.

We pull up to my house, and I sigh in relief when I notice my dad isn't home. He already forgot my birthday, not that I expected him to remember. The last thing I wanted was to deal with him asking me where I was tonight—like he has any right to act like a parent now.

"Thanks again."

He doesn't say a word as I get out of the car and run inside, leaping over the rotten parts of the porch that I have committed to memory. A part of me considers just going to bed, but the club was so crowded that I feel grimy and disgusting. I grab a towel from the linen closet and go into the bathroom.

Throughout the duration of my shower, I can't shake the feeling of Grayson's touch. It lingers everywhere. His hands on my waist. His lips at my ear. The length in his pants as I ground against him. It's taking over my mind and making it hard to focus on anything else.

Sliding my hand between my legs, I press two fingers against my clit—rubbing in a circular motion. I close my eyes and imagine it's Grayson. My head lolls back against the tiles as I try to picture him doing this to me, but I know nothing is close to the real thing. That kiss in the hallway did more than take my breath away. It ruined me for even myself.

Giving up, I turn off the water and climb out before wrapping a towel around my chest. As I reach my room and

125

shut the door behind me, a shadow cast on the wall tells me I'm not alone. I'm about to scream, but something stops me.

"Grayson?" I flick on the light to find him sitting on my bed, staring at his hands. "What are you doing here?"

His eyes meet mine before gazing over my body, reminding me that I'm only in a towel. Within a second, he gets up and stalks across the small room. My back is against the door, and he's so close I can taste him. Our breaths mix together as he runs his knuckles down my arm, and the conflicted look on his face makes my heart hurt.

"Tell me to stop, Sav." He all but whispers. "Tell me to leave. You have to."

I should, that much is clear. No good could come of this. Not when he hates me. Not when his sole mission in life is to destroy me. And yet, I want him here, more than I've ever wanted anything.

"Stay."

Like the crack of a whip, his restraint snaps, and for the second time in two weeks, his lips are on mine. I gasp at the sudden movement. Taking advantage of the opportunity, he slips his tongue into my mouth and intertwines it with my own. He tastes the way he looks—sexy and dangerous, with a small hint of home.

"Fucking hell," he groans as he presses against me. "You don't know how bad I've wanted this. Wanted you."

My head falls to the side when he starts kissing my neck. His mouth is like magic as he licks and sucks on the sensitive skin. I can already feel how rock hard he is. His hand starts sliding up my thigh, lifting the towel just enough. He's tender at first, rubbing me in all the right places. My body is entirely at his mercy, and I'd stay like this forever if given the chance.

"Oh God." I breathe, quivering from the pleasure.

He smirks. "You haven't seen anything yet, baby."

The pet name alone turns me into a puddle of mush. His

126

lips find mine again, and he kisses me, hard yet sweet. Still holding the towel around me, he places his hand over my own and slowly starts to pry it off.

"Can I?" he asks, voice full of sincerity. Like if I told him no, he would respect it. Like I'm in control.

I nod and release the only thing covering me, allowing him to slide it down until it pools on the floor. He lets his eyes sweep across my body and bites his lip.

"You're perfect."

Gripping my hips, he lifts me up and carries me over to my bed. He gently lays me down before pulling his shirt over his head. I need to resist the urge to whine at how physically flawless he is. The term "washboard abs" was invented with this boy in mind. I'm sure of it.

My hand reaches up and rests on his chest, then makes its way down. I feel over every muscle, memorize every dip. He stays completely still until I reach his pants and pop open the button. I pull the zipper down slowly as he watches me.

"Take them off," I tell him. When he still seems unsure, I look him straight in the eyes. "I want this, Gray."

He's fighting something as he takes a few breaths. "Do you know what you're asking? I know you're a virgin, but I won't go easy. I can't. I don't know how."

"H-how do you know that?"

"You told me," he admits. "The night you were drunk and I brought you back to my house."

Fuck me and my drunken admissions. I can only imagine what else came out of my mouth. However, it still doesn't change the fact that I want this, want him. I grab his shoulders and pull him down onto me, pressing my lips to his.

"Take it, Grayson. It's yours. It always has been."

He growls before standing up, pushing his pants and boxers down in one go. His hard cock springs free, making my eyes widen. He's big, probably eight or nine inches, and thick. I timidly wrap my hand around it, and he hisses as his head falls back. Moving to the edge of the bed, he watches me as I stick my tongue out and lick the tip—tasting the small bead of pre-cum that has accumulated.

"Fuck," he murmurs.

I take the head into my mouth and swirl my tongue around it as I pump the rest with my hand. His reaction only encourages me to keep going. I slide him in and out a few times until he hits the back of my throat. Grayson moans, fisting his hand in my hair and pulling me off him.

"You keep doing that, and this won't last long enough for me to take anything."

As I lay back, he steps out of his jeans and climbs onto the bed beside me. He kisses my neck then proceeds to move further down my body. When he reaches my breasts, he takes one nipple into his mouth and sucks, while his fingers tease the other. I arch my hips as I release a loud whimper. I know I should be quiet, in case my dad comes home, but I can't help it. It feels too good.

"Fuck me, Gray. Please, fuck me."

He groans and rests his forehead on my chest. "Christ, Sav. You can't just say things like that and expect me not to combust on the spot." Moving even lower, he blows a cool breath over my belly button. "Soon, baby."

I'm about to argue it when his tongue grazes over my clit, and I instantly see stars. He flicks his tongue a couple times, making me quiver and squirm on the bed, before slipping one finger inside of me.

"You taste so good," he murmurs against me before diving back in for more.

My hand reaches down, lacing into his hair to pull him closer and get more friction. As I start to grind against him, he pulls his one finger out and replaces it with two. The sting is uncomfortable, but only slightly. Like he can sense my discomfort, he applies more pressure and sucks my clit into his mouth. His fingers work to spread me open as his mouth makes me feel things that could put even the best drugs to shame.

Pressure starts to build, and I find it harder to stay quiet. He adds another finger to the mix and moans as his tongue and thumb rub me in ways that push me right over the edge. My orgasm explodes inside of me as I scream his name.

"Holy shit!" I pant while coming down from the intense euphoria. "That was amazing."

He picks his head up and licks his lips, pulling a condom from the pocket of his jeans. "We're just getting started."

I watch as he rips the foil packet open with his teeth and rolls it over his hard cock. Once he's done, he moves closer and lines himself up at my entrance. He inches in just slightly, making me wince at the pain of being stretched open. When he reaches the small bit of resistance, he stops and looks at me.

"Last chance to change your mind."

I shake my head. "Do it."

Coming down to kiss me, he covers my body with his own and thrusts in—breaking through and claiming me entirely. He starts off slow, pulling out and pushing back in until I assure him that I'm all right. Then he quickens his pace.

"Shit, your pussy is so fucking tight." He hisses, pulling up to get better leverage.

The only thing leaving my mouth is a mix of his name and obscenities. He starts going faster, harder, chasing his high and bringing me with him. The pitch of my voice raises, and he grits his teeth as he presses his thumb to my clit.

"Grayson!" I shout as I feel myself on the brink of another mind-blowing orgasm.

"Not my name, baby. Not tonight."

I throw my head back against the pillow while my hips

arch up instinctively, needing just a little more pressure. And like I knew he would, he gives it to me.

"Fuck, Gray!" I scream as I clench around him.

With one last hard thrust, he roars and pulses inside of me—shooting his load into the condom. Just like that, my virginity is gone. Taken by the one person I always imagined giving it to, but under completely different circumstances. All I can do now is hope I don't live to regret it.

14

GRAYSON

AFTER WHAT WAS HANDS DOWN THE BEST SEX OF my life, I ease myself out of her and pull the condom off, tying the end and tossing it into the garbage can before collapsing down onto the bed. The only sound in the room is our labored breathing, but it's not at all awkward. Savannah giggles happily, smiling from ear to ear.

"Holy shit, that was incredible," she whispers.

I smirk and turn to look at her, taking in how good she looks all sexed out. "Pissed you waited so long now?"

It only takes a second of thinking about it before she shakes her head. "No. If I hadn't, it wouldn't have been you." She rolls over to face me. "And you said you didn't know how to go easy."

It's true, I did, and when I said it, I meant it. But hovering over her and seeing how vulnerable she was while still trusting me not to hurt her, it's like something in me knew—she's the exception. She's everything I shouldn't want, and everything I can't resist.

As I let my eyes rake over her body once more, I notice a healing bruise over her ribcage. "What happened?"

Her attention focuses on what I'm looking at, and she

hesitates just long enough to make me suspicious. "Oh, that. Dance injury. It happens."

Every part of me says she's lying—but why would she lie about a bruise? Where else could it have come from? *No, stop. It's not my problem.* I push it to the back of my mind and focus on the here and now. Slipping my arm underneath her body, I pull her closer so her head rests on my chest. I'm already going to hell for this; I may as well enjoy it. She relaxes into me and sighs in relief.

"Will you stay?"

I hum, pressing a kiss to the top of her head but not answering the question. "Go to sleep, Sav."

She doesn't say anything else as her hand rubs small circles over my stomach. It isn't until she stops and her breathing steadies that I'm sure she's no longer awake. I allow myself a few more minutes with her, not wanting to get up just yet. I know once I do, my mind is going to torture me for what I just did.

THE NEXT MORNING, I wake in my own bed, with the taste of Savannah still lingering on my tongue. Last night plays in my mind like a movie reel. The way she moved, the sounds she made, how it felt to finally be inside her, I know one thing for sure—I'm utterly screwed. Now that I know what it's like to have her, divine intervention couldn't grant me enough self-control to resist doing it again.

Swiping my phone from the nightstand, I call the only other person who knows about my true intentions here.

"You slept with her, didn't you?" Tyson asks as soon as he answers the phone.

"How did you know?"

"Because you're calling me at 10 a.m. on a Saturday. You

never call anyone unless it's important." He pauses for a moment and then snickers. "So, how was it?"

I throw my arm over my eyes. "Fucking mind blowing."

"Damn, who would have thought a virgin would be so good? Let me have a pass at her, will you?"

He's kidding, I know that, but it doesn't stop me from growling possessively. "You're not helping, asshole."

He laughs like this shit is the funniest thing in the world to him. "Okay, okay. In all seriousness, though—I don't know why you're making such a big deal out of this. If anything, it only helps you."

"What do you mean?"

"*I mean,* you took her virginity. Girls eat that shit up. It's like every fairy-tale ever taught them that sex automatically means impending marriage."

He has a point, though I don't picture Savannah as the type to watch fairy-tales—not anymore, anyway. "I don't know, man."

"Just, hear me out." He inhales, reminding me I really need a cigarette. "You said she's too strong to break easily, did you not?"

"I did."

"Then you need something to play on, and this could be it. The more you take from her, the worse it'll hurt when you deliver that final blow. And in the meantime, you get to eat your cake and have it, too."

I groan, sitting up and rubbing a hand over my face. "That's pretty messed up."

He snorts. "No more fucked up than her lying and helping throw your dad in prison. Besides, it was impossible for you to keep your dick in your pants *before* you fucked her. You haven't got a chance now."

BY THE TIME MONDAY morning comes, I've already wallowed in self-pity enough to get it out of my system. One thing I'm not sure of, however, is whether I'm going to let myself have Savannah, or if I'll go back to staying away—or at least trying to. What Tyson said made sense, but it still feels like a betrayal to my dad. He said to stay away from her, and what took place Friday night was the total opposite of that.

"Okay, *please* tell me you two finally fucked," Carter requests as soon as I walk into school.

I roll my eyes. "Hey. Nice to see you, too."

"Yeah, yeah, hey. Life's good. Kids are great." He waves the topic off dismissively. "We can get together and paint our nails later. Now, you and Savannah?"

The way I see it, there are two ways I could go about this: I could become a legend by being the only guy in this school to bag Savannah Montgomery, or I can deny it and make her think it wasn't anything more than a meaningless fuck to me. Being as the former could backfire as she sees people praise me for getting with her, I go with the latter.

"Sorry to disappoint. I drove her home, that's all."

He groans loudly, turning to bang his head against the wall. "I was *really* hoping you two screwed the anger out of each other by now."

"Nope." I finish grabbing my books and close my locker. "And besides, even if I did, it wouldn't change anything. I can't stand that bitch."

Spinning around to go to class, I'm face to face with Savannah herself. I do my best to remain stoic, but I'd be lying if I said the hurt expression on her face didn't feel like a punch to the gut. Still, this is exactly what I was afraid of, and exactly what I can't allow to happen. She's nothing but a liar—a traitor in the worst degree—and I need to remember that.

THE DAY DRAGS BY so slowly that I start wonder if my concept of time is distorted. It'd be nice if that were the case, something a simple nap or good night's sleep could fix. Unfortunately, that's not it, and I know exactly what the problem is, or *who,* rather.

Every time I see her, I picture what she looks like underneath that uniform. The sound of her voice reminds me of how she screamed my name as she fell apart. I swear I've spent most of the day half hard inside these already uncomfortable dress pants.

If I can't make it through a few hours without fucking her with my eyes, how am I going to resist her for the rest of senior year? Getting revenge or not, it's not like we could ever be more than this. More than enemies. I would never allow it.

"Grayson?" Kinsley gets my attention in fourth period. "Are you okay? You look distracted."

Savannah turns around to look back at us, giving me a sad smile before narrowing her eyes on Kinsley. It's like they're in a silent pissing war, and only one is aware of it. Still, it looks like the school slut may not be useless after all. I give her one of my best smiles and take her hand in mine.

"I'm okay, babe. Thanks for checking on me, though."

She sighs dreamily. "You're welcome."

Savannah huffs before shoving earbuds in her ears. *Good, she's irritated.*

I THROW THE FOOTBALL down the field, watching Hayden catch it and run it into the end zone. My eyes drift over to the cheerleaders, despite all the times I've told myself not to look. Savannah is running them through a new stunt as they all watch her intently. Liam comes behind her, placing his hands on her waist and lifting her up. The sight of him touching her, even in such an innocent setting, has me seeing deep shades of red. Between being manhandled during cheer and her dance with Brady, she does enough to make me think my desire to lock her in my treehouse at eight years old wasn't such a bad idea.

Every part of me knows I shouldn't want her, but for fuck's sake, she's like a drug. An addiction that I've let myself taste and now can't quit. I think about everything that Tyson said, and maybe he was right. What if I can have the best of both? It's a dangerous line that I'd usually be hesitant to walk, but as long as I can keep my feelings purely sexual, I don't see why we can't do this.

I watch her carefully, waiting for the moment she goes inside—like she does every time they have practice. Her actions are so predictable I could set a watch to it. Sure enough, fifteen minutes later, I get a chance to glance over there and find her gone.

"I'll be right back.," I tell Coach, jogging over to the bleachers.

From where I'm standing, no one can see me unless they're coming from the school. Savannah walks out, not even thinking to look in my direction. I whistle to get her attention, and she turns to me with a confused look on her face.

"What are you doing?"

I smirk. "Waiting for you."

She scoffs, crossing her arms over her chest. "Are there a few screws loose in your head or something? Why the fuck would I want anything to do with you after the shit you pulled today?"

Before she can say anything else, I grab her by the back of the neck and pull her in, searing our mouths together. She squeals in surprise, but doesn't hesitate to kiss me back. Her hands grip the front of my shirt and pull me closer. My tongue tangles with hers in a fight for dominance, though it's a pointless battle—one she never had any chance of winning.

"You're mine, Savannah. I will use you however I want and treat you however I please. If you don't like it, tough. Tell someone who cares." I leave no room for debate. "Now, enough talking. I've done nothing all day but let thoughts of you run wild in my imagination." Sliding my shorts down, I pull my already hard cock out and pump it in my hand. "And we're going to make one a reality, right *fucking* now."

Her eyes widen as she looks around. "Grayson, we can't. What if people see us?"

"Then people see us." I look down at my dick and back up at her. "Unless you want to go get Kinsley for me. I'm sure she wouldn't hesitate to get on her knees."

It's exactly what I needed to say, because she immediately swats my hand away and replaces it with her own. "She comes anywhere near you like this, and you're going to see a side of me that would put even the craziest of psychos to shame."

"Ah-ah." I tut. "What did I say about talking?"

She rolls her eyes before dropping down. The second I feel her mouth on me, it's like I've died and gone to heaven. How did I ever expect to deny myself of this? I reach up and grip onto the bar above me.

"Fuck, you're good at that."

A low hum vibrates her mouth, and I throw my head back as I try to hold in the sounds of pure ecstasy. She pulls my cock out before running her tongue down the underside. Then, she smiles in a way that shows her determination. I don't get a second to wonder the meaning of it because she's taking me in again and shoving me all the way into the back of her throat. The second she gags around me, and proceeds to moan because of it, I'm completely spent.

My grip tightens as I explode, releasing myself inside of her lying little mouth and covering her sins with my own.

She takes everything I give her and swallows it down before licking her lips. It's erotic, and sexy, and has me ready to fuck her into oblivion right here—but I can't.

She stands, pulling my shorts up with her and tucking my softening dick safely inside them. "You ready to go back?"

And just like that, I feel my resolve start to slip. She's not trying to kiss me, or ask what this means. Maybe Tyson was wrong, and if that's the case, I'm in even more trouble than I thought.

"You go first. I'll wait a few minutes."

Her eyes narrow. "Why?"

"Because. No one can know about this." I grin as I wipe some cum from the corner of her mouth. "This is just getting rid of some built up sexual frustrations. Call it childhood fantasies, if you must. It won't last forever, and once it fizzles out, things will go back to how they were." I take a step back. "And besides, I wouldn't want Kinsley finding out."

She glares at me, practically shooting fire from her eyes. "You really are an asshole, you know that?"

"Never claimed to be otherwise, babe."

Shaking her head, she walks away and back to her team. Maybe it was a dick move, throwing her so-called *friend* in her face like that, but I don't want her to confuse this for something it's not. She needs to remember what we are.

Just like I need to remember what I came here for.

THE RAIN POUNDS ON the roof of the school as the thunder cracks loudly outside. The fact that they even had us come in today is surprising, being as they're expecting trees to be knocked over and there's potential for tornados. I'm sitting in second period, the one class I have with just Savannah. No one watching my every move or analyzing the

138

meaning of every glance her way. It's just the two of us, alone in a stupid graphic design class.

Another bolt of lightning flashes. Judging by how closely the thunder comes after, it couldn't have been more than a couple miles away. However, that's not what surprises me.

One of the most vivid memories I have of Savannah from when we were younger is the time she slept over my house during a really bad storm.

I roll over in my bed, trying to drown out the sound of the downpour that's happening outside. The wind blows harshly against the window, and I wonder how much force it would take for it to break. As another rumble of thunder sounds, I hear it mix with the sound of a muffled scream.

Savannah?

Slipping out of bed, I make my way across the hallway and into the guest room. Savi is curled up under the blanket, shaking uncontrollably. I close the door behind me and turn on the light.

"Sav? What's wrong?"

She peaks her head out from the comforter. "N-nothing. I'm o-okay."

Another bang and she screams, immediately going back to her hiding place. I chuckle softly and walk over to the bed, lifting the blanket and slipping under it with her. As I look at her face, I realize she's been crying. The dried tears mix with the new wet ones leaking out.

"Why didn't you tell me you were afraid of thunderstorms?"

She sighs, looking away from me. "I didn't want you to think I'm a baby."

I place my hand under her chin and lift it until our eyes meet. "I would never think that. Now, come here." Putting my arms out, she willingly cuddles into me. "And besides, I'm just as bad with spiders."

A giggle leaves her mouth. "You're worse."

"Am not."

"Are too! The last time you saw one in the treehouse, you screamed so loud I heard it from my room."

I poke her in the side, loving the way she squirms. "That was different. It was huge!"

"Whatever you say, wuss."

That night, we fell asleep together, wrapped in each other's arms, where no storm or spider could ever hurt us.

With one more crack of thunder, everything goes completely black. The only thing brightening the room is the very minimal light coming through the windows. Still, Savannah is yet to flinch once.

"All right," Miss Lawson announces. "Grab your things and head to the gym. It looks like we're going to take shelter in there until the storm clears and the power comes back on."

I gather all my belongings quickly and make sure to stand next to Sav as we leave the classroom.

"When did that happen?"

Her brows furrow. "When did *what* happen?"

"You lost your fear of storms," I explain. "I seem to remember a time when I needed to hold you so you'd stop screaming every time lightning struck."

"Maybe that was just an excuse to get you to hold me."

I hum. "Perhaps, but we were nine, and you were crying."

She chuckles dryly, looking anywhere but at me. "Why do you care, Grayson?"

She's right, I shouldn't. The fucked-up fact that I do is not lost on me.

"Just humor me."

Groaning, she turns around and looks me straight in the

eyes. "About a year after you left, when thunderstorms became the least scary thing I dealt with."

With nothing else to say, she walks away and leaves me alone to wonder what she meant by that. I saw how afraid she was that night, and there is no way it was a ploy to get in my arms. Her fear was too genuine, too painstakingly real to be faked.

My mind instantly remembers the bruise on her ribcage. She said it was from dance, but what if it wasn't? I try to remind myself that her safety and wellbeing aren't my problem, but the second I see Delaney in the hallway, it all goes out the window. She needs someone, and while it *can't* be me, that doesn't mean she should be alone.

"Laney," I call out to her. She stops and waits for me as I catch up. "Hey. You and I need to talk."

15

SAVANNAH

Pirouette. Three rotations. Turnout. Grand jeté.

I throw myself into the moves, using each one to distract my mind from thoughts of Grayson. Lennon follows along with a mastered skill. We both move in sync, showing how compatible we are as a duet. Brady stands off to the side and watches the choreography for any errors while controlling the music.

"Lennon, work on your face. You look pained," he tells her.

She laughs, not faltering in her moves at all. "You try keeping up with her. You'd be in pain too."

I ignore their banter and focus on the routine. In the recital, I have four dances—a solo, a duet with Lennon, a duet with Brady, and a group routine with me as the featured dancer. It may be a lot to take on, but I've never liked anything more. Dancing is my escape, my happy place. When I'm letting my body get lost in a song, it's like nothing else in the world matters.

Arabesque. Front Aerial. Fouetté. Turn. Run. Split. Pirouette. Turnout. Fall. Pose.

As the music ends, I can see how hard Lennon is

143

breathing, while I've barely broken a sweat. She looks at me in disbelief and shakes her head as she falls to the floor.

"That's it. I'm convinced. You're superhuman."

I grab my water bottle from the windowsill and sit down to rest against the wall. "No, I've just been doing this for years. Over a decade even. It's all I know."

Brady plays some background music and joins us on the floor to stretch, warming up for our duet. "I always judge Savannah's mood on how hard she dances.," he offers, and it reminds me of how well he knows me. "Like today, there's something on her mind. Something she's trying to avoid."

"Ooh. Do tell." Lennon rolls onto her stomach and rests her chin on her fist.

I shake my head. "There's nothing *to* tell. I just really want to do well at the recital, that's all."

It's wrong to lie to my best friend, and making Grayson right about me sucks, but it's better than the alternative. If I told Brady that I lost my virginity, and *who* I lost it to, he would lose his shit. Protective is an understatement for what he is when it comes to me. I'm already beating myself up over all this. I don't need his lecture on top of it.

Sleeping with Grayson was a bad move. I know that. It gave him another thing to hold over my head. But, in that moment, with him less than an inch away from me and looking in my eyes like he needed me to ease the pain, I've never wanted anything more.

I thought maybe things would be different after that night. Don't get me wrong, I never expected him to magically fall in love with me and everything to be okay, but I didn't think he'd still be a cold-hearted asshole. Hearing him continue to flirt with Kinsley right in front me stung. I had hoped that at the very least he would stop that, but I was wrong.

When I saw him waiting for me behind the bleachers, I had every intention of telling him to go fuck himself.

However, the second he kissed me, all the willpower I had to resist him vanished. Kissing Grayson is just as exciting and heart stopping as it was the first time, when we were ten years old and sitting on top of his roof, under the stars.

The level of certainty in his voice as he told me that I'm his sent shockwaves straight through me and made me clench around nothing. He could have taken me right then and there, and I probably would've let him. It made one thing very clear to me—turning him down is not something I have the ability to do. It's a scary revelation, because that means I'm completely at his mercy.

I'M JUST ABOUT TO get in the shower when there's a knock at my front door. As soon as I open it, I feel like someone hit me with a bus. Delaney stands on the other side, looking just as shocked as I feel.

"Fucking Grayson," I grumble under my breath and open the door wider to let her in.

She gives me a warm smile as she steps inside and looks around the hellhole I've been so very blessed with. That's the thing about Delaney—she always tries to withhold judgment of others. However, I've known her since I was a kid, and I can almost hear the thoughts running through her head.

"What are you doing here?"

She shoots me questioning look. "I could ask you the same thing."

My eyes roll harshly. "Yeah, yeah. Perfect Savannah Montgomery is really just a poor chick from the wrong side of town. Quit the shit and just tell me why you're here."

Placing a hand on her hip, she shakes her head. "Okay, stop. Just because your life went a little downhill doesn't mean you can be rude to everyone around you."

"*A little downhill?* Look around, Delaney! This place looks like it'll fall apart with too strong of a breeze. I'd hardly call going from living in the house next to yours to this shit hole just 'a little downhill.'" As she remains quiet, I take a deep breath and run my fingers through my hair to calm down. "Are you going to tell everyone?"

"No." She answers without any hesitation at all, catching me off guard. After how I've been the past few years, I wouldn't blame her for a second if she went to school tomorrow and shouted it from the rooftops.

"Why not?"

"Because." She shrugs. "You used to be my best friend, and I miss that. I miss you."

All the emotions from the last couple weeks take over as I start to tear up. I cross the room quickly and pull her into my arms. It's been so long since I had a friend as good as her, and I was wrong to assume she would think any less of me for where I live.

We stand in the middle of the living room, sobbing like babies and squeezing each other like our lives depend on it. By the time we pull apart, our faces are soaked and my mascara is running.

"You look like a raccoon," she giggles, reaching up to wipe away some of the makeup. "I think I just made it worse."

I laugh and go toward the bathroom to wash up. "My room is just down the hall. You can wait in there. I'll only be a minute."

After I rid my face of all things cosmetic, I pull my phone from my pocket and send a quick text to Grayson.

Savannah: You sent Delaney to my house?! Are you out of your mind?

As I walk down the hallway, a response comes in.

Grayson: Depends on who you ask. Have fun.

I roll my eyes.

Savannah: Oh, I will, and jokes on you. She's not going
to expose me.

Grayson: Damn.

I could spend all day overevaluating his sarcasm and
trying to figure out what it means, but that would be
pointless. He's so different from the boy I remember. To
understand him, I'd need to get closer, but that process alone
is dangerous. One of us will end up hurt, and I have a feeling
it won't be him.

DELANEY AND I SPEND hours catching up. She tells me
about how her older sister Ainsley went away to college,
which doesn't surprise me. After graduating valedictorian
three years ago, I'd expect nothing less. She also fills me in
on what Tessa has been up to lately. I'd heard plenty of the
rumors going around, but I never thought they were true—
especially the one about her dating Easton, one of Knox's
best friends.

"What did your dad have to say about that? I can't
imagine he was okay with it."

She laughs. "I mean, if you call getting into a screaming
match with Tess as he told her she's forbidden from seeing
him okay with it, then sure."

"Oh God." I face palm. "That probably only made her
want to date him more."

"Worse. She slammed a door so hard the chandelier fell
from the ceiling and shattered on the floor."

My jaw drops. "She didn't!"

Laney nods. "Oh, she definitely did. And then she went and snuck out her window to go see Easton. My dad threatened to send her to boarding school, but you and I both know it's an empty threat."

"She'd get kicked out anyway," I reply, only half joking.

The front door opens and then slams shut. A wave of dread washes over me as I look at Delaney, eyes wide and pleading. She may already know I'm poor, but I seriously doubt my father is sober right now, so she's about to know all my secrets.

"Savannah!" he shouts, sure enough slurring my name while he stumbles down the hall. "Whose expensive ass car is in front of my house?" Appearing in the doorway, his sights land on Delaney. "Well, I'll be damned—little Delaney Callahan. Look at you! You must be eighteen by now."

Her brows furrow as she looks between the two of us. "Uh, not for another few months."

My father, the sick fuck that he is, blatantly checks her out before frowning. "That's too bad."

"Dad, Delaney was just leaving." I stand up from my bed, praying she follows my lead. I turn and give her a look. "I'll walk you out."

She fakes a smile. "Thanks. It was nice seeing you again, Mr. Montgomery."

He stares at her chest as we slip by him, making me nearly vomit in my mouth. "Yeah, you too. Come by anytime."

I don't think I've ever rushed out of my house so fast, and Delaney is hot on my heels. As soon as reach her car, she looks back at the house and then at me.

"Jeez, Savannah! What in the world happened to *him*?"

I really don't have the answer to that question. Shrugging, I say, "Drugs? Alcohol? Who the fuck knows exactly, but I don't have time to get into it. He'll follow me out here if I don't get back in there soon."

She gives me one last hug before unlocking her car. "I'm really glad we're friends again."

I smile. "Me, too."

When I go back inside, my father is already drinking straight from a bottle of Jack Daniels. He grunts as he sees me, which I'm totally prepared to ignore until he opens his mouth.

"That Callahan girl grew up nice," he tells me. "When's her birthday again?"

Maybe it's the fact that I have a lot to make up for when it comes to her, or that I just got her back in my life, but every protective bone in my body narrows in on him.

"Leave her alone."

He laughs. "You have some nerve trying to tell *me* what to do."

I stand my ground and step closer. "If you want to be a sick disappointment of a man, that's on you, but leave Delaney out of your mess."

Before I know it, he's up and rushing toward me, gripping me by the neck and pinning me to the wall. "Excuse me, you ungrateful little bitch."

"Go ahead, leave a mark where everyone at school will see," I croak out, and he lets go but still stands too close.

He looks down at me, trying to intimidate me with his height. "You're lucky I don't kill you."

"Lucky?" I scoff. "That'd be doing me a favor."

I know it's the wrong thing to say the second I see his face. My eyes look for somewhere else to go, anywhere to escape him, but I'm stuck. Rearing his fist back, he slams it directly into the side of my head, and everything goes black.

I go into Gray's room and find his window wide open. My feet pad across the room as I stick my head out and see him sitting on the roof. I smile and climb out to join him while he looks at the stars.

"I thought I might find you out here."

He grins, making my heart beat faster. "It's so pretty when there are no clouds in the sky."

Tipping my head back, I realize how amazing it looks, all lit up. "Wow, it is."

We sit in a comfortable silence, neither one of us wanting to ruin the moment. Still, it seems like something is bothering him, and I've never been able to feel at ease when he's not.

"What's wrong?"

He shakes his head just slightly, but then sighs. "It's nothing."

"It's not nothing if it's making you sad on a night like this." I nudge him with my elbow. "What is it?"

He's quiet for a moment, as if he's trying to decide whether he should tell me or not. I'm about to ask again when he finally speaks.

"I don't know what I want," he admits. "Maybe it's a new bike, maybe it's my best friend."

What? Did he just admit to liking me? That he wants me? He looks over at me with a sheepish grin on his face, and I realize he did. My face breaks out into a huge smile—one he returns as his shoulders sag in relief. As we both admire the sky some more, I feel his hand slowly rub against mine. I follow his lead, and our fingers lace together.

"I really like you, Savi, and not just as my best friend."

The butterflies that come alive in my stomach may very well carry me away. "I really like you, too, Gray."

His eyes study my face, almost as if he's looking for any sign that I may be messing with him, but he isn't going to find one. When his gaze lingers a little too long on my lips, I start to get nervous. Oh my God, is he going to kiss me?

A million things run through my head as he starts to lean in. Did I brush my teeth this morning? Am I going to mess this up? Will he not like me anymore if I'm bad at this? However, when it all comes down to it, this is Gray—my Gray.

I lean in to meet him some of the distance. Our noses touch first, and my eyes flutter closed. I can feel his breath on my face, warm but stutteringly nervous. Then, our lips brush together. It's slow, and sweet, and everything dreams are made of. When he breaks the kiss and backs away, I can feel my cheeks heat. I rest my head on his shoulder as I replay it in my mind.

Our friendship may never be the same, but I've never been more excited for the future.

I WAKE IN THE morning on my bedroom floor, sporting a killer headache. The huge bump on my head reminds me of last night's events. *Fucking hell.* He must have dragged me in here after he knocked me out and just left me on the floor. I get up slowly then go into the bathroom to find some Tylenol. After swallowing the two pills down, I turn on the shower. I don't necessarily feel like going to school, but the alternative of staying here all day is my only other option. Needless to say, school is the lesser of the two evils.

FIRST PERIOD, I MAKE it a point to sit next to Delaney. I may have made a lot of mistakes in my life, but it feels so good to have my friend again. Brady is great, but Laney was the closest friendship I had, other than Grayson—and it doesn't look like I'm ever getting that one back.

"No, stop," I laugh, pushing her hand away so I can continue applying the highlight to her face.

She huffs, but stays completely still. "I'm going to look like a clown."

"You know, your confidence in me is rather insulting."

A small chuckle bubbles out. "You'll get over it."

"Well, don't you two look cute," Grayson drawls, coming to stand in front of the desks we've pushed together.

Delaney tries to look at him, but I grab her chin and turn her back toward me. "What do you want, Grayson? We're busy."

"Ouch." He places a hand over his heart and feigns injury. "I can't come say hi to my two favorite girls?" I start to think he's gone mad when he corrects himself. "Well, one of my favorite girls, and you."

Switching out the highlight for bronzer, I shake my head. "No, I'd really rather you don't."

He leans over my desk and gets as close to me as he can. "That's not what you were saying on your birthday."

"What happened on your birthday?" Delaney shrieks.

"Shh!" I tell her and then turn to Grayson. "You know, for someone who wants to keep that quiet, you sure have a big mouth."

His eyes glint with mischief as he smiles. It's the same smile that used to make me weak in the knees, and like a fine wine, it's only gotten better with age. He winks at me before going back to his desk and immediately focusing his attention on Kinsley. *Jackass.*

Delaney follows my gaze. When she finds what I'm looking at, she frowns.

"Okay, you *really* need to tell me what is going on with you two, including what he was just referring to."

WHEN I GET HOME from dance that evening, I'm so worn out I can barely move. My headache ended up coming back my third period, and then again as I tried to rehearse the duet with Brady. Between the sharp pain in my skull, and Delaney's advice running through my mind on a loop, I couldn't focus at all. Brady ended up calling it early and telling me to figure out my shit before it costs me my chances at Juilliard. I know he didn't mean to be hurtful, but it stung.

I sit on my bed and hold my phone in my hand, once again thinking about my conversation with Laney. After telling her everything that has happened with Grayson, not foregoing the massive detail of him taking my virginity, she seemed hesitant to give me her honest opinion. It took promising that I won't stop talking to her again before she told me that I shouldn't be allowing him to walk all over me —and she's right.

The more power Grayson has, the stronger he becomes. After some of the shit he's done, he doesn't deserve the time of day from me, let alone my body. No matter how much I may want him, I need to protect myself, and that means stopping this sick game before it's really even started.

My fingers move across the keys quickly, as if I'm ripping off the Band-Aid. Without giving myself a second to change my mind, I hit send and ignore the uncomfortable feeling in my stomach.

It had to be done.

16

GRAYSON

CARTER POINTS AT A PAGE IN THE PLAYBOOK, explaining it to Jace like him understanding it matters. He's the kicker, and as skilled as he is at it, the only thing he needs to concern himself with is getting the ball through the goal posts. Still, he and Carter argue the technicalities on everything.

The original plan of tonight was to come up with some new plays. The past few years, North Haven has dominated on the football field, but only because HG's previous quarterback graduated, and, until me, they hadn't found anyone good enough to defeat them. This year, however, all that is going to change.

I take a sip of my beer as to the two idiots in front of me bicker. I swear, if I didn't know any better, I would think they have some secret romance going on. They argue like a married couple.

"Seriously, can we go back to coming up with plays? Not everyone wants to sit here all night and listen to you."

Carter rolls his eyes and flips the page, starting to place the Xs and Os where they go. My phone vibrates on the table and I see a text from Savannah. Before anyone has a chance to see it, I grab it and swipe it open.

Savannah: Friday night was a bad judgment call, and Monday on the field should have never happened. Whatever was going on between us is over. It won't happen again.

Reading her words, anger boils inside of me. The thought of her turning me down and denying me of what's mine makes my chest tighten. It's like I automatically feel like slamming my fist into the nearest wall. Who the hell does she think she is by ending this? Things between us will be over when *I* say they're over, and not a minute sooner. Didn't she hear me the other day?

In the worst timing ever, Jace returns from getting a drink. He glances at the phone clutched tightly in my hand. He doesn't get to see much before I flip it face down onto the hardwood.

"Dude, you're an absolute legend for bagging Savannah."

I shake my head. "I told you, nothing happened."

"I know what you *said*, but clearly, that was a lie. Anyone can see how badly you two want each other. And hey, all power to you. I've been trying to get with her for *years* and never had any luck." He smirks as he takes a sip of his beer. "Maybe you and I could tag team her one day. No homo shit though."

This guy really has a death wish, doesn't he? Between the way that Savannah is trying to brush me off like I'm the easiest thing in the world to quit, and this tool's hopes that I'll let him anywhere near her, I'm ready to explode.

I chug the rest of my beer before loudly slamming it back down on the table. "All right fuckers, I'm out. I've got shit to do."

They eye me suspiciously but don't say anything as I get

up and walk out. My car roars to life, and as I pull onto the street, I press the pedal to the floor. She doesn't know the monster she's just awoken.

PULLING UP TO SAVANNAH'S house, it looks like no one's home. However, a small light coming from two rooms near the back tells me that's not true. I get out of my car, going around and popping off the screen to her window. *Oh Savannah, don't you know better than to leave this unlocked?* Climbing through, I notice she's not in here. However, the sound of water running in the bathroom tells me her whereabouts.

The way I see it, I have two options. I can either wait for her here and have a total replay for what happened last time —a tempting idea— or I can do what I wanted that night. I decide on the latter and follow the sound of the noise.

Steam billows out the small crack in the bathroom door, and I can only imagine how hot the shower she's taking is. I step inside and close the door behind me before stripping down to nothing. She's yet to notice anyone else is in here as she hums along to one of her favorite songs—a song I believe she has a dance routine to.

The second I rip open the shower curtain, she lets out an ear-piercing shriek. Then, her eyes widen in disbelief.

"Grayson? What the fuck are you doing in here?"

"I told you. You. Are. Mine," I growl. "Whenever and wherever I want you."

She backs up as I step into the confined space with her. "Don't I get a say in this?"

I smirk. "No baby, and if you try to deny me, you'll see just how far I'm willing to go to get what I want."

Like a lion with its prey, I pounce—grabbing her and spinning us around so her back is against the wall. Our wet bodies collide, and my mouth meets hers in a passionate, sinful kiss. All the resistance she had in that text message and when I first stepped into the room, disappears without a trace. The only thing left is her, and me, and our burning desire to rip each other to shreds.

"Don't ever try to tell me this shit won't happen again," I tell her as I move to kiss her neck.

She moans, dragging her nails down my back and clinging to me in any way she can. I cup her pussy in my hand and use my middle finger to tease her clit. The vibrations of her body give away everything she's feeling. As I slip the digit in, I realize she's just as tight as the night I took her virginity. *Oh, this will be fun.*

Not giving her any preparation at all, and being consciously aware that I'm lacking a condom, I lift her up and line my cock up with her entrance. She waits for the painful intrusion she knows is coming, and when I slam myself inside her, she bites her lip and whimpers.

The feeling of her squeezing around me bare is one that can never be matched. I grip her waist with both of my hands and start to bounce her on my dick. As the pain starts to subside, she moves with me. With her hands on my shoulders for leverage, she keeps her legs wrapped tightly around my hips.

"Oh my God," she breathes, feeling the ecstasy in the moment.

"Last time I checked, baby, there's no god here."

The two of us move in tandem, getting carried away by our actions and quickening our pace. Before I know it, I'm pounding into her ruthlessly and she's taking every inch of what I give her. Her moans start to become louder, and her voice raises a few octaves—a telltale sign that she's about to come undone.

I wrap my arm around the back of her to make sure she doesn't fall and move one hand to tease her clit. Within seconds, her body starts to convulse with pleasure, and she releases with a silent scream of my name. The feeling of her orgasming around me was one thing when we were separated by a thin piece of rubber, but without it, it's unreal. I grit my teeth as I hold it in, letting her ride out her own high first. Then, once she starts to come down from it, I slip out and press on her shoulders. She gets on her knees and looks up at me, eyes wild yet innocent as she opens her mouth. With a few jerks of my hand, I explode, shooting everything I've got all over her face.

She swallows down what ended up in her mouth then proceeds to wipe her thumb through her cheek and suck on that too. I don't think I've ever seen anything so hot and erotic in my life.

I put my hand up to help her stand, and as she washes her face, I climb out of the shower—taking the towel she brought in for herself and using it to dry my body.

"What are you doing?" She asks.

I make quick work of getting dressed and just as my hand is on the doorknob, I turn to find her staring back at me. "I came here to prove a point. I got what I wanted, and now I'm leaving."

It's cruel, and most likely unnecessary, but there isn't an ounce of me that regrets it as I leave her to process my words. *Grayson 3, Savannah 0.*

THE NEXT DAY AT school, I half expect Sav to act differently. To give me sad eyes in the hallway, or confused glances during class. However, none of that happens. If I didn't know any better, I'd think that nothing was going on with her at all. She stays smiling, talking to Delaney and laughing with Emma. The things I said to her last night must have made no difference at all.

"Hey, Savannah!" Carter grins deviously as he calls her over. "Come here for a minute."

She walks to where we're hanging out on the steps of the school and gives him a curious look but refuses to let her eyes meet mine. "What's up?"

"Settle a debate for Jacey and me here." He winks at me. "True or False. You and Grayson fucked."

She turns to look at me, her expression taunting—threatening to expose our secret little sexcapades. I raise my brows at her and she rolls her eyes. "False. I wouldn't risk getting whatever shit he's most likely caught from Kinsley already."

If I wasn't there last night, and didn't have the scratch marks across my skin to prove it, even I would believe her. I chuckle and shake my head to play into the lie.

"I told you shitheads. Nothing happened."

They both look surprised, but still, Jace remains unconvinced. "I don't know. You two were at each other's throats for a while there, and then you drove her home on her birthday, and, suddenly, all that tension is gone."

Oh, trust me, it's anything but gone. I feel it now, as I stand here, inches away from her while she's unable to be touched. If anything, it's stronger. Simmering inside and ready to reach up and choke me at a single moment's notice. I need to be careful of the things I do and say, or she's going to end up being the one with all the power.

Savannah shrugs and sits down next to Paige. "I just realized he's not worth my time, that's all. After the club, he drove me home and dropped me off, where I went inside *alone* and went to sleep."

It's not the furthest thing from the truth. I *did* drop her off, and she *did* go inside alone, until I turned my damn car around like something from Fast and Furious and waited for her inside her room. She's simply leaving out the details between when she went in and when she fell asleep.

160

"All right, all right," Carter caves. "You two didn't bang. Fine."

I can't help but chuckle. "Why do you sound so disappointed?"

Jace ruffles Carter's hair and grins. "He lives in this world where Savannah is completely untouchable by anyone other than Brady Laurence. If *you* got with her, then maybe he has a shot."

"Fuck off, that's not true," Carter argues, but Savannah is grinning from ear to ear.

"Aw, my little Cartercakes." She reaches forward and pinches his cheeks, making him blush.

It's as innocent as something you'd see between kids at a playground, but tell that to the green-eyed monster inside of me, who wants to grab Carter by the throat. I look away and try to calm myself down, but it isn't easy. She needs to keep her hands to herself.

"Well, well. If it isn't my good friend Savannah." I glance over to see a kid, who looks about fifteen, coming toward us.

He's not wearing a uniform, which means he's from NHH, and judging by the look on her face, they're anything but *good friends*. She rolls her eyes and tries to seem unaffected, but I can tell she's nervous.

"What do you want, Trey?"

He looks like a douchebag as he comes and plasters himself against her side, way too close for my liking. "I thought you'd want to introduce me to your friends."

"I'd really rather not."

"Oh, come on," he presses. "Don't be like that, neighbor."

Everyone looks at him, confused, except me. I'm ready to kill the fucker.

"What is he talking about, Sav?"

She looks to me for saving, but even I'm not sure what to do. In perfect timing, Knox jogs across the street. He calls out Trey's name, and it looks like this kid is about to piss himself.

"Sorry, guys, this little fucker likes to start shit," he explains, grabbing him by the back of the neck and dragging him back across the street.

Carter glares at Knox. "Keep your trash on the other side of the street, Vaughn."

"Yup! Will do!"

Savannah sighs when she notices the threat is gone, and the conversation returns to normal, but I'm not completely satisfied. Had he outed her secret, I would have nothing left on her. Judging by her recent actions, she's unfazed by what we have going on behind closed doors. That secret is mine and mine alone. The only one that gets to fuck with her is me, and this little dipstick needs to learn that.

I take out my phone and send a quick text to Knox.

Grayson: I want to see that shithead in 20 minutes. No witnesses.

Watching him from where I stand, he reads my message and nods.

AFTER SEPARATING FROM EVERYONE else and waiting in my car for a bit, Knox sends me a location. When I get there, it's just him and Trey—whose fear can almost be smelled, it's so palpable. He turns around, and his eyes widen when he realizes who I am.

"I'll keep a lookout," Knox tells me, snickering and shaking his head as he walks away.

As I stalk toward Trey, he tries to take a few steps back. "Listen, man. I'm sorry. I didn't mean anything by it. I was just messing around."

I grip him by his shirt collar and slam him up against the brick wall. "Tell me what the fuck you know."

"I don't know anything," he pleads. "Just that I moved into a shitty neighborhood and found out that the most popular girl of Haven Grace Prep lives right next door. That's all, I swear."

Trying to pry my arm off, he doesn't get anywhere. I pull him off the wall only to push him right back into it, grinning evilly as he bangs his head. "You leave her the fuck alone; do you understand me? And if I find out you're telling *anyone* what you know, I'll make it so no one hears from you again."

He nods rapidly, and I drop him to the ground. Feeling satisfied, I leave him to tend to what is probably a killer headache. Knox is around the corner, and when he sees me approach, he smirks.

"That was fast."

I pull a cigarette from my pack and place it between my lips before offering him one as well. "He's a whiny little bitch. Doesn't do confrontation well, does he?"

Chuckling, he kicks a rock by his foot. "No. He just talks a lot of shit."

"That's what I'm worried about." I take my keys out of my pocket. "Keep an eye on him. Make sure he doesn't try anything else."

"Already planned on it," he tells me. "But answer me this."

"What?"

I swear, if he's another one of those people who want to ask me a bunch of questions on my relationship status, I'm going to walk back to Trey and use him as a human punching bag.

"Does she know?"

My brows furrow. "Know what?"

He smirks, as if he has all the answers to all the world's greatest questions. "That you're in love with her."

My eyes widen, and the concept alone has me sputtering

on the smoke inside my lungs. I cough violently, and when I finally calm down, I look him straight in the eyes.

"You've got it all wrong, man."

Now it's his turn to look confused. "Well, from where I'm standing, that's exactly what it looks like. You beat up her fake boyfriend—nice work by the way—and now, you were just protecting her honor with Big Mouth back there."

I laugh darkly and shake my head. "No, I'm protecting what's mine. Savannah's heart isn't what I'm after. It's her demise."

SAVANNAH

I sit on my porch as I wait for Delaney. Shivering, I wrap my jacket tighter around me. Usually, Brady would already be out front, but he called this morning to tell me he came down with a stomach bug. I considered walking, until the temperature instantly made me shy away from the whole idea.

"If it isn't Princess Savannah." Trey's irritating voice catches my attention. "What's wrong? Your chariot never arrived to pick you up?"

I roll my eyes. "Ha. Ha. You're just so witty."

"Look at you, thinking you're so much better than me. Newsflash, sweetheart, you live in the same shit neighborhood that I do."

"What's your point?"

He grins. "Well, the only difference between you and me is that everyone knows I'm poor. I don't believe they know about you, though."

If he's trying to get under my skin, it's working. "What do you want?" I ask, grimacing at the way he looks me up and down. "Okay, gross. What are you, fifteen?"

"And *all* man, baby."

I don't know whether to laugh or vomit. "That's never going to happen. I'll ruin my own reputation before I let your grimy hands come anywhere near me."

He looks defeated before changing his demands. "In that case, I want something else. Something to entice me to keep your little secret."

"Oh yeah? And what's that?"

"Money. I think ten grand should be enough."

"Ten thousand dollars?" I laugh dryly. "Look around, Trey. Does it look like I have that kind of money?"

Taking in the sight of my house, he shrugs. "Maybe not, but your boyfriend does."

"Brady isn't my boyfriend."

"Not him." He shakes his head. "The angry one. Tall, broody, blond hair."

Grayson. "He's not my boyfriend either."

His eyes rake over me one more time. "Well, I'd be happy to go back to my original proposition."

Delaney pulls up, and I thank the heavens above, but as I go to move around him, he continues to block my way. I put a hand on his chest and push him back.

"Look, let me make myself *very* clear. I don't have money for you, and I'm not a fucking prostitute."

He steps forward, getting in my face. "Well, you better figure it out, princess. Wouldn't want to lose your perfect reputation, now would you?"

With that and a wink that makes me feel sick to my stomach, he backs up. I get in Delaney's car and welcome the warmth.

"Thank you so much. Brady is sick this morning," I tell her.

She smiles, but eyes Trey suspiciously. "Is everything okay?"

166

I nod. "Yeah. He's just the annoying little shit from next door."

Ending the conversation, I reach over and turn up the volume on the radio. The two of us sing along obnoxiously, with dance moves and all. My voice cracks as I try to hit the high note, making Delaney cringe from the sound.

"Seriously, it's a good thing you can dance. You're no better at singing now than you were as a child," she teases.

"Hey!" I pout. "I resent that."

"Resent away, darling." She pulls into the parking lot and the two of us get out. "All right. I'll see you in first period."

She goes to walk away, when I reach out and grab her wrist. "Wait. Come with me to my locker."

"You mean with all your jock friends? I don't know. They're not exactly my crowd."

"Okay, one, you don't have a crowd—no offense. And two, you'll be fine. I promise."

I don't give her a second to fight me on it as I loop my arms with her and walk into the school. Being as we're a little late, everyone is already near my locker. It takes a little tug for me to get her to continue down the hallway, but she eventually sighs and gives in.

"Hey, Sav," Jace greets me.

"Hi. Guys, this is Delaney. Laney, this is Carter, Jace, Wyatt, Hayden, and you already know Grayson." I grumble the end of it, and then turn to the girls. "And that's Emma, Paige, Becca, and Kinsley."

Emma beams one of her friendly smiles at her. "You're in our first period class, aren't you?"

Delaney nods. "Yeah, though I don't think we've ever talked, really."

Carter, being the pig he is, smirks and looks her up and down. "I can't understand why."

"Haven't you reached the limit for the number of girls

you've fucked this school year? And it's only November," Grayson asks while laughing.

"My sex life has no limit, young Hayworth," he quips.

Jace chuckles and fist bumps Carter, as if sleeping around with tons of women is something to be proud of. Meanwhile, Kinsley is standing as close as she can to Grayson with a sour look on her face.

"Well, as long as you don't plan on putting her on the cheer team." She crosses her arms like she has any say in the matter. "Our team is perfect as is."

I stare her down in a way that tells her she doesn't want to test me. "I can think of one change I'd like to make. Keep up that attitude, and she'll be *your* replacement."

Once the bell rings, we all make our way to class. It's obvious how uncomfortable Delaney is with being late, but she sticks to my side as she and Emma make small talk. It's nice to see her making new friends. Without me, she's always tended to stay with her sister. She's too shy to make friends of her own. However, with the downhill spiral Tessa seems to be on, it's probably a good thing that she and I are back to being friends.

As we enter the classroom, I'm happy to see Mr. Englewood is out today. I let Grayson have my old desk that he's claimed since the day he got here and sit next to Delaney. The substitute, whose name I can never seem to remember, puts on a movie and then proceeds to play on his phone, giving us free range to do as we please.

The whole period is eighty minutes of pure boredom, and halfway through, Delaney and I decide to entertain ourselves by playing MASH. I do her first, writing down Carter, Jace, Hayden, and Wyatt as the guys, and leaving out Grayson—for obvious reasons. She catches on quickly and smirks at me.

"So, did you take my advice? Did you tell him you two can't hook up anymore?"

I snort. "Yeah. It went over really well."

"Uh-oh." She watches me curiously. "What happened?"

"Well, I texted him and said things with us were a mistake and won't happen again."

"Yeah?"

"And then he proceeded to show up at my house while I was in the shower, break in, and tell me that I don't have a say in the matter. That I'm his and there isn't a damn thing I can do about it."

Her eyes widen. "Sav, he didn't...."

I shake my head. "No. God, no. I was a more than willing participant, sad to say."

"Okay, good." The tension leaves her shoulders in an instant.

The fact that I'm completely unable to resist him is not something I'm proud of. Our situation is far from perfect, especially with him holding my secret over my head like he has been. However, I'm weak when it comes to him. He has me—hook, line and sinker.

A giggle from the other side of the room gets my attention. Delaney and I look over to see Kinsley hanging all over Grayson, as usual. He's sitting on top of her desk while cracking jokes with Hayden. As if he can sense he has my attention, his eyes meet mine. There's something in them, something sinister, and he winks before focusing back on Kinsley.

"If he's so adamant about you two hooking up, why is he over there with her?" Delaney questions.

I pull my gaze away because it hurts too much to watch. "Let's just say Grayson isn't the guy he used to be."

"Clearly." She turns back to me and sighs, seeing the gloom written all over my face. "Okay, plan B. After class, we're going to see someone. I have an idea."

THE BELL RINGS, AND Delaney pulls me up out of my seat in a hurry. We leave the classroom and turn left where I normally go right. I don't know where she's bringing me, but she seems pretty determined. It isn't until I see who's waiting at the end of the hallway that I start to reconsider letting her take the lead.

"Uh, Laney, I'm not sure about this," I tell her, but it's too late.

Tessa looks up at me and her eyes narrow. "What are you doing with *her*?"

"Well, for one, she's my friend," Delaney defends. "And two, she needs guy advice."

"What?" Tessa and I shout in unison.

She chuckles softly. "Well, I'm out of my depth here. I know literally nothing about what to do in your situation. Tessa, on the other hand, knows plenty."

Tessa snorts. "Yeah, I'm not helping her."

She goes to walk away, but her sister grabs her wrist. She rolls her eyes as she's pulled back.

"Tess." Delaney says her name, her tone half plea and half warning.

Looking between us, it's clear she doesn't want to do this, but for Laney, she caves. "All right. What's going on?"

"Grayson," Delaney spits out without hesitation, making my eyes widen. "They're hooking up in secret, but at school, he's all over Kinsley."

"Delaney!" I whine, looking at her with wide eyes.

I wasn't supposed to tell *her* about Grayson and me, let alone her sister. If this gets back to him, I can only imagine what he'll do.

"I thought something was up with you two at that party."

Being as the damage is already done, I may as well get her thoughts. "Since the day he moved here, he's been... different. He hates me with a fiery passion and wants to ruin my life. I'm not even making that up. He's literally told me that."

Tessa smiles, as if it's funny to her, but with a look from Delaney, it dissipates. "Go on."

"Well, on my birthday, we had sex. I thought it was just a one-time thing, and I really wasn't sure what to think about it, but since then, we've fooled around a couple more times. He tells me I'm his, or more like demands it, but then he goes and flaunts Kinsley around like she's God's gift to men."

She grimaces. "You mean that little psycho who told the whole school you raped her brother?"

"That's the one."

Delaney's jaw drops. "Wait, what?"

Tessa waves her off dismissively. "Not the time, Laney. I told you, you live under a rock." She turns her attention back toward me. "As far as I'm concerned, and as much as I love Grayson, it sounds like he needs a dose of his own medicine. Make him feel what it's like to see the one you want with someone else."

"You mean *I* make *him* jealous? Is that even possible?"

The corners of her mouth raise in a devilish smirk. "While you were drunk and dancing at that party, he didn't take his eyes off you for a second. Trust me, it's possible."

I SPEND ALL OF second period ignoring the not-so-subtle looks from Grayson and thinking about what Tessa said. She's right. I've noticed him get jealous a lot, especially when I pretended to consider giving Jace my virginity. He looked like he was ready to burst, and when he followed me to my locker after, we had our first kiss—the one that ruined me for everyone else.

"Where's your friend?" Carter asks as soon as I reach our lunch table.

"You mean Delaney?" He nods.

Jace rolls his eyes. "Someone has a little crush."

I can't help but laugh. "Sorry, babes. There's no chance of that *ever* happening. She's practically a nun."

Smirking, he shrugs one shoulder. "It's always the innocent ones that turn out to be the biggest freaks."

I cringe. "Okay, I so didn't need to hear that."

Grayson plops down next to me, a little too close for comfort. "Didn't need to hear what?"

"Carter's secret fantasies about the Callahan twins," Jace informs him.

"Both of them?" I shriek.

The sound of Gray's laugh pulls at my heartstrings. "Tessa would probably screw you for the hell of it, but you definitely don't have a shot in hell with Delaney."

"That's what I said, before his dirty mind took it to places I never wanted to go."

Carter pops a fry into his mouth with a smile. "A guy can dream."

Kinsley comes and sits down, with Becca and Paige at her side. The three of them look like something out of Mean Girls, only less pretty. They all take out their juices, reminding me they're on a "cleanse"—something they tried to get Emma and me to do with them, but we declined. Let one of them pass out during cheer due to lack of food and watch what happens.

"So, Savi," Kinsley starts, and the nickname sends a wave of anger through me.

I narrow my eyes on her, my expression cold. "*Don't* call me that."

"Why not? Grayson does." The look on her face tells me she knows exactly what she's doing, and she's doing it intentionally.

Faking a sweet smile, I rest my arms on the table. "*Grayson* has been calling me that since we were five, and while I don't particularly like it, he gets a certain leeway. You, on the other hand..." I don't need to finish for her to know what I'm insinuating.

"Whatever." She rolls her eyes and tries to recover by focusing on something else. "Gray, are you still coming over today? My parents won't be home until late."

It's as if she just plunged a knife straight into my chest, hearing her call him the name reserved just for me. What's worse is the way he smiles.

"Yeah, I'll be there."

I try to ignore the pit in my stomach, but it's no use. The games he plays, throwing his extracurricular activities with Kinsley in my face on a constant basis, only to show up at my house and stake his claim on me—it's time they come to an end. Tessa was right. He needs a little dose of jealousy.

IT DOESN'T TAKE LONG for me to get the chance to show him who he's fucking with. We're all in third period, working on a project together, when I get up to throw something away. By the time I come back, Grayson has moved from sitting on one of the desks to the chair I was just using.

"Really?" I deadpan. "Where do you expect me to sit?"

He smirks. "I can think of one place."

Looking down at his lap and back up at me, I know what he's doing. He's trying to make a fool out of me. By me sitting on his lap, it would look like I'm okay with him touching me. It would basically send a silent message that he's the one in control here, and I refuse to do that. Instead, a stroke of genius passes through my mind.

"Oh, good idea." I tell him and then turn to stand in front of Jace. "May I?"

His eyes widen in surprise, and he moves his hands out of the way. "Be my guest."

I plant myself right in Jace's lap, ignoring the way Grayson glares from where he's sitting. I look at him and smile sweetly, which was probably the wrong thing to do, because it looks like he's about to blow a fuse.

"Fine, have your fucking seat," he growls, standing up and going back to sit on the desk.

I shake my head. "No, it's fine, really. I'm good here."

We continue to work on the project as I stay where I'm at, much to Grayson's disapproval. He's so focused on the way Jace's hands keep ending up on my thighs or my waist that he doesn't even notice when Kinsley tries getting his attention.

"Grayson?" She tries for the fifth time.

"What?" He snaps.

She recoils from the tone of his voice, looking surprised that he spoke to her like that. "I need you to sign your name on the sheet."

He rips the paper from her hands and angrily scribbles his name across it. Meanwhile, Jace starts poking my side, only to realize I'm ticklish. His one arm holds me to his chest as his other hand attacks.

"Stop!" I squirm, and judging by the way he throws his head back and bites his lip, he's enjoying this a little more than originally intended. "Oh my God, you're such a pig."

He chuckles. "Well, what do you expect? I've got the hottest girl I know on my lap, moving her ass back and forth."

Going to stand up, he tightens his hold on me to keep me in place. I can feel Grayson's stare burning into us, and while a part of me is concerned for Jace's wellbeing, another part is enjoying having the upper hand for once. He gets to experience what he's made me feel for the last few weeks.

Moving his mouth as close to my ear as he can, Jace

174

whispers, "He's not going to kill me, is he? He kinda looks like he's going to kill me."

Sure enough, I look at Grayson, only to see him already staring back at me—and if looks could kill...

I chuckle and shake my head. "I don't think so." Keeping my eyes on him for another moment, I hum. "But maybe hire a bodyguard to be safe."

CLASS LETS OUT, AND Jace gives me a hug before going to fourth period, promising we'll pick back up where we left off. It's obvious he's just helping me make Grayson jealous, but it's working, so I have no complaints.

I go to my locker to switch out my books when a deep and angry voice echoes into my ear.

"What the fuck do you think you're doing?"

Turning around, I find Grayson no less than six inches from me. I feign innocence and give him a sweet smile. "I have no idea what you mean."

"Cut the shit, Savannah. You know *exactly* what I'm talking about."

I'm eating this up as I play the part. "Oh, you mean with Jace? I don't know. I think I might give him a chance. He's sweet, and hot as hell. Haven't you noticed?"

He punches the locker next to my head and gets in my face. A part of me starts to wonder if maybe I took it too far, but then I remember all the times he flirted with Kinsley in front of me. And Lord only knows what they've done behind closed doors.

"Doesn't feel good, does it?" I cross my arms over my chest.

He shakes his head and takes a step back, a devious smile spreading across his face. "Tell Delaney you don't need a ride home today."

"What? Why?"

"Because you're coming with me." He brings his lips to my ear, and his warm breath causes me to shiver. "I'm going to fuck the thoughts of Jace right out of you. By the time I'm done, the only name you'll remember is mine."

18

GRAYSON

By the end of the day, I'm on edge with the need to get Savannah out of here and back to my house. I already know my mom isn't home, having left to spend the weekend visiting my Aunt Lauren. She offered to wait for me so I could go with her, but I declined. I have more *pressing* matters here.

The image of Sav on Jace's lap is burned into my brain, taunting me at every turn. She had every opportunity to sit on mine, and she chose him. I know it wasn't because she wants him. She was doing it to get a rise out of me. Well, it worked. She's got my attention—every fucking bit of it.

Everyone starts heading for the doors, with Jace giving Savannah a hug that lasts just a little too long. Her eyes meet mine from over his shoulder, and I can see the amusement in them. Once they're gone, she turns to me.

"Did you tell Delaney you have a ride home?"

She nods. "Did you tell your little slut you're not coming over today?"

"Nope. She's not my concern, though. Teaching you a lesson is."

Standing her ground, she looks as unfazed as ever. "Do your worst."

She follows me out the back door of the school and over to my car. Some people stare as they see us, wondering why the two people who seem to hate each other would be leaving together. I'm almost positive this is going to get back to Carter and Jace, but frankly, I don't give a shit. They *should* hear about it. Maybe then they'll know not to fuck with what's mine.

The drive home is quiet, with neither of us willing to cave. She stares out the window with that same confident look on her face, not faltering for a second. There's a point she wants to prove, and she isn't backing down.

I pull into my driveway, and the two of us get out. Unlocking and opening the door, I gesture for her to go in first. She looks around at the house she knows as well as I do, then turns to me.

"No one's home?"

Shaking my head, I step closer. "The house is mine, *all weekend*."

She holds my gaze and pulls her bottom lip between her teeth. "What are you going to do with so much alone time?"

"You."

"Me?" A small yet condescending giggle leaves her mouth. "And exactly what do you plan on doing to me?"

"I'm going to blur the lines of pleasure and pain, and make you beg for mercy as I bring you to the edge—over, and over, and over again." I bend down to nip at her earlobe, gently sucking it into my mouth. "Go upstairs. I want you on my bed and waiting for me by the time I get up there."

"And I want *you* to end whatever friends with benefits shit you have going on with Kinsley."

I almost laugh, knowing I haven't touched that girl since Savannah's birthday—when she destroyed my sex life and claimed me for herself without even knowing she did it. But

178

this, right here, is about control, and I'm not willing to give that up any time soon.

With one arm wrapped around her back, I pull her into me. "Do I look like I take orders from you?"

"You get what you give," she retorts. "For every minute that you spend focused on that bitch, I'll be flirting with Jace."

She's infuriating, pushing at all my buttons and making it hard to keep my cool. I lean down and press my lips to hers in a ravenous kiss that shows her just how close I am to snapping. When I back away, she's momentarily dazed.

"Upstairs," I repeat, and she rolls her eyes before finally listening.

"Bossy."

I go into the kitchen and grab two bottles of water from the fridge, not wanting any excuse to leave my room for the rest of the afternoon. I shut off the light and make sure the door is locked before I make my way upstairs to my room. As I enter, I find her standing there, looking around the room she used to spend much of her time in, tauntingly similar yet different all the same.

Placing the bottles down on my dresser, I move to stand in front of her. She looks up at me through hooded eyes, and I tuck a loose strand of hair behind her ear. She's breathtakingly beautiful, and if things were different, I would spend every day of my life worshiping the ground she walks on. Instead, the only way I'm able to have her is like this— sexually, meaninglessly, and without any hopes for the future.

"Seeing you today, sitting on his lap with his hands all over you, I couldn't breathe. I wanted to rip you right out of his grasp."

She almost seems remorseful as she frowns. "That's the way I feel every time you're with Kinsley. It's like you want to be with her."

"Is that what *you* want, to be with Jace?"

"No." She shakes her head. "I flirted with him because I knew it would make you mad."

"Well, consider it a success—I'm mad." I push her down so she's lying on my bed and hover over her. "And you're going to make it up to me."

I press my mouth to hers, and my whole body comes alive at the contact, the way it always does. She hums into it, grabbing the back of my neck and pulling me closer. My hands roam up her petite waist and make their way under her shirt.

It's cruel, really, having to see her every day in this uniform. It's like every one of my adolescent fantasies come to life. She looks like a naughty librarian with her skirt and knee-high socks. All I've wanted for weeks is to strip it off her—piece by piece.

She opens her mouth to allow me in, and our tongues tangle together. Tasting her is like heaven, knowing how sickeningly sweet she is. I slip my hand up her skirt and pull her panties to the side. The second my finger slips inside, she lets out a moan that goes straight to my dick.

"You're so ready for me," I tell her as her juices coat my finger.

It's been no more than a minute, and I'm already hard as steel inside my pants. She reaches between us and rubs her hand over my clothing. I need to get them off. It's too painful, too restricting. I push myself off her and pull my shirt over my head, before sliding my pants down. She lets her eyes rake over my body, whimpering from the intense attraction between us.

"Like what you see?" I tease.

She glares at me and rolls her eyes. "Shut up. You know you're hot. I'm not about to boost your already inflated ego."

I start to undress her, slowly—like we have all the time in the world, no matter how much it tortures me. By the time

I'm done, she's left in only her bra and panties. I stand in front of her and admire the sight. It's no wonder everyone wants her. She's got the body of a goddess.

"Like what you see?" She throws my own words back at me and I chuckle.

"Abso-fucking-lutely."

It only takes another second before I'm back on top of her, grinding down to rub my hard cock against her through the thin material. It's such a tease, and only makes me want her more, but it's also driving her wild.

"Grayson," she pleads as I suck a mark into her collarbone.

I pick my head up to look at her. "Yeah, baby?"

"I want you."

Shaking my head, I place a short kiss at the corner of her mouth. "And I want you to keep your ass off other guys' laps."

I reach over to my nightstand, pulling a pair of handcuffs out of the drawer before turning to her. Her eyes widen when she sees them, but in a way that shows her exhilaration. I gesture for her to move up higher on my bed, and then kneel beside her. I place a cuff on one wrist and then wrap it around one of the poles on my headboard. As I put the other cuff on the remaining wrist, she tugs on the restraints—testing them and finding she can hardly move at all.

"Good?" The last thing I want is to leave marks on her flawless skin.

She nods, and that's all the permission I need. I move toward the end of the bed and crawl between her legs, kissing from one knee, up her thigh. She squirms with pleasure, letting out small breathy moans in the process. Then, when I finally reach my destination, I move her panties to the side and blow a cool breath of air over her pussy.

"This," I tell her, slipping my finger inside just enough to tease her, "is all mine. Let me find out anyone else came near this, and there will be hell to pay."

She groans and throws her head back, obviously turned on by my possessiveness. However, I hope she knows I'm not the slightest bit kidding. Even just knowing Jace *thinks* about fucking her is enough to send me on a rampage.

I hook my thumbs into the waistline of her panties and pull them down her legs. She's already dripping by the time I discard them on the floor and get back to business. I watch her reaction as I run my tongue over her clit. She groans, pulling on the cuffs and making them clink against the wood. When she arches her hips to try to find some friction, I back away.

"Lay still, or I'll stop and leave you like this."

"You wouldn't."

I smirk. "Fucking try me, baby."

With a whimper, she does her best to stay motionless. I add a finger, shoving two inside of her. The fact that she remains so tight tells me I'm the only one allowed to do this, and fuck if I'm not loving it. I lick into her, and her taste coats my tongue. It's just as good as the first time, if not better, because this time, she's at my mercy. I don't need to hold back in fear of physically hurting her. Today, I'm taking everything I want.

I suck her clit into my mouth, and she screams out. It's harder than any time before this, and judging by the sounds she's making, she doesn't have any complaints. My fingers fuck into her, fast and ruthless. Yet, when her voice goes up an octave and she seems like she's about to come undone, I stop.

"W-what?! Keep going."

I grin deviously. "I told you, this is about *my* pleasure, not yours. This will be a whole lot easier if I don't have to keep reminding you of that."

Standing up, I pull my boxers off and let my cock free. She

stares at it hungrily and licks her lips, silently telling me exactly what she wants—which happens to be where I was going with it anyway. I climb over her, placing my knees on either side of her chest. I line myself up at her mouth and she opens. Her tongue darts out and licks the head of my dick before I rock my hips to enter.

She sucks me off like a fucking professional, with just the right amount of suction and swirling her tongue around the head as I pull back. It feels too good. I lace my fingers into her hair and start to thrust, fucking her mouth the way I've wanted to for weeks. She stares up at me with watery eyes as she gags around my length. It's hot, and dirty, and puts all my wet dreams to shame.

Before this ends sooner than either of us want, I pull out and move to grab a condom. Just as I'm about to rip it open, she stops me.

"Wait." I shoot her a confused look. "Don't. I want to feel you."

"Sav…"

She shakes her head. "You didn't use one in the shower, and it felt incredible. And besides, you said today was all about you, right? Tell me it doesn't feel better without one."

After a very quickly settled internal debate, I throw the condom onto the floor and get back on the bed.

The second I push myself into her pussy, I need to tighten every muscle in my abdomen to keep from cumming on the spot. Unlike the shower, there's no water to wash away the slickness of her pussy. It's just her and me, skin on skin.

I grip her hips and start pounding into her—hard. She's an absolute mess as I fuck her relentlessly, and I know it would only take a little pressure on the right bundle of nerves for her to let go, but there's a lesson to be learned here. Besides, I don't know if I'd be able to hold back if she came around me right now, and I'm far from ready for this to be over.

Pulling out of her for a second, I flip her over. Her arms are crossed, and she doesn't look the slightest bit comfortable, but there are no complaints as I put her on her knees, thrusting into her from behind. It's rough, with much better leverage, and she's in sexual bliss. Her moans are so loud that I'm starting to wonder if the neighbors can hear. It's a good thing no one is home. The sounds coming from her mouth sound like they came straight from a porn flick.

"Fuck, you feel so good." I tell her, only to get a jumbled mess of words as a response.

Again, just when she's about to reach her high, I stop. She drops her head down and lets out a low whine that only has me smiling. To see her so frustrated is exactly what I was looking for. I give it a couple seconds for her body to relax again, and then I'm back to thrusting harshly inside of her.

"Please let me cum. I need it, Grayson," she pleads.

I slap her ass so hard it'll probably leave a mark. "Do you still want Jace? Do you think he can fuck you better than I can?"

"No. No, no, no."

"Who do you belong to, Savannah?"

"You," she answers without hesitation. "Always you."

"Better fucking believe it, baby."

I pull out and flip her back around, immediately going back in, only this time I press my thumb against her clit and watch as she lets go. Her face contorts into the hottest expression I've ever seen as she comes undone and explodes around me. That alone is enough to bring me to my breaking point.

At the last second, I pull out and cum all over her stomach. Spurts of white cover her torso, and if I didn't think she would kill me for it, I'd take a picture. She looks so fucking hot, and *so* fucking mine.

I collapse onto the bed next to her, leaving her covered in my essence and cuffed to the headboard. She's stuck, like my own personal sex slave. What I wouldn't give to be able to leave her there...to have her on demand for whenever I'm feeling like I need to get off—which is fucking constantly since I moved here and came face to face with her for the first time in years.

Getting up, I go to grab a towel from the bathroom and come back to clean her off. She lies there in a post-sex haze, watching me yet falling asleep at the same time. Once she's not going to drip on my bed, I toss the towel into the laundry basket and get the key from my drawer. I remove one cuff at a time, but even though her hands are freed, they stay above her head.

"Are you okay?" I question.

"Mm-hm."

A part of me wonders if I should bring her home, but I'm not quite sure I'm done with her yet. Instead, I climb in bed next to her, and before I know it, we're both out cold.

I WAKE IN THE middle of the night, chilly and alone. A frigid breeze comes through the open window, one I remember being shut before I went to sleep. I pull on a pair of sweatpants and walk over to it. Savannah is sitting on the roof, and *fuck*, she's dressed in my clothes. I climb out, careful not to slip, and join her.

"What are you doing out here? It's freezing."

She smiles as she stares up at the stars. "This was always my favorite place in the world. I've missed it."

Memory lane is *not* a place I'm willing to go with her, so instead of saying anything, I hum and admire the sky. Neither of us speak for a while, both lost in our own thoughts. I can remember the last time I was up here with her like it was yesterday. That first kiss meant everything to me—a ten-year-old kid who thought his dreams were about to come true, before they were all ripped away. It's a bittersweet feeling.

"We should go back in, before we get sick," I suggest.

Shrugging her shoulders, she finally looks at me. "I'm not tired."

"Oh, don't worry," I smirk. "I can think of plenty we can do to wear ourselves out."

THE SOUND OF MY phone vibrating against the nightstand pulls me from my peaceful slumber. I go to reach for it but am stopped by the weight pressing down on my chest. After hours of what can only be described as sexual heaven, we fell asleep—wrapped up in each other. I slip out from under her and grab my phone before leaving the room.

"Hello?" I practically whisper to make sure I don't wake her.

Tyson chuckles into the phone. "You know, I was going to ask why you weren't here, but I think I just figured it out."

I groan and go downstairs to the kitchen. "Fuck off. You don't know anything."

"So, you mean to tell me there isn't a blonde in your bed right now?" He may be an asshole, but he's the one person in my life that I'd never lie to. When I don't answer, I can practically hear his grin. "That's what I thought. So, you two are still fooling around, huh?"

"Yeah, all thanks to your fucking stellar advice. Thanks, dick. Now I can't focus on what I'm supposed to be doing because every time I look at her, I want to fuck her against every surface of the room."

He laughs. "Yeah, it may have been a little ill-advised, I'll admit. Though, in my defense, I think I underestimated your feelings for her a bit."

"I don't have *feelings* for anyone," I retort.

"Sure, you don't, buddy."

I roll my eyes. "Will you shut the fuck up and tell me what to do? How am I supposed to hurt her when all I can think of is fucking her senseless all the damn time?!"

Letting out a sigh, he takes a moment to answer. "Okay, maybe you should just relax on the revenge front for a little bit."

"What?"

"Don't jump down my throat, shithead. Just listen. Maybe you just need to ride this out. You spent your entire childhood pining after this girl, and with what you've been through, you've earned the right to live out that fantasy," he explains. "So, let yourself enjoy this, and once it's run its course, get back to what matters."

I run a hand over my face. "Wouldn't that be exactly what my dad didn't want? For me to be involved with her?"

"When you were ten, maybe, but you're not a little boy anymore, Grayson. You're eighteen and more than capable of not becoming a pawn in her father's games. I mean, unless you're afraid you're going to fall in love with her."

Snorting, I shake my head. "Fuck you. You know I don't fall in love with anyone."

"Good. Just make sure you don't let that happen, and you'll be golden."

The sound of someone coming into the room catches my attention. Savannah leans against the doorway, wearing only my T-shirt, and I'm immediately drawn to her.

"Ty, I have to go. I'll text you later."

He snickers. "Have fun."

Without saying goodbye, I hang up the phone and look her up and down once more. She's gorgeous, in that *doesn't even need to try* kind of way, and all I want is to mark every inch of her skin.

"Hi." She greets me, not coming any closer.

I get up and walk toward her, placing my hands on her waist. "Hey."

"I'm going to go get dressed, and then I'll have Delaney drive me home."

In a careful move, she arches up on her tiptoes and kisses me. It's quick, and as sweet as she is, but it only makes me want her more. I'm battling between what I want and what my father wants, when finally, one wins.

She goes to turn away, but I stop her with a gentle hand on her cheek. "Don't."

19

GRAYSON

SAVANNAH AND I SPEND THE ENTIRE WEEKEND together. Both of us are insatiable, which leads to having sex in as many places around my house as we can manage. The kitchen, the den, the shower. We even wonder if we could get away with it on the roof, but for safety reasons, and the sake of Delaney, who could probably see us from her bedroom window, we decide against it.

When we're not a sweaty mess of tangled limbs and breathy moans, we watch movies and make a failed attempt at baking a cake. What can I say? She tastes so much sweeter. The two of us laugh like we haven't in years, and by the time I drop her off on Sunday night, we're both exhausted.

AT SCHOOL ON MONDAY, I can already feel the shift in our dynamic. I'm not constantly battling between ruining her life and ripping her clothes off. She sends subtle looks my way, with a look in her eyes that tells me she's replaying this past weekend in her mind. It's torture to have to want her this bad and need to wait, but I fucking live for it.

By midday, Jace has kept his hands to himself, and Savannah has stayed off his lap. However, I know that if she gets the slightest inclination that I'm rubbing Kinsley in her face again, there's going to be more of what she pulled Friday afternoon. Since I'm not able to handle that without risking a criminal record for breaking Haven Grace's favorite kicker, I know I need to tell Kinsley it's over.

With a text message to meet me at my locker before lunch, it's the perfect spot to end this without giving Savannah the satisfaction of thinking she's won. Familiar dark brown hair comes walking down the hallway. Judging by the smile on her face, she has the wrong idea on what this is.

"Hey, you," she simpers, throwing her arms around my neck and going to kiss me.

I turn my head just in time. "No, stop." Removing her hold on me, I take a step back. "I didn't ask you to come here so we could hook up."

"Then, what?" As she studies the expression on my face, I can see the moment it clicks. "Grayson, that's not funny."

"Who's joking?"

Crossing her arms, her anger shows. "Are you kidding? Do you even realize the mistake you're making?! I'm the best you'll ever have, you know that? How could you do this to me?"

The more she yells, the less patience I have. Finally, when she shoves me, I've had enough.

"Okay, stop. You're acting like we were serious or something. Newsflash, we weren't. All that happened between us was a couple of blowjobs, and that was over a month ago. Don't act like you didn't see this coming."

She's caught off guard, and clearly doesn't like being put in her place, but as her eyes land on something behind me, her expression hardens. "What the fuck are you looking at?"

Pushing past me, she storms away. I don't need to turn around to see who's standing there—I can feel it. The buzz in

190

the air, the sexual tension so thick I could choke on it, the pull in my chest that demands I go to her. Of course, it's Savannah, and she heard everything I was hoping she wouldn't.

"Shouldn't you be in lunch?"

She chuckles before going to her locker. "Shouldn't you?"

I finally turn to face her. "I had something to take care of."

"So I heard." The smile on her face does nothing to hide her amusement. "Breakups are tough."

"Oh, shut up. You knew it was fake the whole damn time."

She closes her locker and walks backward with her hands in the air, smirking happily. "Hey, I didn't say a word."

I can't help but laugh as I shake my head and run after her. She squeals and tries to evade me, but my arms wrap around her waist, pulling her into me. The giggle that leaves her mouth is one that I want to bottle up and put in my pocket for a rainy day. For a day when all this is over, and she's left the broken mess I intend for her to be.

I WALK INTO THE backyard, heading straight for the treehouse. Savannah follows behind, but isn't exactly a fan of my idea to explore the abandoned structure.

"Seriously, come on. You'll be fine."

She shakes her head. "No. Look at it, Gray. That thing is twelve years old, and hasn't been played in for eight. Besides, imagine all the spiders that are in there."

I roll my eyes and place hands on her hips, hoisting her up on the ladder. "There aren't any spiders. I already came out here to check. Up you go."

As we climb inside, the wood creaks from our weight. Not only was she right about it being old, but we're also a combined hundred-something pounds heavier than we were.

Still, it holds steady as we get inside. It's nostalgic, being in here with her, but not at all awkward.

I lean against the wall and cross my ankles, looking around at the drawings that are still hanging on the wall. They're faded, and some have been ruined by rain getting in, but the tape has managed to hold. I chuckle as I find the one I made my mom laminate for me.

Treehouse Rules:

1. *No girls allowed except Savi.*
2. *Everyone must know the password.*
3. *No grown-ups.*
4. *All secrets shared in the treehouse, stay in the treehouse.*
5. *The password is puddles.*

"Remember how mad Tess and Laney would get when they weren't allowed up here?" I ask, gesturing to rule number one.

Savannah snickers. "How could I forget? They told me we couldn't be friends anymore unless I let them in."

"Did you?"

"No. You would have been so mad at me, and besides, they only stopped being my friend for ten minutes."

It goes back to being quiet as we both look around until I can't help but laugh.

"What?" she questions, confused.

I bite my lip and shake my head. "It's nothing."

"Bullshit." Moving across the small room, she sits next to me. "Tell me."

My eyes focus on my hands. "I've just had a dream or two of us having sex in here."

"Did you really?" she chuckles.

"It wasn't as old and rickety as it is now, but yeah."

Before I know it, she's straddling my lap and bending down to kiss my neck. I run my hands down her back, humming at how good it feels to have her lips on my skin. When she starts to unbutton my pants, I grab her wrists.

"What are you doing?"

She smirks. "Making your dreams come true."

Excitement rushes through me as I lift her shirt over her head. I don't think there is a single thing this girl can do that wouldn't turn me on. However, as I admire her body, another bruise catches my eye.

"What happened?" I rub my thumb over it, and she hisses at the contact.

With a mastered skill, she masks over the pain I know she just felt. "It's nothing. Just a bruise from a cheer stunt. I'm fine."

"Savannah—" I try, but it's no use.

She leans down and presses her lips to mine. "I told you, *I'm fine.* Now shut up and fuck me."

THE BLEACHERS ARE FILLED with students and parents. I stand in the tunnel with the rest of the guys, waiting for the announcer to introduce us. The energy in here is enough to get us all pumped up and ready to slaughter this other team.

"And for the home team." The announcer begins. "Leading their season undefeated, with four wins, it's The Haven Grace Warriors!"

As we run out to the shouts and applause, the cheer team is lined up on either side and waving their pom-poms. I hold my helmet in my hand as I jog past Savannah, sending her a quick wink and loving the way she blushes. Her eyes roll playfully, and all I can think about is stripping her out of that uniform.

The game is intense. Our defense is incredible, but our offense isn't playing the way we should be. Feeling exhausted, I sit down on the bench and pull off my helmet to take a drink. I'm watching the other team come close to getting a touchdown when the mascot comes over and hands me a piece of paper. I thank him hesitantly before opening it.

Win this game and I'll make it worth your while.
- S

Glancing behind me, she winks and bites her lip in a way that renews all my energy. I stand up and put my helmet back on my head, running onto the field as soon as they miss the field goal. *Talk about motivation.*

WE ALL WALK INTO the diner, with Carter and Jace singing *"We Are the Champions,"* even though it was a regular season game. I'm almost positive they were drinking on the way here, but it's none of my business. After we fill most of the tables, the waitress comes over and congratulates us on the win. Only five more games until we face off against NHH, and fuck if I'm not ready for it.

Savannah sits in the booth across from me, still sporting the uniform I haven't gotten a chance to fuck her in yet. Hopefully, that'll change tonight. During every game, I've had a difficult time keeping my eyes on the field, but this one was so much worse.

Over the past couple of weeks, Savannah and I have spent every free moment we have with each other. Stolen moments in empty hallways and sneaking away to guest rooms at parties, we're both as greedy as the other—taking everything there is to give and then some. I've been waiting for the sexual chemistry between us to cool off, but it's only burned hotter. At this point, I don't know if things will ever calm down.

We're halfway through our meals when my phone vibrates in my pocket. I pull it out and smirk at the name.

Savannah: I want you so bad I can barely sit still.

I damn near choke on my milkshake. Taking out my wallet, I throw some cash down on the table and stand up.

"All right, I'm out of here."

"You're leaving already?" Carter slurs.

I nod. "Unlike you assholes, I played hard tonight." I focus my attention on Savannah. "Sav, you need a ride home?"

"Yeah, that'd be great. Thanks," she plays along.

They eye us suspiciously as we say our goodbyes and head out the door, but I couldn't care less. The only thing I'm focused on is getting Savannah on my cock. We get into my car, and I'm so sexually strung out that I fumble with the keys. Sav chuckles and runs her fingers through her hair.

I pull out of the parking lot and get about halfway to my house when she puts her hand on my crotch, rubbing me through my jeans. I growl and try to keep my eyes on the road, but I don't have much self-control when it comes to her.

"You keep doing that, and I'm going to pull this car over and fuck you right here."

She bites her lip and leans over the center console to nip at my earlobe. "What if that's exactly what I want you to do?"

And just like that, I'm swerving onto the shoulder and gripping her skirt-covered hips as she rides me in the driver's seat.

"GRAYSON?" MY MOTHER CALLS from downstairs. I hop off my bed before sliding down the banister. When I reach the bottom, my mom stands in the doorway of the kitchen with a big smile on her face.

"What?" I ask.

She shakes her head and reins it in. "Nothing, can you run to the store for me? I'm about to start making dinner, but we need milk."

I nod. "Let me just go grab my keys and my phone."

There are probably about five stores closer that have what I need, but I drive right past them. Savannah is at the dance studio, and having an excuse to go into town, I'm definitely taking advantage of it.

I pull up in front of the familiar building and automatically spot her through the window. She moves her body with such skill that even people walking by stop to watch for a minute, but she remains unfazed. It's not a dance routine I recognize, and I've seen a lot in the past couple months. It can only mean one thing—she's improvising.

For the first time, I go inside to get a better view. She's so wrapped up in the sound of Camilla Cabello booming through the room that she doesn't even notice I'm here. She spins around and bends in ways that would probably break me if I tried. It's mesmerizing to watch her, enchanting and beautiful how she completes every move with an unmatched perfection.

On one particular turn, I slot myself in front of her. Dancing may not be my specialty, but she takes the lead in ways that make it easy for me. She drags her hand across my body as she walks around me, leaving a lingering burn everywhere she touches. I spin to face her and lift her by the waist. Her legs go around my waist and I press her up against the wall, not giving a flying fuck about the potential for an audience. My hand finds the back of her neck, and I pull her into me, crashing our lips together.

Her nails dig into my back, and the music fades away. As our tongues tangle together and we breathe each other in, all that matters is us—until a familiar voice interrupts the moment.

"What the fuck."

20

SAVANNAH

THE SOUND OF BRADY'S VOICE PULLS ME FROM THE panty dropping moment with Grayson, and as I turn to look at him, I can see the betrayal all over his face. Unwrapping my legs, I slide down the wall until my feet are on the floor.

"Brady, I can explain."

"Explain what?" he shouts. "How you lied to me? How you've been sneaking around with *him*? I know you've been through some shit, but you're not this fucking stupid." Turning to Grayson, he shoves his finger in his face. "You! Get the fuck out of here before I call the police. I don't want you anywhere near her."

Grayson turns an angry shade of red. He steps closer, looking ready to snap Brady like a twig. "What I do with her is *none* of your business."

The two of them stare each other down, and I'm afraid one is going to swing before I push myself in between them. "Gray, don't. Just walk away, please."

"Yeah, *Gray,* listen to your girlfriend."

"Brady!" I snap. His taunting is only making the situation worse, and I already saw the damage Grayson caused to his face the last time they got into it.

"What?" He glares at me. "Are you forgetting that a couple months ago, he wanted to destroy you? How he found out your secret and threatened to expose you with it? Or—here's a question—did you forget that he damn near tried to kill me? Why are you acting like none of that ever happened?"

I press my back against Grayson's chest, keeping him away from Brady. "I-I don't know."

He throws his arms in the air, defeated. "I won't sit here and watch you ruin your life. Involving yourself with a monster like him is the stupidest thing you've ever done."

"That's not fair."

Shaking his head, he walks back toward the door. "You should leave." He pauses and his eyes focus on me. "Both of you."

"Brady," I plead, but it's no use as he walks out the door.

I move to follow him, when Grayson's fingers wrap around my wrist. "Don't."

"Let me go, Grayson! I have to talk to him. He needs to listen."

He pulls me into his arms and holds me as I break. "You just need to give him some time to cool off. Come on." Leading me toward the door, he grabs my phone off the bench. I look back at the office I know Brady is in right now. "You can call him tomorrow."

THREE DAYS AND FIFTEEN PHONE calls later, I've come to realize that Brady isn't going to call me back. I hang up and slip my phone into my pocket just as Grayson comes behind me, poking my sides and scaring the shit out of me. I screech and look around to make sure no one just saw that.

"What are you doing?"

He chuckles, smiling in the way that makes my heart melt, and grabs my hand. "Come with me."

"Why?"

"What the hell do you mean, why? Since when do you need a reason to come with me?"

I roll my eyes. "Since you started randomly grabbing me in the hallway."

"What can I say? It's the things you do to me."

He pulls me down the hallway and into the janitor's closet, closing the door behind us and immediately pushing me up against it. His mouth is on mine, kissing me so hard it's like he's trying to suck the life out of me. It's brutal, harsh, and desperate.

I claw at his shirt, knowing we only have a little bit of time before someone realizes we've gone missing. Grayson's hands lift my skirt and pull my panties down before unbuttoning his pants. He pulls the condom from his pocket and rips it open with his teeth.

"Planned this, did you?" I ask suspiciously.

He smiles. "I was hopeful. Seeing you in that uniform always gives me dirty thoughts."

"Good to know," I chuckle.

He lifts me up and sinks me down onto his cock, filling me entirely. I grip onto the nearest shelf as he fucks into me. His mouth sucks a mark into my shoulder. Meeting him thrust for thrust, the only sounds filling the room are our heavy breathing and skin hitting skin.

"God, why haven't we done this sooner?"

I bite my lip to try to conceal my moans, but when he starts to go harder, it becomes more difficult. As my orgasm hits unexpectedly, I scream out. Grayson's hand comes up to cover my mouth and muffle the noise as he lets go, emptying himself into the condom. He holds me for a minute and gives himself time to relax before pulling out and gently putting me back on the ground.

I pull my panties up and into place. "You mean that couldn't have waited another couple of hours?"

He smirks. "Are you complaining?"

"Not even a little."

As I go to walk out, he grabs my hand. I turn back to face him, confused, when he pulls me into him. With a gentle touch on my cheek, he presses his lips to mine in a soft, innocent kiss. It's the first time he's kissed me first without the intentions of it going further, and my heart stutters because of it.

"What was that for?"

He shrugs and releases me, stepping back. "Just really wanted to kiss you. Now go, I'll see you in class."

FOR THE REST OF the day, my mind is clouded with thoughts of Grayson. Ever since the weekend we spent alone at his house, things have been different between us. There are still moments where I see the darkness brewing in his eyes—when he looks at me like I'm Satan reincarnated—but they're few and far between.

Despite how close we've grown lately, he's always made sure I know that we're just fooling around. It hurt the first couple times, but eventually, I became numb to it. That part of our relationship has never faltered, but today, with the way he kissed me before I left the janitor's closet, I can't help but hope that maybe he's starting to come around.

I'd be lying if I said I haven't developed feelings for Grayson. Strong feelings. The kind that keep you awake at night. That make you want to rip your heart straight from your chest and throw it at their feet. I've never let myself acknowledge them, in fear that the pain of unrequited love might rip me to shreds, but they are there—simmering under the surface and threatening to break free.

I STORM OUT OF the house, slamming the door behind me. I'd rather wait on the porch in the cold than deal with my drunken father for another minute. From the second I came home today, he's been on my ass, from asking me for money to accusing me of stealing his drugs. I can't handle him. Thankfully, tonight I'm going to a party and then spending the night at Grayson's.

As if my night couldn't get any more frustrating, I'm scrolling through my phone when an irritating voice meets my ears.

"Do you have my money yet?" Trey asks.

I roll my eyes and turn to face him. "When are you going to get it through your head? I don't *have* any money, and Grayson sure as hell isn't going to give it to you. I don't know what else I can say to make you understand."

"Well, you better start giving me something or spreading your legs, because otherwise, I have no reason not to tell everyone that your riches are actually rags in disguise."

Getting fed up, I decide to call his bluff. "You know what? Fine. Go tell everyone. Shout it from the damn rooftops for all I care. See how that goes for you." I stand up and get in his face. "No one is going to believe you. Especially not when I tell them you're just a bitter little sophomore who couldn't take no for an answer."

In perfect timing, Grayson pulls up with Delaney in the back seat. I shove past Trey as I walk toward the car. As soon as I get in, Gray is glaring at Trey, looking like he's ready to rip him limb to limb.

"What was that about?" he asks.

I shake my head and buckle my seatbelt. "Nothing I can't handle. Let's go."

THE PARTY IS INTENSE, with girls in skimpy dresses passing around Jell-O shots and tubes of alcohol. I take one and roll my eyes as she walks away. Leave it to Jace to not only hire waitresses, but make them wear clothing that barely covers their vaginas.

"I just don't understand why they couldn't be dressed in something a little less revealing."

Carter shushes me, pressing his finger to my lips. "If you love me at all, you won't ruin this for me."

We all laugh at his antics. It's no secret that he's already buzzed, having been drinking since before anyone got here. Jace always complains that he comes over under the guise of helping set up, but ends up staying by the keg the whole time.

"Laney," he slurs. "My dear Saint Delaney, are you sure you don't want a drink?"

She shakes her head. "I'm good, Carter. Thanks anyway."

He sighs. "Well, then, how about a lap dance instead?"

Practically choking on air, her eyes widen. "Uh, I um…"

"How about you give me one instead, big boy?" Grayson jumps to her rescue like a knight in shining armor.

Carter frowns, mumbling something about not being gay under his breath before walking away to go find more booze. I watch him carefully before turning to Jace.

"Shouldn't you stop him?"

He grins and shakes his head. "We've been giving him colored water for the past hour and making him think they're shots. He'll sober up soon."

HALFWAY THROUGH THE PARTY, I'm finally starting to relax. After the argument with my dad, and then having to deal with Trey on top of it, I'm grateful for the chance to let

204

loose. Tomorrow I'm sure I'll have to figure out what I'm going to do about the pain in my ass that won't seem to go away, but tonight is mine.

I'm standing across the room when Grayson waves me over.

"Lay on the bar, beautiful," he says, complimenting me in front of everyone for the first time. "We're doing body shots."

It's dangerous and risky. I know if we have any desire to keep things private between us, I should run in the other direction, but with the way he's looking at me, I can't resist. I let him lift me onto the hardwood and lay back. He raises my shirt and tucks it under my bra. The level of comfort between us doesn't go unnoticed as Jace spikes his full cup of beer on the floor.

"I fucking knew it!"

Carter laughs as Delaney looks at Jace like he's gone mad. "Knew what?"

"That they've been hooking up!" He turns to us. "I called that shit months ago, but you two denied it so hard!"

Grayson makes no move to deny it, but the conversation of us going public with whatever this is needs to be had in private—with none of our friends inserting their opinions.

"Because I let him lift up my shirt? It's body shots, not a damn marriage proposal."

He remains unconvinced, but my attention is pulled from him as Grayson licks a stripe across my neck and sprinkles salt on it. Placing the lime between my lips, he pours the shot into my belly button—immediately slurping it back up. He licks the salt from my neck before taking the lime from my mouth. It's hot, erotic, and has my every nerve ending on fire.

With his help, I hop down and turn to him. "All right, hotshot, my turn."

He smirks as he pulls his shirt over his head and climbs onto the bar. "Do your worst."

Never having done one before, I repeat his actions, and as I take the lime from his mouth, he looks shocked that I was daring enough to do it at all. Once everyone goes back to doing their own thing, and the attention is no longer on us, he brings his lips to my ear.

"That was so fucking hot."

The sexual chemistry between us has always been explosive, but with alcohol, it's worse. Before we end up all over each other in front of everyone, I grab Delaney and go to join Becca and Paige on the dance floor. As my body moves to the beat of the song, it reminds me that I need to get back in the studio. Brady has yet to return any of my calls, but the recital is only a week away. I didn't want to ambush him into talking to me, but I will if I need to.

Suddenly, the music cuts out, and the sound of someone slow clapping echoes through the room. I turn around to see Trey walking toward me. My eyes widen, realizing the threat I made earlier may have been a stupid one.

"What are you doing?"

He smirks. "I'm applauding you for your academy level performance that has had everyone here fooled for years."

"Trey," I plead, but he clearly doesn't care.

"What? You don't want them to know?"

Jace comes into the room, wondering what happened to the music, when his eyes narrow on Trey. "What the hell is going on in here? I don't remember inviting any North Haven trash."

"Well, then you'd probably be keen to know one of your own is exactly that."

Looking ready to punch this kid in the face, Jace shoves his shoulder. "Listen shit-brick, you better explain what the fuck you're talking about and fast, before I have my security escort you out—and they tend to get a little rough."

Trey turns to me. "Savannah? Do you want to tell them, or should I?"

I look to Gray, but he's too busy glaring daggers into the side of Trey's head. Quickly going over it in my mind, I have two options. I can either give in to his insane demands and potentially ruin things between Grayson and I, or I deny it and hope everyone believes me over him.

Making a split-second decision, I stand my ground and swallow down my fear. "I have no idea what you're talking about."

"Suit yourself." He rolls his eyes and focuses on Jace. "Your little princess isn't as well off as she appears. In short, she's dirt poor."

Everyone breaks out into hysterical laughter, as if the idea is completely outlandish. It's exactly what I wanted, and I relax a little, thinking this is going to play out in my favor.

"Okay, it was one thing for you to harass me after I already turned you down, but to come here with a lie like that? It's pathetic, even for you."

Glaring at me, he pulls something out of his pocket and my stomach drops. "See, I thought you might not believe me, so I brought proof." My blood runs cold as he passes a handful of pictures to Jace. "See for yourself."

Carter and Jace flip through a couple before looking at me in disbelief. Jace shakes his head and walks away, while Carter appears genuinely hurt.

"Seriously? I thought we were friends. How could you?"

Tears fill my eyes as I feel my entire world crashing down around me. "Carter!"

"Don't. Just, don't."

AS I IGNORE DELANEY asking if I'm okay, I get out of the car and use the spare key to get inside Grayson's house.

Going straight into the basement, I start taking all my anger out on his punching bag. *Right. Left. Right. Right. Left.* By the time two strong arms wrap around my waist, my knuckles are already bleeding.

"It's over," I wail. "The only thing I had left, and he took it, for spite."

"It'll be okay."

"It won't. No one is ever going to look at me the same. If they don't hate me, they'll feel sorry for me. Kinsley is going to have a fucking field day and take over as captain. Jace and Carter will probably never talk to me again. And they probably shouldn't." I turn in his arms, looking up at him through the tears. "Make me forget. Please. Even just for a moment, I need to forget."

Grayson searches my face for something unbeknownst to me before grabbing the back of my neck and pressing our lips together. I throw everything I've got into the kiss, trying to portray how I feel about him. It's messy, with my tears making our mouths wet, but as he fucks me right there on the workout room floor, there's nothing else I need. As long as I have him, I'll be okay.

I LAY WITH MY head on his chest while his fingers run through my hair. I don't know what this means for us. Everything has been so different between us lately, but if I'm the joke of the school, dating me would be social suicide. The thought of possibly losing him a second time makes me feel sick to my stomach. Which reminds me...

"Can I ask you something?" I question, and he hums, telling me he's listening. "Why didn't you tell me you were moving?"

"What?"

"When we were younger, I came back from my

grandmother's, and you were just gone. Why didn't you say goodbye?"

He sits up abruptly and pushes me off him. "I know what you're referring to, but why the fuck are you asking me this? You fucking know why."

"If I knew, I wouldn't be asking," I protest. Why is he getting so mad about this? It's just a simple question. "Did you not want to? Did your dad not want you to tell me?"

In a split second, he snaps and gets up in my face. "Don't you dare fucking talk about him, do you hear me? You don't get to even think his name!"

As he backs up and tries to calm down, I can't help but feel concerned. "What the hell happened to you between then and now? Who made you so cold? Because you're sure as hell not the boy I remember."

"Stop! Stop acting like you don't know! I saw the fucking video! I heard the interview!"

My brows furrow. "What video? What fucking interview?" I try to take his hand in mine but he rips it away. "Grayson, talk to me!"

"Why? Why the fuck do you even care?"

"Because I'm in love with you!"

The declaration slips out before I even have a chance to stop it, and both our eyes widen at the revelation. However, the hope of him being happy about it dies as he shakes his head and looks away from me.

"You need to leave." It's so low that I almost wonder if I heard him right.

"W-what? Grayson, no. Don't do this."

His gaze meets mine, and the fire burning in his dark blue orbs is enough to scare even me. "I said leave! Go! Get the fuck out!"

Grabbing my clothes, I hurry upstairs and rush to put them on before racing out the door. The freezing December air does nothing to comfort me as tears pour down my face. I run across the street and knock on the door of the one person who can help me.

"Sav?" Delaney asks as she sees me. "Are you okay? What the hell happened?"

I shiver, half from the cold and half from sobs that rip through my body. "I n-need a ride."

21

GRAYSON

I PACE BACK AND FORTH BEFORE GRABBING ONE OF the weights and throwing it against the mirror, watching as it shatters. Seven years of bad luck, right? Add it to the fucking list.

Why did she have to bring up my father? And to have the audacity to act like she doesn't know the reason I moved away that summer. Like she wasn't the catalyst of that whole shitshow.

Things between us were good until she had to go and make them personal. It was easy, separating my sex life with Savannah from the part of me that wanted to get revenge for what she did to my family. The little girl who ruined my life was a traitorous liar, while the one in my bed was a goddess. But when she dropped that emotional truth bomb, everything hit me like a truck. No matter how much I try to separate the two, they're always going to be the same.

As unexpected as her confession was, what caught me more off guard was the rush of emotions that washed over me when she said it. *Euphoric. Blissful. Happy. Ecstatic.* Hearing her say those words is everything I've longed for since I was eight, and ten years too late. All I wanted was to be with her, until I learned the truth of what happened to my father. The love I once felt was replaced by a raging fire that could never be put out.

Sleeping with her is one thing, but falling in love with her is something I could never allow. To be with her would be the worst form of betrayal. How could I let myself be with the person who indirectly caused my dad's death? It's simple, I can't.

If I've learned anything the past couple months, it's that resisting her is not something that comes easy to me. I need to stay away from her. To gain some distance while I get my head on straight. It'll be hard—I can already feel the gaping hole in my chest where she should be—but it's what I need to do.

I take out my phone and dial the one number I haven't called in weeks.

"Hey. Can we talk?"

22

SAVANNAH

THE MUSIC FILLS MY EARS, ERASING ALL THE thoughts from my head as I throw myself into each move. Tears flow from my eyes and blur my vision, but I keep going. Everything that happened tonight, the pain and the disappointment, none of it matters in this moment. Here, I can be free. Here, I'm okay.

Flashing blue and red lights reflect across the room as they fill the dark night outside, but I don't stop dancing. This is the only thing holding me together. If I stop, I'll break. I've put myself back together so many times in the last eight years. I'm not sure I have it in me to do it anymore.

Brady enters the studio, followed by two police officers. I must have forgotten to turn off the silent alarm. However, as his eyes see the tears in mine, he stops.

"It's all right. I know her." He tells them as I leap through the air. "You can go."

Leaning against the doorway, he watches me carefully. The tears haven't stopped, and therefore neither have I.

It's late—nearly two in the morning—but it's as if time doesn't matter. Not in here. Not like this.

As the song fades to an end, Brady turns off the sound

213

system, but I still continue to dance. He comes closer with careful steps, watching me like a caged animal that could attack at any moment. The second it all catches up to me, I come crashing down, and he instantly pulls me into his arms.

Sobs rip through me, making my chest hurt with every breath. The waterworks soaking his shirt don't seem to faze him, however, as he holds me close and continues to whisper comforting words into my ear.

It's okay. I've got you. It's going to be all right.

But it's not, and it won't, because how could things be okay when the one person I love most in this world doesn't love me back? I have nothing.

DESPITE WANTING TO STAY cooped up in my bedroom, I show up to school on Monday morning. Delaney stays by my side, giving me strength to get through this. As we walk through the doors, everyone stops to stare. They whisper to their friends, talking about how I have a lot of nerve coming back here, or how they thought I dropped out—believe me, I wish I could.

Reaching my locker, I see Carter, Jace, Hayden, Wyatt, and Emma. With a nudge from Wyatt, they all turn to look at me, but none of them say a word. Laney keeps a comforting hand on my back as I grab my books. I'm about to leave when the urge to say something makes it so I can't move.

"I just want you guys to know, I'm really sorry. I may have lied about my home life, but everything else was real."

Emma looks like she's about to cry, but still, I'm met with silence. I sigh, heading toward first period when a sight worse than the most painful nightmares appears in front of me. *Grayson and Kinsley.*

They walk toward us, and no matter how much of me screams to look away, I can't. As he stands there, with her

214

pressed firmly against his side, gone is the hatred that burned in his eyes. There's no trace of the angry glares that have sent chills down my spine, or the stares of pure want and need that awakened my soul. All that's left is pure indifference, and somehow, that's worse.

"Let's go, Sav." Delaney whispers, pulling me away, but I can't. I won't. Our love story doesn't end like this.

I turn around and head back down the hallway, ignoring the calls of my name. When I reach Grayson, I go to grab his arm.

"Grayson, I need to talk to—"

"Ew!" Kinsley shrieks as she turns around. "Keep your dirty hands off my boyfriend, you lying bitch."

I recoil, narrowing in on the one word that makes it hard to breath. "B-boyfriend?"

Grayson won't look at me, while Kinsley smirks. She turns to him, taking his face in her hands, and pulling him down for a kiss. It's forced, not at all the way he's kissed me, but hurts all the same. Just like that, the last part of me, something I didn't even know was still whole, shatters into a million tiny pieces.

"Run along now. No one wants you here," she sneers, wrapping an arm around Grayson's waist.

I can't get my feet to move until Delaney pulls me away.

Boyfriend. He's her boyfriend. I told him I'm in love with him, and his response was to become Kinsley's boyfriend.

Did I imagine the last six weeks, when we spent the days laughing about the stupidest things, and the nights lost in each other under the sheets? Was I crazy to think we stood a fighting chance? All I know for sure is that I can't stay here.

Delaney follows me as I push through the front door. "Where are you going?"

"Don't know, don't care."

She grabs my wrist and gives me a concerned look. "Do you want me to come with you?"

I shake my head. "You're in the running for valedictorian. Don't let me ruin that. I'll be okay. You go."

Sighing, she wraps her arms around me and gives me a tight hug. "Text me if you need me."

"I will."

SITTING IN THE COLD in only my school uniform, I should be uncomfortable, but I can't feel anything besides the pain of my heart breaking. I swing back and forth as I ignore the world around me. How could I have been so stupid? From the second he came back here, he made it clear that he wanted to hurt me. The anger that radiated from him was paralyzing, but his smile was infectious.

Maybe this was his plan all along. To get me to fall for him then rip it away. Perhaps ruining my social status wasn't enough for him, so he left it to someone else while he focused on what would hurt more. He took everything—my virginity, my heart, my hope. Claiming it all for himself, he took from me until the only thing I had left was the blood in my veins. If he could, I'm sure he'd take that too.

"There you are." Brady says, coming up and wrapping his coat around me. "I've been looking for you for hours. You must be freezing."

"I'm fine." My voice is like stone, completely void of any emotion.

He sighs. "Well, you can't get sick. We need you this weekend." Gently prying my hand from the swing, he takes it in his. "Come on."

"It hurts, Brady. It hurts so bad."

"I know. We're going to go make it better."

I GIGGLE, APPLAUDING AS he throws a cheeseball up in the air and catches it in his mouth. The thirty-six that he missed lie scattered across the studio floor. After finding me at the park, Brady brought me back here and called for reinforcements. Twenty minutes later, we had all the junk food Jacob could grab in a quick trip to the grocery store, and the most comfortable sweats I've ever worn in my life.

"All right, turn the music up," I tell him, watching as he grabs the remote and raises the volume.

The sounds of "Haunted" by Taylor Swift fill the room, the perfect melody for what I'm feeling right now. It's loud and irate, exactly the feelings I need. I start a pirouette and spin until I'm dizzy. The moves are messy but firm as I take out my anger, and by the time I'm done, my labored breathing feels like healing.

Brady switches the song to Shake It Off, and the two of us dance around the room like idiots, laughing hysterically and not giving a shit if people are watching through the window. Sometimes, what you need is just to let go for a bit, and a friend to let go with.

WE'RE JUST FINISHING OUR duet to *Señorita* when Brady shuts off the music and turns to me. The look in his eyes shows he's in "big brother knows best" mode instead of the supportive friend mode he just spent half the day in.

"All right, Sav. Time to go," he tells me.

My brows furrow. "What do you mean? Go where?"

"It's Monday. You have cheer practice."

With my jaw practically on the floor, all the air leaves my lungs. "Have you lost your ever-living mind? I can't go there."

He sighs and grabs his sweatshirt. "You have to. If you

don't, it's like you're handing over captain to Kinsley without putting up a fight."

"They're going to vote me out anyway."

"Then they vote you out," he counters. "At least then you know you didn't just give it to her."

A low whine emits from my throat. "Haven't I been humiliated enough for one week?"

"Almost." Brady jokes. "Let's go, you'll thank me later."

AS I WALK INTO the gymnasium, all eyes focus on me. Kinsley is running them through stunts that are far more dangerous than their skill level allows, but when she realizes they've all stopped, she turns around to see what they're looking at.

"What the hell are *you* doing here?" she sneers.

I look around at my team, finding only Emma staring back at me with something other than disgust on her face. It's obvious where I stand, but Brady was right, I can't just hand it over.

"Last time I checked, I'm still captain."

The irritating laugh she lets out goes right through me. "Weren't you listening this morning? *No one wants you here.*"

I stand strong and square my shoulders, refusing to let her get to me. "I really don't care what you say, Kinsley. You can't just waltz in here and demand captain. That's not how it works."

She narrows her eyes at me before smirking. "Fine, we'll put it to a vote then." Turning to the rest of the team, my chest tightens. "All those in favor of overthrowing Savannah and making me captain?" Everyone raises their hand except Emma, and Kinsley focuses back on me with a devilish grin on her face. "There, now it's settled, and the first action I'm taking as captain is kicking your fake ass off this team."

It's a very formative experience, seeing everyone I thought was my friend turn against me so easily—though I brought this on myself. I give them a sad smile before nodding once. If I didn't think it would make me look worse, I'd smack the smug look right off Kinsley's face.

"Now let's go," she announces. "Practice is ending early today. I have plans with my *boyfriend*."

The word doesn't fail to sting, and I know that was her intention. As they all walk toward the locker room, Emma stands there, watching me sadly.

"Em, come on, or you can join her," Kinsley calls.

Mouthing a silent apology, she goes with them. I don't blame her. Cheer is that girl's whole life, and she's good at it. No part of me would want her to give that up.

I send Brady a text and walk out to the football field, sitting on the bleachers as I stare at the empty turf. I spent almost four full years on this field and put all my energy into cheering on the football team. It's upsetting to know I won't finish out the season for my senior year.

Memories of the games we've played this year flash through my mind. When Jace kicked a field goal from sixty yards away. Hayden intercepting a throw and weaving his way all the way down to score a touchdown. Grayson running a Hail Mary play at the end of a game, and Carter catching in the end zone,—continuing their undefeated streak. It's all bittersweet.

The ruffling of my hair grabs my attention, and I turn my head to see Wyatt smiling at me. Carter kisses the top of my head while Jace sits down and pulls me into his arms. Even Hayden stands there with his arm around Emma, grinning as he shakes his head at me.

"You don't hate me?"

Carter sighs, leaning forward to rest his arms on his knees. "It turns out, you're a pretty hard person to stay mad at."

Relief floods through me. "I'm so sorry. I never meant for it to get so out of hand."

"Why did you lie in the first place, though?" Emma asks.

I shrug. "Before I started here, I knew one thing—wealth meant power. What I wanted was to fit in. Then one thing lead to another, and I was the girl everyone idolized. I thought that if people knew the truth, I'd be the laughingstock of the school."

Carter shakes his head. "We never liked you for your money, princess. It was your bitchy attitude and ability to put people in their place that won us over."

"And you're hot, so that helps," Jace quips as I lean against him.

Using my sleeve, I wipe away the few tears that have managed to escape. "I really do love you guys."

"We love you, too," Carter responds. "Now if only we could figure out what the hell is going through Grayson's mind. *Kinsley?* Seriously?"

I shake my head. "I don't want to talk about him."

He frowns. "Not yet?"

"Not ever."

I JOG DOWN THE street, running to escape from all my demons. My father. Kinsley. Grayson. The faster my feet move, the further away they feel.

The music flows through the earbuds and into my ears. It's therapeutic, really, how a song has the ability to make you feel that much better. The lyrics are like an outlet, not only for the songwriter, but for the listener—kind of like my dancing. It's always been a way for me to tell a story—to deal with the pain and heartache, and just let it out.

I come to a halt as an idea clicks in my mind. Then I turn

around and race back to the studio. I get there in record time and burst into the room. Brady eyes me carefully.

"I want to change our duet."

He seems unsure. "Okay? What part?"

I shake my head. "All of it. I want to change the dance, the song, everything."

"Have you gone completely insane? The recital is in four days!"

Standing my ground, I can already picture the dance in my head. "I don't care. I need to do this."

23

GRAYSON

Kinsley sits across from me, ranting about everything under the sun. Can't she see that I don't care what color nail polish Becca had on today? She's making it hard to enjoy my milkshake—which is really something, because this diner has unbeatable shakes. Still, I pretend to listen and nod my head at all the parts I think are important.

Dating her isn't something I want, but I have to. It's a necessary move, albeit one that creates more problems for me than it solves. She's the kind of person I normally can't stand to be around, but she's the only one who can accomplish what I need. Making her my girlfriend isn't to keep *me* away from *Savannah*, it's to keep *Savannah* away from *me*.

I know that if she's standing in front of me, begging for me to talk to her, I won't stand a chance. I'll cave in five seconds flat and hand her my heart on a silver fucking platter. No, I can't let that happen. Keeping her at a distance is what's best for both of us.

"You should have seen it," Kinsley smirks. "She looked so stupid standing there all alone as we all walked away." Giving her a confused look, she can tell I wasn't paying attention. "Savannah. Focus, Grayson."

I shake my head. "Don't. Don't talk to me about her."

"Uh, okay," she says hesitantly, taking a sip of her water. "You know, if I didn't know any better, I'd think you two had something going on."

"What the fuck did I just say?" I snap. "Do you just not know how to listen? I said *don't* talk to me about her."

She scoffs and rolls her eyes, picking up her phone and scrolling through it. Suddenly, the door swings open, and a livid Delaney comes storming toward me, followed by Tessa, who gives me a warning look.

"Grayson Matthew."

Wow, I'm in middle-name-level trouble. "Who told you that?"

"It doesn't matter. I need to speak to you." With a look at Kinsley, she clarifies. "Alone."

"Uh, excuse me," Kinsley sasses. "Rude, much? Can't you see we're busy here?"

Laney glares at her. "Do I look like fucking care?"

Both mine and Tessa's eyes widen. Being a Goody Two-shoes since she was little, Delaney Callahan doesn't use profanity unless she's *really* pissed.

Kinsley pouts as Delaney focuses her attention back on me. "Grayson, *now!*"

"I'd listen to her," Tessa advises. "She's been on the war path all damn day."

Deciding to appease her, I tell Kinsley I'll be right back and slip out of the booth. Laney shoots one last dirty look at my girlfriend before following me to the parking lot. As soon as we get outside, she looks like she's going to hit me.

"What on earth is wrong with you?" She shouts. "How could you do that to Savannah?"

"I didn't do anything to her," I defend, but we both know that's a lie.

"Like hell you didn't. I was there Friday night, picking up the broken pieces you left her in!" She pauses for a second but doesn't let me get a word in before she continues. "And then you run right to Kinsley? Seriously, Grayson? *Kinsley*?"

I throw my hands in the air. "I had to, okay? I fucking had to!" Rubbing my hands over my face, I walk over to sit on the step. "I *can't* care about her. Not the way she wants me to."

"You already do. If you didn't, you wouldn't have told me where she lives," she retorts. "You knew damn well I was going to keep her secret. So, don't even try playing like you were hoping I'd do your dirty work."

"It doesn't matter. The past can't be rewritten, and she can't undo what she did. We will never be a thing."

Her brows furrow. "Okay, we'll pretend like I know what *that* means." She runs her fingers through her hair and sighs. "I just don't want to see you two throw away something that's been thirteen years in the making. When we were little, you two were the one thing I was sure of."

I smile sadly. "Things were different then, Laney. So much has changed."

"Except for the fact that you're still crazy about each other," Tessa chimes in, but as soon as I look at her, she raises her hands in surrender. "Sorry, I'll shut up now."

"No!" Delaney argues. "Tess is right. I saw it myself, the way you two have been with each other the past few weeks. The way she's talked about you." She sighs. "It's everything you hope to find, and you're throwing that away."

A groan rumbles from deep in my throat. "What the hell do you want from me?"

"I want you to admit that you're in love with her!"

"Of course I'm in love with her!" I laugh dryly. "I have been since I was fucking nine years old."

She calms her tone, as if she feels like she's getting through to me. "Then tell her that. Whatever it is, you two can get through it."

225

I shake my head. "We can't. Not with this." Standing up, I pull my keys from my pocket. "I'm sorry, Laney. Tell Kinsley something came up and I'll pay her back for the bill."

"Grayson—" she calls as I go to walk away. I turn back to glance at her, and she looks just as defeated as I feel. "If you change your mind, I have a spare ticket to Savannah's recital on Friday night. I think you should come."

With no true intentions of taking her up on that, I nod once and head for my car. It was naive to think I could handle staying around here. The wounds are too fresh for us to coexist right now—too deep for us to avoid causing the other more pain. I need to leave, at least for a little while.

DRIBBLING THE BASKETBALL, TYSON charges at me but he lacks the coordination I have. I spin, going around him and shooting it—nothing but net. The air feels hot in the oversized gym as I fan myself with my shirt. Ty grabs the ball and checks it to me before trying to make it to the hoop. He goes to take the shot, but while he might be two years older, he's a good six inches shorter. I reach my hand up and block it, laughing as he scowls.

"You're a little shit, Grayson."

I give him a knowing look and smile. "I'm not sure you're really in the place to call someone a *little* anything."

He rolls his eyes. "Fuck off. Are you done running from your problems yet? You've missed what, three days of school already?"

"Since when do you give a shit how much school I miss?" I steal the ball and take it outside the three-point line.

"Since I promised your mom I'd look out for you."

Just as I shoot, my phone starts ringing on the bench. I walk over, seeing Kinsley's name and vomit-inducing picture on the screen. Hitting ignore, I go back to playing the game.

"That's like the eighth time she's called today." He looks down at his watch. "And it's only noon."

"What's your point?"

He chuckles. "I don't have one. I just never expected you to change your noncommittal ways for some overly obsessive trust fund baby who won't hop off your dick for five minutes." He stands against my side as he tries to block me. "I honestly thought you'd end up dating Savannah."

I shove my elbow into his stomach, barreling my whole body into his and knocking him over before shooting the perfect three-pointer, but I'm not about to celebrate.

He narrows his eyes at me and pushes himself up off the floor. "What the hell, man?"

"Why the fuck does everyone insist on talking to me about her?" I shout.

"I don't know, maybe because we can all see what you're not willing to admit."

Getting up in his face, I'm ready to deck him. The only reason I haven't is because he's my cousin. "Yeah? And what's that?"

He squares his shoulders and mirrors my glare. "That you're less of a person without her. You're angry and irrational. You walk around acting like the world screwed you over, and you'll stop at nothing until you burn the whole damn thing to the ground." His frustration is evident as he shoves past me and heads toward the door. "Your father may have wanted a lot of things for you, but I don't think any part of him wanted *this*."

Alone to drown in my own destruction, I lie down on the gymnasium floor and stare at the ceiling. Every part of me knew better than to get involved with her. The plan was simple—find her weakness, her Achilles' heel, and destroy her with it. It couldn't have been any more straightforward, but it all went to hell the moment I kissed her. That one taste of what things could have been derailed me in an instant.

Standing there, watching as Trey revealed her secret to everyone, I felt conflicted. One on hand, I was pissed. That information was mine, the only thing I had that could cause her pain. On the other, I was relieved. She got what was coming to her, but my hands remained clean, or at least as clean as they could be with everything I'd already done. Seeing her break down, however, hit me with a feeling I never expected—sympathy.

Savannah and I used to be that one constant in my life—the one thing I knew I could count on. It's like we were written in the stars...destined to be together. Even growing up apart from her, I always hoped we'd find each other again someday. It wasn't until I found proof of my father's warning that I finally understood why he wanted me to stay away from her. I drank so much that day, my mom was afraid I'd need my stomach pumped.

The next morning, I had made two vows to myself—I'd never give someone the ability to hurt me that way again, and I'd get my revenge on the ones who betrayed him. Betrayed me. I just never expected I'd end up as broken as she is. Tyson may have a point after all.

I TAKE A DEEP breath as I reach up and knock, loosening the tie around my neck just a little. No part of me is sure about this, or about what I plan on doing afterward, but it's a step. The door swings open, and I'm met with two wide green eyes. Delaney takes in my appearance and smiles.

"Still have that extra ticket?"

She nods. "Just let me grab my purse."

As she steps out and closes the door behind her, I realize I've never seen Delaney so dressed up before. Her light brown hair is kept out of her face with braids and diamond clips. The black dress she's wearing sparkles as it reflects the light, low cut and revealing. Being as she's the closest I've got to a little sister, let someone try hitting on her tonight. I've been needing an outlet for this pent-up frustration.

THE VENUE IS FILLED with supportive friends and family, but I'm sure we're the only ones here for Savannah. Delaney and I sit several rows back from the stage. Personally, I don't want Sav to see me here, and Delaney agreed—explaining that the sight of me may catch her off guard and cause her to mess up.

We watch dancers come and go from the stage for what feels like hours, but Savannah is yet to be seen. Even a routine I've watched her rehearse with Lennon is performed as a solo. I look over at Delaney, confused, but she only shakes her head and smiles. Finally, the director of the dance studio comes out onto the stage. She's a middle-aged woman, and the female form of Brady.

"Thank you so much for coming tonight," she says into the microphone. "The final performance is one that even I didn't get to see until just last night. It was choreographed entirely by the dancer herself and perfected in only a matter of four days. So please, put your hands together for the immensely talented Savannah Montgomery, performing *Broken Memories*."

Everyone applauds and Delaney straightens in her seat, but the stage remains empty—until the music starts to play. It's a simple music box tune with a layover track of children laughing. Two small kids walk across the stage, holding hands and nudging each other playfully.

Suddenly, the tune becomes sinister, and two older dancers come out to rip the little boy away. The girl searches frantically, running back and forth with a fearful look on her

229

face before walking backward off the stage, opposite the side the boy was taken.

Love Me or Leave Me by Little Mix starts playing, and for the first time all night, Savannah steps out. She looks flawlessly gorgeous in her white costume, with her hair down and curled. A white gold necklace, similar to the one I gave her, lies against her chest.

She moves her body across the stage with a delicate ease, leaping through the air like she has the ability to fly. Her spins are perfectly executed, and as she turns out of them, you can see the pain in her eyes.

Brady stands toward the back corner of the stage with his back to the crowd, unmoving and firm, even as Savannah pounds on his back and pulls at his jacket.

She returns to throwing her body into every move, following each one with another in a way no other dancer could. She's not just putting on a performance, she's spilling her soul.

As the second verse starts, Brady begins to move. It's like they're facing off, both angry and unwilling to cave. Then, the bridge hits, and he's in her face. She swings at him with each hand, only for him to catch both her wrists—a reenactment of our first kiss. Her body falls limp as he holds her and spins them around.

Straightening, she turns to face the audience, and Brady lifts her by her waist. It's a brilliant move that not only shows their strength but their trust in each other. The two of them move around the stage in synchrony until they're face to face again. As the last notes play, she watches with pleading eyes as he grabs the small pendant and rips it from her neck, before turning and walking slowly off the stage.

Savannah collapses to the ground, reaching for him with one hand, and grabbing her chest with the other. The entire place is silent as tears flow from her eyes. With a painful finality, she lays her head on the stage, and the hand that was grasping for Brady relaxes.

It's as heartbreaking as it is beautiful, and in an instant, the entire place is on their feet. The screams and cheers are deafening as she's commended for such a jaw-dropping performance. There isn't a single person in the audience unmoved—including me. Especially me. While they all saw a dance, I saw a story. The story of us.

24

GRAYSON

ALL NIGHT, I CAN'T GET THAT DANCE OUT OF MY head. The way she moved. The pain etched into each of her perfect features. Even just watching her, my heart broke. She took our tragic story and managed to turn it into something beautiful. Turned it into art.

There are a million different reasons why we should or shouldn't be together, and I can't seem to make sense of any of them. The only thing I know is that this isn't something I can figure out on my own. I need to talk to Savannah—lay everything out on the table, and see where we go from there.

It's half past three when I decide I can't wait any longer. Grabbing my keys, I get in my car and drive toward her house. The whole way there I can hardly sit still. We haven't spoken to each other since the night of Jace's party, when she confessed to being in love with me, and I responded by kicking her out of my house. The look on her face as I screamed at her to leave is still burned into my mind, tormenting me late at night when I can't sleep.

When I pull up to her place, what can only be described as a ratty, beater car is sitting out front. It's a slightly familiar one; I'm guessing her dad's. Every time I've come to pick her up, if that car was parked outside, she'd be waiting on the porch by the time I got here. I have yet to come face to face with him again after all this time, but I'm not about to shy away. I need to talk to Savannah.

As I get out of the car and walk toward the door, I hear glass breaking, followed by shouting coming from inside.

"Don't ever speak to me that way again, do you understand me? You live under my roof! You treat me with respect!" a man yells.

I'm just about to knock when the door swings open and Savannah's father stumbles out of it. He looks like shit, not half the man I remember him being. His hairline is receding, he's paunchy, and he smells like he bathed in a bottle of whiskey.

"Fucking ungrateful little bitch," he mumbles.

As if he didn't realize I was there at first, his eyes meet mine and widen drastically. The two of us stand there, staring at each other in a silent face-off, until he shakes his head and drunkenly staggers down the steps and to his car. It's obvious he shouldn't be driving in his condition, but I have more pressing matters to deal with. I just hope that if he kills himself, he doesn't take anyone else with him.

The door is left halfway open, and I peek my head in before entering. Savannah is crouched down on the floor, sweeping up what looks like the broken pieces of a beer bottle. Her hair is a mess, as if someone had their hands in it, and her shirt is ripped.

"Sav?"

Her head whips toward me, and that's when I see it—the fresh gash on her forehead and handprint on her cheek. In a split second, it all becomes crystal clear. All the bruises I noticed over the last few weeks…her comment about dealing with things much scarier than thunderstorms…how nothing I did seemed to have any effect on her.

Her father has been beating her this whole time.

"What do you want, Grayson?" The cracking in her voice tells me just how defeated she is.

"Why didn't you tell me?"

She laughs dryly as she stands and empties the dustpan into the garbage. "And when did you expect me to do that? When you were looking for anything you could use to ruin my life, or when you were screaming at me to get out of your house?"

I step closer and reach out to touch her, but she dodges it. "I can help you."

"I don't need any help."

My brows furrow. "Savannah, he's hurting you!"

"And you haven't?" She snaps. "Don't try playing the knight in shining armor now! You've been no better than he is!"

"Don't be like that."

She scoffs. "Be like what? Truthful? Honest? What you did to me hurt so much more than anything my father has ever done." Turning around, she doesn't even look at me as she says the next words. "Go. I don't want you here."

It's like someone plunged an icepick straight into my chest. As everything tightens inside me, I feel like I can't breathe. She'd rather get thrown around than let me help her, and why should she? I've done nothing but make things harder for her. School was the one place she could act like everything was okay. Like her life wasn't a fucking train wreck. It was the only time she felt safe and hopeful, and I took that away from her.

I've always been meant to protect her, and instead, I caused her the most pain.

I PULL UP TO the studio, not even bothering to park in a space or turn off my car before I'm storming inside. It only takes a minute to find Brady, standing with the same guy I saw helping him after our little scuffle outside the bar. I grab him by the shoulder and spin him around. His demeanor changes when he sees me.

"What the hell do you want?!"

"Did you know?"

He looks at me as if I've gone crazy. "Know what? That you're a bastard?"

"About Savannah's dad!" I scream. "Did you know he's been using her as his own personal fucking punching bag?"

"He's been what?" His instant outrage is enough to tell me he's been just as clueless as I have. "And how do you know this?"

I pace back and forth. "Because I just went over there to talk to her, and heard him screaming at her! There was broken glass everywhere, and she's got a nasty cut on her forehead and his handprint on her face."

"What are you doing *here* then? Why aren't you helping her?"

"She doesn't want me to! Not that I blame her. She has every right to hate me, but him…?" I shake my head as my fury builds. "No. He already ruined my life. He doesn't get to ruin hers too."

Heading toward the door, Brady calls after me. "Where are you going?"

"To find the piece of shit," I answer. "I'm going to fucking kill him."

THREE HOURS OF SEARCHING for the son of a bitch, and I come up empty. Wherever he is, I hope he knows what a shitty fucking person he's become. It's one thing to stab his best friend in the back, but to beat on his own daughter? There's a special place in hell for assholes like him, and if I'd found him tonight, I'd have been the one to put him there.

As I'm driving home, I come across the familiar plot where the playground used to be. It's overgrown now, but my mind immediately goes to the waterfall. The time we spent there was everything to me, and while it might be freezing outside, it may just be the one place to help me clear my head.

The path is completely overgrown, telling me that no one else has been here in a while. It isn't until I get deep into the woods that I can hear the flow of water. Clearing out spider webs and foliage, I finally reach the opening. I step through the bush and take in the sight in front of me.

It looks the same as it did eight years ago, only older. Moss covers the bottoms of the trees, and the waterline is higher than I remember. Sitting down on one of the rocks, it's so cold I can see my breath, but the rage inside burns so hot that I can't feel it.

Taking out my phone, I've got three missed calls and seven texts from Brady. They're all different variations of telling me to calm down and to think rationally. It's amusing, how he thinks he has any influence on me or my actions. The reality is simple: if her father hadn't evaded me this afternoon, he'd be rotting at the bottom of a ditch somewhere.

I roll my eyes and go to put the device back in my pocket, when it slips from my hand and slides down the rock— clanking on something before hitting the ground. My brows furrow as I reach to grab it and spot a glass bottle. It's old, and has obviously been here for a while, but the seal seems to have remained strong. When I pick it up, I realize it's filled with rolled up pieces of paper.

The only two people I've ever known to be here are

Savannah and myself, and judging by the looks of it, that still rings true. I hold the bottle over one of the rocks and slam it down. The glass breaks with ease, freeing the papers inside. As I unroll the first one, I find my suspicions were right. Handwriting I'd recognize anywhere is scribbled across it.

Gray,

Where did you go? I came home from Nana's and you were gone! Daddy said you and your family moved away. I miss you. Why didn't you tell me? Why didn't you say goodbye? Just come home. Come back for me.

Savi

I flip to the next one.

Gray,

Why haven't you called me yet? I know you know my number. Does where you moved to not have phones? I wish someone would tell me what's going on. I really miss you. I don't know what to do without you. You're my best friend, Gray. I just keep hoping one day you'll come back.

Savi

And the next.

Gray,

Delaney told me today that your dad died. Are you okay? I wish I could be there for you. I'd hold you really close like you did for me the night of that bad storm. The new phonebook came the other day. I tried to look for your name, but it wasn't there. If by some chance you come back here, I hope you find these and call me. I miss you.

Savi

Gray,

Things are getting scary. Daddy is acting weird, coming home all the time smelling gross and falling down all over the place. He's started leaving me home alone a lot. He says I'm a big girl now and I can handle it, but I'm scared. I don't know what's going on. Why haven't you come back yet? Why haven't you called? Do you have a new best friend? Is it because we kissed? Because we can pretend it never happened. Just come home.

Savi

The last one is short, only three lines, but enough to raise goosebumps across my skin.

Grayson,

I'm scared.

Things are getting worse.

If something happens to me, I love you.

Savannah

The overwhelming emotion threatens to choke me with the truth. She didn't know. Whatever was done to record that video, she wasn't the willing participant I thought she was. All this time, I thought she was playing the victim. She really didn't know.

What have I done?

MY FIST POUNDS ON the door as I will for it to open. When it does, Delaney stands on the other side, her face full of concern. I try to keep my composure, but anyone with eyes can see that I'm breaking.

"Tell me what to do," I plead. "She hates me, and she has every right to, but please. I need you to tell me what to do."

She sighs. "All Savannah's ever wanted was you. If you can't give her that, you need to stay away. It's all or nothing."

"What if I can? What if I want to?"

Searching my face for any signs of ill intentions, she nods and opens the door further to let me in.

25

SAVANNAH

I PULL DOWN THE MIRROR IN BRADY'S CAR, ADDING more concealer in an attempt cover up the cut on my forehead. I tug a lock of hair down over it when I'm done. It's not a perfect job, and if someone looks too closely, they'll notice. However, it's enough to not bring attention to it. The last thing I want is for people to ask me what happened.

After Grayson *so courteously* told Brady about what my dad has been doing to me, Brady stormed over to my house and demanded I stay with him and Jacob for a while. At first I resisted, not wanting to impose. I take up enough of his time with dance and giving me rides to and from school. Taking up space in their house felt like encroaching on their relationship, and I would never forgive myself if they split up because of me.

Unfortunately, Brady wouldn't take no for an answer, and Jacob joined him. They told me that the only alternative to not going with them was to call the police. Being as I'm already enough of the school's charity case at the moment, I really didn't want everyone to find this out, too. So, I packed a bag, and we left.

"You going to be all right today?" he asks.

"Why wouldn't I be?"

"I don't know. I mean, with Grayson being back from wherever he fucked off to, and now knowing about your shithead of a father."

Putting away the makeup, I flip the visor closed. "It's nothing new for me, Brady. Nothing I can't handle."

A proud smile stretches across his face. "That's the Rocky I know and love."

"Yeah, yeah. Love you too. I'll see you after." I hug him and open the door.

"Have a good day at school, sweetie!" he says in his best falsetto mom voice, making me laugh.

As I walk into the school, I realize a lot of the attention is no longer on me. People don't smile at me the way they used to, but they also don't shoot me dirty looks anymore either. I go down the hallway and toward my locker, waving at Carter and Jace. Unfortunately for me, Kinsley is standing there, too, with Becca and Paige.

"You know, I'm really thinking we should request her locker be moved. I don't want to be forced to look at trash so early in the morning," she quips.

Carter scoffs. "Savannah may not be rich, but she's better than you in every other aspect. You want to see trash, look in the mirror."

It's sweet how he defends me, but it only motivates her to keep going. She's been doing this since last week, being as she didn't have her *boyfriend* here to distract her. Maybe with him being back today, she'll finally leave me the hell alone.

Her look of disgust flips instantly to a sweet smile as she looks beyond me. "Hey, babe," she coos.

I roll my eyes. *Speak of the devil, and he shall appear.*

Continuing to focus on putting away my books and grabbing the ones I need for class, I'm startled when someone slams their hand on the locker next to mine. It's so loud that everyone in a nearby radius goes completely silent.

I start to think Kinsley may have thrown something at me, but when I look up, I see Grayson. He's hovering over me, with his face only inches from mine.

"What are you doing?"

He grazes the knuckle of his index finger down my jaw. "What I should have done the day I got here."

In one swift move, and with everyone's attention on us, he brings his lips down to my own—kissing me like it's breathing the life into him. I start to move my mouth with his, for no reason other than sheer habit. It isn't until Jace makes a whooping sound that I snap out of it. *What the hell am I doing?*

I push him away, immediately slapping him across the face so hard that the sound echoes throughout the hallway. He stretches out his jaw, but before he has a chance to say anything, I slip by and leave him standing there—hurt and rejected, just like I was. *Welcome to the club, motherfucker.*

DELANEY CHUCKLES AS SHE pops a piece of bagel into her mouth. We're sitting in the library, skipping first period to have some much-needed girl time. One of the perks of her being the principal's favorite is that she can get out of class for just about anything. As long as there's record of her staying on school property, she's set.

"I can't believe you slapped him."

I quirk a brow. "Are you saying he didn't deserve it?"

Shaking her head, she takes a sip of her water. "No, he definitely did. I'm just surprised. I didn't think you had it in you."

"Laney, I told him I'm in love with him, and he proceeded to kick me out of his house and date my worst enemy. As far as I'm concerned, he's lucky slapping him is all I did."

"Okay, touché," she concedes. "But is that it, though? You two are just done?"

It's a loaded question, one with so many answers it makes my head spin. In theory, I want nothing to do with him. He tormented me for weeks before giving me false hope that there may be a happy ending for us after all. That small taste of what used to be—better than what used to be, even—felt like heaven. It gave me hope for the future and made all the shit I've dealt with worth it, only for him to rip it away again the same night I lost everything else. And then slapped me in the face when he showed up with Kinsley on his arm.

I should hate him for everything he's done, but that's where I hit a roadblock. Because he's still Grayson. He still has the ability to make me come alive with something as simple as a look. The feeling of his lips on mine is still like finding water in the desert. And he's still the only guy to ever own my heart—something I honestly believe may never change.

"I don't know," I tell her truthfully. "But, if wants any chance at winning me back, he's going to have to grovel."

She snickers. "I'd expect nothing less." The mood in the room changes, and her expression becomes serious. "Now, because I wouldn't be your best friend if I didn't bring it up, are you okay?"

I'm about to ask her what she's referring to, but the look in her eyes says everything. I throw my head back, groaning. "He told you."

"The bigger question is why *you* didn't."

I take a deep breath and give her an apologetic smile. "I didn't tell anyone. Not Grayson. Not you. Not even Brady," I explain. "I thought it was something I could handle, and I didn't want everyone worrying about me. It's humiliating."

She sighs, moving to wrap her arms around me. "We're your friends, Sav. We're supposed to worry."

My head rests against hers, and for the first time in a

while, I feel like things might turn out okay. There are no more secrets. My reality isn't looming over my head, threatening to pop up at the most unexpected moments. And the best part? I'm not alone. Yeah, things definitely aren't so bad right now.

I'M SITTING AT MY desk, waiting for second period to start, when Grayson walks through the door. His eyes search the classroom before they land on me. I prepare myself for his wrath as he makes his way over, but instead the anger I expected, he's completely calm. He places his hands on my desk and leans in, dropping the level of his voice so only I can hear him.

"If you don't want to forgive me yet, that's fine, but one day you will. I won't stop until you do." He moves his lips to my ear and whispers, "We were always meant to be together. You may not believe that anymore, but that's all right. I'll believe in it enough for the both of us."

With that, he backs away and goes to his seat—leaving me speechless.

THE NEXT DAY, I arrive at school to find flowers in my locker. Twelve long stemmed pink roses that, given any other situation, would take my breath away. Unfortunately, this isn't one of those situations, and keeping the roses would send him the wrong message. So, I pass them out to girls who look like they might need just a little cheering up.

ON WEDNESDAY, HE LEAVES the necklace he took from

me on my desk during second period. It's in a black box, and I can see he got the chain fixed from when he broke it. I run my finger over the engraved plate before closing the box and putting it in my purse. Despite how badly I want to put it on, I won't give him the satisfaction of seeing it hanging back around my neck.

THURSDAY BRINGS A DIFFERENT surprise. In the morning, I find a drawing taped to my locker. A picture of two little kids holding hands, with "Savi and Gray" written at the top, separated by a heart. I must have been in third grade when I drew this.

"He drew you a picture?" Delaney asks, confused.

I shake my head. "I drew it for him when we were like eight. I can't believe he kept it."

She watches me fold it up carefully and put it in my bag. "Think he's done enough groveling yet?"

"Not quite."

ONE OF THE BENEFITS to Grayson working tirelessly to win back my affection is that Kinsley has yet to say a word to me since Monday morning. I don't know what he threatened her with, but having been on the wrong side of his madness before, I can only assume it scared her into silence.

I'm sitting at the lunch table, doing some homework I missed last week, when someone places a bottle in front of me. I put my pen down and take it in my hands. When I realize what it is, there isn't anything I can do to hold in my laughter.

Blackberry Snapple.

"What's that?" Jace questions. I slide the bottle toward

him, and he grabs it to read the label. "Isn't this the drink you sent Kinsley on that wild goose chase for?"

I nod, and out of the corner of my eye, I can see Grayson trying to conceal his smile. *No, not happening.* While the gesture is sweet, he doesn't get to win me back with a drink. He'll have to try harder than that.

Standing up, I keep my attention on Jace. "You can have it. I don't even like the stuff."

It takes everything in me to ignore the feeling of Grayson's stare as I exit the cafeteria.

BY THE END OF the day, I can see his patience is starting to weaken. With every attempt being thrown back in his face, it's obvious he wasn't expecting it to be this difficult.

I'm standing at my locker when I can sense him behind me. His hand grazes down my back as his voice meets my ears.

"When are you going to forgive me?"

I turn around, using every muscle in my body to resist falling right back into his arms. "I told you, I'm not."

Our friends, and everyone around for that matter, watch us curiously. Grayson doesn't seem to mind, though, as he moves just a little bit closer.

"But I miss you, and I know you miss me, too."

"The *you* that I miss doesn't exist. Not anymore, at least. I'm not sure I even know you."

He sighs, resting his forehead on my shoulder. "That's not true. You know me better than anyone."

"Well then, it's just that I can't trust you anymore."

With a gentle push against his chest, he backs up, and I close my locker before walking down the hallway. Everyone keeps their eyes on me, and those who don't, start to when Grayson calls my name.

"Savannah, wait. Please."

I turn around, feeling completely defeated. "What Grayson? What could you *possibly* want now?"

"What I've always wanted—you." He comes closer and only stops when he's a couple feet away. "The last few weeks, the last eight years even, have been nothing but hell. Between getting ripped away from each other when we were just kids, and being reunited under the most fucked-up circumstances known to man—it's all taught me one thing for sure: my life is better with you in it."

We've attracted an audience, but I don't think he cares, because his attention is solely on me.

"Since I got here, we've been at war over the two things neither of us can live without—power and control. Now, I've already lost you once, and you'd have to be out of your mind if you think I'm going to let that happen again, so screw it."

He drops to his knees in front of me, and everyone around gasps.

"You can have it. Christ, I'd pull my heart out and hand it to you if I thought it would do me any good. The only thing I want is you, because I'm in love with you. I knew it when I was fucking nine years old, and I damn well know it now. You're it for me, Savannah. There's no one else, and I don't want to live a life without you by my side."

My stomach is in my throat as I gawk at Grayson, having heard everything I've always dreamed of him saying. The headstrong, punch-throwing, bigshot quarterback is on his knees in front of me, and all I see staring back at me is the little boy I swore I was going to spend the rest of my life with.

"Get up."

"Not until you forgive me," he argues.

"Gray." The nickname alone is enough to spark hope in his eyes. "Get off the floor and fucking kiss me."

Not needing to be told twice, he jumps up and pulls me in

248

to cover my mouth with his own. He takes everything he can while still giving me all of him. It's needy, and passionate, and has the ability to restart my heart all on its own.

"I love you, so fucking much," he tells me, and I don't think I'll ever tire of hearing him say it. "You really forgive me?"

I nod. "But I have one condition."

"Anything."

Taking a step back, I keep my eyes locked with his. "I want you to explain *everything*."

26

GRAYSON

HOLDING SAVANNAH'S HAND IN MINE, WE NAVIGATE through the woods to the one spot I can really call ours— hidden away from the prying eyes and ears of everyone else. If there is any place we should have this conversation, it's here. She deserves to know the truth. I just fear the fallout.

"Do you remember the first time I brought you here?"

She looks up at me and smiles. "How could I not? *You're not taking me out here to kill me, are you?*"

"Don't be stupid," I tease, reciting it back to her with a nudge.

As we walk through the clearance, I can tell by her expression that it's been a while since she was last here. She runs her hand gently across the tree we carved our initials into. You can barely see them now, but we know they're there. Once she's done looking around, she comes over to sit beside me and takes a deep breath.

"Okay, I'm ready."

I reach out to hold her hand, knowing that telling her this could change a lot for her. How she sees her father, though he's done most of the damage on his own. How she sees herself. This conversation could break her even more than she's already been.

"Are you sure? There are things you don't know. Things that maybe you *shouldn't* know." I warn, but she remains firm and shakes her head. "Alright, where do you want me to start?"

"The day you left."

———

I watch as the rain drips down the window, the weather looking like exactly how I feel. Not only is Savannah gone this weekend, but I can't play outside. Even sitting on the roof is off limits until it dries up and it doesn't look like that'll be happening any time soon.

Savi will be coming home tomorrow, though, and I can't wait. Since we had our first kiss on Thursday, I've been even more excited to see her than I normally am. If our parents knew, they'd probably say we're too young to have feelings for each other, but what do they know?

"Grayson, dinner!" My mom calls.

I pull myself away and head for the stairs, using the banister to slide down. My mother stands at the bottom with a disappointed look on her face.

"One day you're going to fall doing that, and I don't want to hear you cry about it when you do."

Something I've learned about my mom, is that she's a sucker for how cute I am. So, I smile sweetly and give her a hug. Just like I planned, she caves. The two of us go into the dining room where my dad is already waiting.

"Hey Gray." He greets me. "You've been spending all weekend in your room. You sure you're okay?"

I nod. "I'm just bored, and I really miss Savi."

"Well, how about tomorrow we go down to the indoor batting cages? Would that cheer you up?"

Just the idea has me instantly in a better mood and I lunge to give him a big hug. "Can we play a game after dinner?"

"Sure. How does Uno sound?"

"The one that regular one or the one that spits cards at you?" The difference matters.

Letting out a light laugh, he and I both know we each want the one the other doesn't. I eye him intently and wait for his decision.

"The one that spits cards at you." I start to celebrate when he stops me. "But only if you promise to take it easy on your mother."

"Deal."

We all sit down for dinner. The smell of homemade mac and cheese wafts through the air and makes my mouth water. My dad thanks my mom with a quick kiss before digging in. It's as delicious as it always is and the cheesy garlic bread that goes with it is my favorite.

Dad starts to clean up the table while I get the game from the closet when there's a knock at the door. My mom glances out the peep hole and has a confused look on her face as she answers it. Five police officers stand on the other side.

"Mrs. Hayworth?"

"Yes?" She replies.

One of the officers holds up a piece of paper. "We have a warrant to search the premises."

They push their way through, instantly starting to look through things. My father comes out from the kitchen, finding myself and my mom panicked as she holds me close.

"What's the meaning of this?!" He roars, bringing all the attention to him.

Two of the men share a few whispers before heading straight to the den. I follow them and when I see them going for my secret spot, I panic. They're going to tell my parents about Savannah's picture! She told me not to let them see it!

"Hey! Get out of there! That's mine!"

However, when they open it, it's not only filled with all my hidden treasures, but with money. They stand up, going straight to my father and turning him around to handcuff him.

"Landon Hayworth, you're being arrested for Forgery and Embezzlement. You have the right to remain silent. Anything you say can and will be used against you in a court of law."

"Dad!" I scream. I try to get to him, but my mom holds me back.

"Theresa, call our lawyer! Have him meet me at the station."

Tears stain our cheeks as we watch my father get dragged out of our house and thrown into the back of a police car. His eyes meet mine as they drive away, and he mouths a silent I love you.

"My Aunt Laura came to pick me up and my mom spent the next two days with the lawyer, trying to get my dad out of jail. According to the warrants, they had proof of my father stealing a lot of money from the company he worked for. Over three million dollars was moved in his name and completely unaccounted for. What they found under the floorboard was only a little under four hundred thousand."

I pause to get ahold of my emotions. Savannah seems shocked by just the fact that he was arrested, but I've only just gotten started.

"There was a trial, but I was too young and my mom wouldn't let me go. Eventually, he was found guilty on all charges and sentenced to spend seven years in a Federal Penitentiary. I got to go see him a few times, but six months later he was stabbed to death during a prison riot."

"Oh my God." She gasps and covers her mouth. "Grayson, that's horrible. I'm so sorry."

I shake my head. "You didn't know, but I'm not done yet."

"It gets worse?!"

Nodding, I start to rub my thumb over her hand in a soothing motion. "Before my father died, he was very adamant about one thing—he was innocent of the crimes he was accused of. That was one of two things that always stuck

254

out in my mind. The other was that you and your father were dangerous, and I needed to stay away from you."

"Me? I was only a kid," she protests.

"Once I turned eighteen, I started looking into his case, and I found some inconsistencies that made me look even further. I remembered his warning and focused on researching your father. It turns out that during a business trip to Vegas, your dad discovered the thrill of gambling. Only, instead of doing it responsibly, he fell down a rabbit hole. He spent all of his savings, and when he ran out of money, he borrowed from some bad people. From what I've seen, he was betting big and only winning small amounts back. When the loan sharks came to collect, he didn't have it, so he started to steal it from the company our fathers worked for."

Her eyes show just how clear everything is starting to become.

"He didn't," she pleads, already seeing where I'm going with this.

My head drops. "The company found out within a matter of a few months, because of the high amounts that were going missing, and your dad set mine up to take the fall. He must have had help, because the whole case was practically rock solid, so I'm guessing he paid someone to cover his tracks. However, the biggest piece of evidence..." I pause and take a deep breath, knowing this is going to hurt her. "The biggest piece of evidence was a video. The deposition of a ten-year-old girl, saying she saw Mr. Hayworth stashing money under the floorboard in the den."

Like a damn breaking, her tears flow like the waterfall in front of us. "No. No, no, no. I didn't. Please, tell me I didn't."

I press my forehead against hers. "I'm so sorry, Savannah. I thought you knew."

"I had no idea, I swear." She holds her head as she sobs.

"No wonder you hated me. You should! I'm a terrible person!"

"No." I take her face between my hands, forcing her to look at me. "You were a child, manipulated into doing something by someone who should have been protecting you. This is *not* your fault."

I hold her as she cries, both of us fully understanding that the events that tore us apart were out of our control. I may have come back here with the intention of getting revenge, but instead I got something so much more. *Her.*

"I really want to stay with you, but I promised Brady I'd help him with something at the studio." She sniffles, wiping her eyes.

I nod and place a kiss to her forehead. "It's okay. I'll drive you. But Sav?"

"Yeah?"

"I love you."

As she exhales, her face breaks into a smile that takes my breath away. "I love you, too."

AFTER DROPPING SAVANNAH OFF at the studio, I go home to find my mom in the living room. Home videos of me as a child play on the TV screen. As I see myself run around in a batman cape, with a paper towel tube as a sword, I laugh.

"I was so weird."

"Yeah. You were always my favorite, though."

A small laugh bubbles out of my mouth. "Favorite out of one. Look at me accomplishing greatness."

I walk over to the pile of movies and put a different one in. As my mom presses play, I sit down next to her.

"Savannah, let's go," I tell her, getting impatient.

"I'm coming, I'm coming." She walks into the frame in her white leotard. "Jeez, Gray. You can't rush perfection."

Tessa and Delaney stand next to us, smiling as Savi walks toward me with fake flowers.

"Okay," Laney starts. "We are gathered here today to join Grayson and Savannah is holy mattress-mony." She turns to me. "Do you, Grayson, take Savannah to be your wife? To love even when she's sick and gross?"

"I do."

She smiles and turns to Savi. "And do you, Savannah, take Grayson to be your husband? To love even if he's a stinky butthead?"

Savannah giggles. "I do."

"Well, then, by the power vested in me, by the piece of cardboard that Tessa and I drew this morning, I now pronounce you husband and wife. You may now share a juice box."

Savi takes the first sip and hands it to me to do the same. Then, we exchange pipe-cleaner rings and wave at the camera.

"Aw." My mom presses a hand to her chest. "You two were the cutest."

I can't help but smile, hoping one day that fake wedding becomes a real one. "Yeah, we were."

A HALF HOUR LATER, I'M working on an essay when my phone rings and Brady's name appears on the screen. For a second, I wonder if Savannah's phone died. She had mentioned coming over after they were done.

"Hello?" I answer.

"Hey, Grayson." Brady sounds less than thrilled to speak to me. "Can I talk to Savannah real fast? I just want to know if she's going to be home for dinner, and she isn't answering her phone."

Everything goes ice cold in an instant. "Wait, what? I

dropped her off at the studio almost an hour ago. She said she had to help you with something."

"I haven't been at the studio all day, and she and I definitely never made plans."

It only takes a second for everything to click. Her knowing everything. How heartbroken she was about it. The determined look in her eyes when I dropped her off. *No.*

"Fuck!" I jump up out of my chair and grab my keys off the desk, skipping most of the steps as I leap down them. "Meet me at her dad's house! I think she's in trouble."

27

SAVANNAH

I sit in the big office chair as I wait for my dad to get off the phone. He's pacing back and forth while a man in a suit watches me from across the table. Daddy looks frustrated. I hate when he's like this.

"Just put $5,000 on the Broncos," *he says into the phone.* "Yes, I'm good for it. I'll have you the money by tomorrow." *Hanging up, he releases a breath and changes his expression. He comes over and kneels in front of me.* "Now Savi, my sweet, sweet, little Savi." *He tucks my hair behind my ear.* "You need to tell the nice man what we practiced, okay?"

I frown. "But it's a lie, and you said it's bad to lie."

"I know, baby, but it's okay just this once, because if you don't, Daddy is going to need to go away like Mommy did."

The idea of losing my dad makes my heart hurt. I already have to live the rest of my life without my mom. I don't want to live without my daddy, too.

I nod, and he steps back behind the camera. The man in the suit smiles at me, but he doesn't look very nice, so I don't smile back. He presses a button on the camera and then turns to me.

"Okay, Savannah. I'm just going to ask you a few questions about the night you stayed at your friend Gray's house, okay?"

259

Shaking my head, I correct him. "His name is Grayson. Only me and his dad get to call him Gray."

He chuckles. "I'm sorry, the night you stayed at your friend Grayson's house. Is that better?"

"Yes."

Looking down at a notebook in front of him, he reads the next question from the page. "You said in the middle of the night, you woke up and needed a drink, is that right?"

"Mm-hm. I was thirsty so I went downstairs for a glass of milk."

"And when you went down to get a drink, what did you see?"

I look to my dad, knowing this is the part where I'm supposed to lie. He gives me a reassuring nod, and I recite the answer he told me. "I saw Mr. Hayworth putting money under the floorboard in the den."

The man in the suit looks back at my dad for a second and they both smile happily. "Did you look in there after he was gone?"

Shaking my head, something about this makes me feel sick to my stomach. "I just saw there was a lot of money in there."

How could I have been so stupid to never put the pieces together? Less than a year after that interview, Grayson disappeared. My dad wouldn't tell me where they went, just that they moved away and weren't coming back.

That asshole knew exactly what he did. He knew the lives he was ruining. His best friend's. Grayson's. Mine. The only person he's ever cared about is himself. Even while he was working to cover his tracks and frame Grayson's father for a crime *he himself* committed, he was still making bets with the stolen money.

A part of me hopes that the reason for all the drugs and alcohol in the last seven years was to cope with the guilt of what he did. At least then it would seem like he has some kind of conscience. If he doesn't feel any remorse for what he's done, then I'm not sure I ever really knew him at all.

I look up at my house, knowing that monster is inside. All of this comes down to him. Grayson's father was taken too soon, because of him. Gray has had to grow up without a father, because of him. Mrs. Hayworth has had to raise her son without her husband, because of him. I lost my best friend, because of him. He's the one who ruined everything, and I'm going to take him down once and for all.

Pressing a button on my phone, I slip it in my pocket and walk through the door. My father is standing in the kitchen. He scoffs when he sees me, and his upper lip raises in disgust.

"Where has *your* ass been for the last week?"

"At Brady's." I try to keep my voice calm.

"Yeah?" He looks me up and down. "Are you sure you haven't been hanging around that Hayworth kid?"

My eyes narrow. "What if I have?"

"Then you better cut that shit out right now. I don't want you anywhere near that boy."

"Why? Because you're afraid I'll find out about what you did to his father?" The way the color drains from my dad's face shows his guilt. "Yeah, I know all about it. How you gambled away all our money. How you stole from the company you spent five years working for. And even how you set your *best friend* up to take the fall."

"You don't know what you're talking about," he counters, but it's as weak as he is.

"Oh, come on. Don't try to be all noble now. Go ahead. Gloat. Getting away with something like that had to make you feel like a badass."

His stare bores into me, his body tense and motionless. "I did what I had to, and your little ass should be grateful for that."

"What you had to?" I snap. "You made your best friend take the fall for a crime he didn't commit! He died in there! Grayson's dad is dead, and *you* did that."

"You're damn fucking right I did!" he roars, slamming the whiskey bottle down on the counter. "And I'd do it again! I got more money out of that score than I've ever seen in my life. It's not my fault the fragile little shit couldn't handle himself in prison."

I can't believe the words that are coming out of his mouth, but even worse is what's written on his face. He looks proud—*pleased with himself* for getting away with millions while his closest friend lost his life. There isn't the smallest ounce of remorse, and *that* causes my blood to boil.

"You're a monster," I tell him. "A despicable, sad excuse for a man."

His eyes darken, like the anger in him is starting to bubble to the surface. "You should be worshiping the ground I walk on. The shit I did kept *you* out of foster care. If I had gone to jail, you would have had *no one*!"

"I would've been better off!"

He laughs dryly and walks around the counter to stand in front of me. "If your mother could see you now—the greedy, unappreciative little bitch you are—she would be appalled."

"Fuck you!" I hiss. "I'm going to make you pay for what you've done. Being as I was unknowingly one of the key pieces of evidence in the case, I'm sure the FBI will *love* to know how you manipulated a little girl into lying under oath."

"You wouldn't dare."

"Oh, I definitely would." Turning to leave, I take one step toward the door. "Enjoy your drink. It's going to be a while before you get to have another."

Before I can get away, he grabs me by the hair and pulls me back. "Over my dead body."

His fist plows into my face with brutal force, sending a shooting pain through my jaw. He uses his grip to slam my head into the counter and throws me to the floor. The kick to my stomach is like getting hit by a truck. I try to shield myself, but as he swings his foot into me again, I can feel my wrist snap.

"You stupid, *stupid* little girl," he sneers as he continues his beating. "I should have taken your ass out years ago." Another blow to my face, and the metallic taste of blood fills my mouth. "Finally getting rid of you will be the best day of my fucking life."

The pain across my entire body is so severe that I'm finding it hard to stay conscious. No matter how motionless I am, however, he doesn't let up. The kicks and punches still come just as hard, with no sign of letting up. *He's going to kill me.*

As the reality sets in, I think of those closest to me. Brady. Delaney. *Grayson.* Are they going to be okay? What will they think happened to me? Will my father get away with this too? It's a horrible feeling, knowing I'm about to die. The only thing I have to look forward to is getting to see my mom again.

Everything starts to go hazy as I hear the faint sound of the door flying open.

"Get off her!" a person screams, and by some miracle, the hits stop coming. "Oh my God, Savi. No, no, no! Fuck! Stay with me, please."

Grayson? I try to open my eyes, but I can't. It's too hard. I'm too weak. Losing the battle to stay awake, the darkness takes over, and the pain fades away.

28

GRAYSON

I PRESS THE PEDAL TO THE FLOOR, BREAKING EVERY traffic law known to man as I speed across town. Every time I try to call Savannah, it goes straight to voicemail. My mind immediately imagines the worst, and my heart plummets at the thought of it. If something happens to her, I will never forgive myself.

Her dad's piece of shit is out front, which means he's clearly home. I throw my car in park and race up onto the rickety porch, bursting through the door. What I see knocks my whole world off its axis. Savannah is curled up on the floor in the fetal position as her father viciously kicks her. My rage spikes to a level that scares even me.

"Get off her!" I roar, running to her side. Her father, the coward that he is, uses my distraction to flee. I know I should chase after him, but I can't leave Savannah. Not now. Not like this. "Oh my God, Savi. No, no, no! Fuck! Stay with me, please."

There's blood everywhere, and the fear of her dying becomes alarmingly real. I take out my phone and call 9-1-1, telling them to get here as fast as possible. Savannah is unconscious, and her pulse is weak.

I just got her back. Don't take her from me again. Please. I need her.

By the time the ambulance arrives, my clothes are stained with red—my hands covered from holding pressure on her wounds. The paramedics give me odd looks. They probably think I did this, like I'm some abusive prick who knocks his girlfriend around. I don't pay any mind to it as they lift Savannah onto a stretcher and wheel her out the door. A police cruiser pulls up and two officers get out, all grim business as they eye her prone form.

"We're going to need a statement from you, but I'll have someone meet you at the hospital for that," the officer tells me, and I nod a silent thank you.

Brady pulls up just as we get outside. His eyes widen drastically as they load Savi into the back of the ambulance.

"Savi! What the hell happened?"

I try to keep my cool, but every time I even think of that bastard, my vision blurs with fury. "Her prick of a fucking father. That's what happened." Just before they close the doors, I stop them. "Wait, I'm coming with her."

"Are you family?"

I shake my head. "I'm her boyfriend."

He gives me a sympathetic look. "I'm sorry, son. Only family is allowed in the ambulance."

"Are you fucking kidding me? Her family did this to her!"

The urge to fight everyone who stands in my way of her is strong, and I think Brady can see that because he steps in front of me.

"Grayson, it's fine. Get in my car, and I'll drive you there."

"No." I start walking toward my car. "I'm driving myself."

"I don't think that's a good idea," he argues. "You're angry. Frantic. If you're not focused enough, you could crash. Do you think Savannah would want that?"

As the ambulance drives away with the most important part of my life, I grab Brady by the shoulders and pin him to

266

my car with an arm at his throat. "Don't fucking tell me what Savannah would want! She wouldn't fucking *want* any of this!" Alarmed officers yank me back and I shake them off, hardly able to stand being in my own skin.

"You're right. I'm sorry," he croaks.

I know I'm taking my wrath out on the wrong person. Instead of apologizing, however, I turn around and walk toward his SUV.

THE TRAFFIC IN CALIFORNIA is irritating on a normal day, but when we're trying to get to the hospital and don't have flashing lights and sirens, it's excruciatingly worse. I don't even wait for the car to come to a stop at the hospital entrance before I jump out and run inside.

"I'm looking for Savannah Montgomery. An ambulance just brought her in."

The woman at the desk seems taken back by my panic. She looks at my blood-stained clothes with shock before shaking herself out of it and typing something into her computer. My whole body is shaking. I can't handle not knowing where she is or if she's okay.

"According to this, they brought her into surgery," she tells me, and my stomach churns. "I'll notify the doctor that you're here, and he'll have someone come out to speak to you soon. Just have a seat."

I stand completely still, unable to move as her words play through my head. *Savannah's in surgery. That piece of shit beat her so bad that she needs fucking surgery.*

Brady gently grabs my arm and leads me over to one of the chairs in the waiting room. He then goes and gets a pack of disinfectant wipes from one of the receptionists and hands them to me.

"To clean your hands," he specifies, and it reminds me that they have her blood all over them.

It probably looks like I committed a murder, and if I wasn't so concerned with knowing if Savannah is okay, that's exactly what I'd be doing right now. That son of a bitch has done nothing but ruin the lives of those around him for his own sick personal gain. I know my focus needs to stay on Savi, but I'm going to make sure that fucker pays for this.

IT FEELS LIKE HOURS pass before a man in dark blue scrubs comes into the waiting room.

"Savannah Montgomery?"

I leap out of my seat, and Brady follows me up to him. "Is she okay?"

"She's stable. Her spleen was ruptured, so we needed to go in surgically and remove it. She has a broken wrist, along with a few cracked ribs and a pretty severe concussion. Had she not gotten here when she did, we may have lost her."

"Jesus Christ," Brady breathes.

The doctor glances at my bloody clothes and concern etches across his face. "Did you let the paramedics check you out too?"

"No, it's not mine." I know how bad that sounds, but I don't give a shit about his opinion of me. "Where's Savannah? Can I go see her?"

He nods and leads us through a set of double doors. "She's in the ICU. I suspect she'll probably be there for a couple days." Pressing the button on the elevator, we walk inside as soon as the doors open. "She's still out from the anesthesia, but she should wake up within an hour or so."

Turning into the room, all the air leaves my lungs. Savannah is lying on the bed, hooked up to all different kinds of monitors. She looks so weak and helpless, the total opposite of everything she stands for. I swallow down the lump in my throat and press a kiss to her forehead.

"God, Savi. I'm so fucking sorry. I should've known you'd confront him. I never should have told you."

Brady places a supportive hand on my shoulder, and for once, I don't push him off. "She's going to be okay."

"That's not the point." I pull a chair closer to the bed and hold her hand as I sit down. "I should've been there to protect her."

AFTER A VERY DIFFICULT phone call with a panicked Delaney, and a half hour interview with an officer asking what happened, Savannah finally starts to stir. Her eyes blink open, and she groans from the light. Once Brady shuts it off, her blue eyes meet mine.

"Hey, gorgeous."

She smiles tiredly. "Hi."

Her voice is hoarse, and I can tell by the look on her face that even something as simple as breathing hurts. I wish I could take that pain away—put myself in her place so she wouldn't have to feel an ounce of it.

Brady sighs in relief when he hears her voice and sees her respond to his face with a smile. "I'll go get the doctor."

Savannah looks around for a second before furrowing her brows at me. "Where's my phone?"

It's an odd request, but I'm assuming she just wants to keep Delaney in the loop. "Probably with the rest of your things. It's okay. I called Laney already. She's on her way."

She looks as if she's going to say something else, but the doctor comes in to do an exam. He checks her pupils and the strength in her limbs before upping her pain medicine to something a little more comfortable for her. The second he steps out, the same officer from earlier enters.

"Miss Montgomery?" he asks, and she nods. "I'm Officer Jenson with the North Haven PD. Do you mind if I ask you a couple questions about what happened today?"

I stand, knowing he's going to ask me to leave, but she grabs my hand. "Can he stay?"

"If that would make you more comfortable, I don't see why not." She relaxes, and I sit back down, lacing my fingers with hers. Officer Jenson pulls out his notepad. "So, let's start with the most important question. Who did this to you?"

"My father," she answers confidently.

"And what brought this on? Did you two have an argument?"

A humorless laugh bubbles out of her and she winces. "This isn't the first time he's laid a hand on me. He's a drunk, a drug addict, and a horrible human being. The only difference between today and all the times he's hit me before is that his goal today was to kill me."

The officer looks startled. "Did he tell you that?"

The moment she nods, my every fear becomes alarmingly real. She could have died today, and I would have been left without her. I already know what that's like, and I'm not willing to go back to it.

Savannah spends fifteen minutes giving the officer a step by step account of what happened. When he's finished writing things down, I notice two more officers appear in the doorway.

"What happens from here?" I question.

"Well, we're currently out looking for Mr. Montgomery, but we haven't been able to find him yet." He explains. "So, until we do, there will be round the clock security outside your room."

Sav's jaw drops. "It's *that* serious?"

"Given your statement, and the extent of your injuries, your father is being charged with attempted murder, and we take that *very* seriously."

"Attempted murder?" Delaney shrieks as she comes in. Her eyes narrow on me. "You said she was injured, not almost killed!"

Brady enters behind her. "I tried to keep her in the waiting room. She's like a freight train."

Laney looks over Savannah, and she instantly starts to cry. "My goodness, look at you."

"I'm okay," she tries, but not a single person in this room believes her.

Going to the other side of the bed, Delaney gives Savannah a gentle hug. "What the hell happened? Your dad did this to you?"

"Yup." She pops the p, not lacking any bit of her usual sass. "He's such a standup guy."

The two of them talk, once again going over the events that make my heart nearly stop. It doesn't get any easier, no matter how many times I hear it. Still, I constantly rub my thumb over Savi's so she knows I'm here for her. If I had lost her today, I don't know what I would have done with myself. I was silly to think that I could ever live a life that doesn't completely revolve around her, let alone one without her in it at all.

"Uh, Grayson?" Delaney gets my attention. "Why do you look like a walking Halloween decoration?"

I look down and realize that I'm still covered in blood. It's as if Savannah didn't realize it either, because her eyes double in size when she sees it. Knowing it's her own probably makes it so much worse.

"Yeah, man. You should probably change your clothes," Brady suggests. "Want me to drive you back to your car?"

I shake my head. "I don't want to leave her alone."

"I'll stay with her," Delaney offers.

I'm conflicted, not wanting to leave her side at all, but they're right. I glance at Savannah, making sure she's okay with me leaving for a bit. If she asks me to stay, there isn't a thing in the world that could pull me from her side.

"It's fine, babe. Really."

I kiss her softly and rest my forehead against hers. "I love you."

"I love you, too," she says with a smile, and Laney beams, rainbows nearly shooting from her chest in joy.

Brady says a quick goodbye to Savannah, promising he'll come back in the morning, and the two of us head out. It's a quiet trip to the car, but as soon as we get in, he turns to me.

"You know, I still don't like you. I don't think you deserve her, and you're lucky as hell she doesn't hate you for what you've done. That being said, you saved my best friend's life today, and that's something I'll never be able to repay. So, thank you."

He extends his hand toward me and I shake it. It's a truce of sorts. A ceasefire. I don't think he and I will ever be friends, but Savannah means almost as much to him as she means to me, and I respect that.

LATER THAT NIGHT, DELANEY and I are quietly scrolling through our phones while Savannah rests, when Officer Jenson returns. He has a solemn look on his face as he gestures for me to join him in the hall. Laney joins me, and the three of us step into an empty room.

"Did you find the bastard?" I question urgently.

He nods and looks down at the ground. "We did."

"And? Did you arrest him?"

"No."

"Why the fuck not?" I shout. "You said yourself her injuries and her statement are enough to charge him! What are you waiting for?"

His eyes meet mine and hold my heated stare. "Mr. Montgomery is dead. He committed suicide."

29

SAVANNAH

It's a strange feeling, knowing both your parents are gone. When I was younger, and my dad told me that my mother had died in a car accident, I was beside myself. I don't think I stopped crying for an entire week. All the happiness in my life had vanished completely, until Gray brightened everything up again. But now, lying in this bed while Grayson and Delaney break the news about my father, I don't feel any of that.

"Baby, say something," Grayson pleads.

I take another moment to let it sink in, waiting for the devastation to come, but it never does. When it comes down to it, I lost my father the day he decided to put gambling before his daughter. The man I've lived with for the past eight years was *not* my dad.

"Sucks for him. I've heard hell is a horrible place."

Delaney's jaw drops while Grayson snorts. He leans forward and places a kiss to my forehead, relieved by the fact that I'm okay. To be honest, I'm more than okay. I'm relieved.

Officer Jenson knocks on the door. "Is it okay to come in?" I nod, and his attention centers on Grayson. "We're going to need someone to identify the body. Usually we prefer it to be family, but Savannah's injuries prevent her from coming down to the morgue."

"I can do it," Grayson says, and then he turns to me. "I'll be back in a little bit."

"Okay."

The two of them leave the room, and my head falls back against the bed. Suddenly, something important pops back into my mind.

"Laney."

She looks at me with that same warm smile she always has. "Yeah?"

"Can you get my phone for me? I need it."

It takes a few minutes, and asking a nurse, but she finally finds it and hands it to me. The screen is cracked, probably from when he threw me to the ground, but it still works. I open the voice memos app and smile brightly when I see it's there. Pressing play, my father's voice comes through the speaker.

"Where has your ass been for the last week?"

"At Brady's."

"Yeah? Are you sure you haven't been hanging around that Hayworth kid?"

"What if I have?"

"Then you better cut that shit out right now. I don't want you anywhere near that boy."

"Why? Because you're afraid I'll find out about what you did to his father? Yeah, I know all about it. How you gambled away all our money. How you stole from the company you spent five years working for. And even how you set your best friend up to take the fall."

"You don't know what you're talking about."

"Oh, come on. Don't try to be all noble now. Go ahead. Gloat.

Getting away with something like that had to make you feel like a badass."

"I did what I had to, and your little ass should be grateful for that."

"What you had to? You made your best friend take the fall for a crime he didn't commit! He died in there! Grayson's dad is dead, and you did that."

"You're damn fucking right I did. And I'd do it again! I got more money out of that score than I've ever seen in my life. It's not my fault the fragile little shit couldn't handle himself in prison."

I turn it off before it reaches the point where he attacked me, and Delaney's eyes widen.

"Is that...?"

Grinning, I flip to my contacts and call the one person who can get me what I need. My father may be gone, but he doesn't get to die without his sins being exposed.

"Hey, princess. What's up?" A familiar voice comes through the phone.

"Hi, Carter. I need your dad's number. I have something he's going to want."

A FEW DAYS LATER, I'm finally released from the hospital. It still hurts to do even the simplest of things, like move or breathe, but the doctor was okay with discharging me as long as I promised to rest. Grayson wheels me down to the car and helps me inside.

"I hope you like my bed. You're going to be spending a lot of time in it."

My brows furrow. "I'm staying with you?"

Glancing between me and the road, he gives me an incredulous look. "You think I'm going to let you out of my

277

sight? Savannah, I almost lost you. My heart broke into a million pieces when I found you bleeding on that floor. The threat may be gone, but the memory is still very real. It's going to be a while before I don't panic at the thought of not being able to keep you safe. You'll have to bear with me."

A wide grin spreads across my face. "Such a caveman."

He chuckles. "You know it, baby."

When we pull up to Gray's house, he comes around to the passenger side and lifts me out of the car. I tell him to put me down but he doesn't listen, carrying me through the door and safely depositing me onto the couch.

"Stay right there. Don't move," he demands. "I'm going to get your meds from the car."

He leaves, but I'm not alone for long before his mom comes in. Her eyes widen when she looks at me—stitches on my face, my wrist in a cast, bruises in multiple places. She comes over and sits down.

"Oh, honey. Are you all right?"

"I've been better, but I'll live. That's more than I can say for him."

She frowns. "I was sorry to hear about your father."

"Don't be," I tell her honestly. "The death of your husband and the death of my father are not the same. Mr. Hayworth was a good man who deserved to live a long, healthy, and *free* life. My father was not. Please don't confuse the two."

Knowing what I know now, about the key part I played in her husband's wrongful conviction, the fact that she's so warm and welcoming, shocks me even more than before. She would have every right to hate me, the same way Grayson did for a while, but she doesn't. She treats me the same way she always has, with love and respect. I'm lucky to have her, and her son, in my life.

I STAND IN FRONT of the casket in my black dress, but not a single tear is shed from my eyes. He's been gone for a week, and I'm yet to feel even the slightest bit of grief. The only reason he's getting a funeral in the first place is because my grandparents insisted on it. Regardless of not hearing from their son for nearly a decade, they were devastated to hear about his death. I, however, just want to get this part of my day over with.

The priest talks about what a loving friend, son, and father he was, and it takes everything I have not to laugh. Grayson stands beside me, smirking when he sees the expression on my face. He's my saving grace, my best friend, and my rock. No matter what I've been feeling lately, he's there to listen to it. I don't know what I would do without him.

The funeral ends, and my grandmother finally releases my hand. I hug her briefly before excusing myself. As we make our way toward Grayson's car, people stop to give me their condolences. I fake a smile and thank each one of them. However, when we finally get through the large group, a familiar face catches me off guard.

"I didn't think I'd see *you* here," I tell Knox.

He shares a look with Grayson that has me questioning its meaning, but I brush it off the moment he speaks. "I'm sorry for your loss, Savannah."

"Don't be. I'm not."

Both him and Grayson chuckle while Knox's gaze rakes over me. "You lose a fight with a train?"

"Something like that," I tell him, looking at my phone for the time. "Babe, we really have to get going."

He looks at me curiously. "Are you in a rush to celebrate?"

I smirk. "Yes, but not what you think."

We say our goodbyes to Knox and head to the restaurant. The whole ride there, Grayson keeps glancing at me, but I've had enough practice in keeping my face completely emotionless. What he's getting today is long overdue, and the fact that it's the same day as my father's funeral makes it that much sweeter.

As we walk in, I recognize the man as soon as I see him. His perfectly tailored black suit doesn't have a single wrinkle on it, and his son is the spitting image of him. I grab Grayson's hand and lead him over to the table.

"Mr. Trayland."

He smiles and stands up to embrace me. "Savannah. It's great to see you again."

After he and Grayson introduce themselves, the three of us sit down. There isn't anything that could hide the confusion on Gray's face, and if I wasn't so eager for this, I'd let him stay that way for a bit.

"Grayson, I'd just like to apologize on behalf of the criminal justice system for the grave injustice your father suffered." He slides a small envelope across the table. "I know it doesn't bring back your dad, but I hope it helps give you some closure."

Gray rips open the envelope and pulls out the letter from inside. His mouth moves as he silently reads the words on the page. Finally, when he gets to the most important part, tears spring to his eyes.

"H-he was exonerated?"

Mr. Trayland nods. "As of yesterday morning."

Wiping his eyes with the back of his hand, he shakes his head. "I don't understand. How?"

"When Savannah confronted her father, she recorded it and captured a full confession. With that, we were able to reopen the investigation and prove your father's innocence."

Grayson turns to me with so much emotion that I can't resist breaking down with him. "You are the best thing in my life," he says honestly. "I love you. Thank you."

As Mr. Trayland excuses himself, Gray and I stay in the middle of a crowded restaurant, wrapped in each other's arms. He presses kisses to the top of my head and declares his love for me a million times over. I may not have all the answers, but there's one thing I know.

Apart, we're two broken souls just trying to make it through, but together, we're flawlessly whole.

EPILOGUE

SAVANNAH

Out of all the parties Jace throws throughout the year, I think New Year's is my favorite. It's the one time of year he doesn't make it exclusive to students and alumni of Haven Grace Prep, which makes it the biggest event in town. No one asks questions or judges anyone else, and everyone has a good time.

"I'm still trying to figure out how you broke your wrist." Carter eyes me curiously.

I roll my eyes. "I told you! I punched a guy in the face!"

"Sure, you did, princess. Sure, you did."

Everyone laughs, but he drops the topic. Good, it's not like I ever intend on telling them what really happened. I don't want their pity. I'm doing just fine on my own.

Since all the bruises have healed and I'm finding it easier to get around now, I told Grayson I could go stay with Delaney. Her parents offered to let me move in. However, the second it came out of my mouth, the look on his face threw the idea right out the window. The plan is for me to stay with him until graduation, when I'll *hopefully* be moving to attend Juilliard in the fall. I don't want to leave any of my friends, Grayson especially, but dancing has always been my dream. And besides, I have a feeling Gray is going to follow me anywhere.

"Savannah?"

I turn around to see most of the cheer team standing behind me, Becca and Paige included. My eyes widen when I see Becca with crutches and a boot.

"Oh my God. What happened?"

"We're *so* sorry. You have to come back to cheer," she pleads. "We need you to be captain again. Kinsley is the worst and has us trying stunts that are going to kill us."

I sigh. After seeing the way that she was making them practice, I knew something like this was bound to happen. She doesn't understand that you need a certain skillset to perform stunts of that difficulty. You can't just throw a girl in the air and expect her to know how to do it. Still, after everything I've been through lately, I simply don't want to go back—but, I may have a solution.

"I can't. You already have a captain."

Paige looks defeated. "Sav, please. Kinsley can't keep doing this."

I shake my head. "Not Kinsley." Reaching behind me, I grab Emma's hand and pull her closer. "This, is your captain. She has more skill and knowledge when it comes to cheer than you can begin to imagine. You'd all be crazy to not take advantage of that."

Leaving them to talk, I walk away and over to where Delaney is leaning against the counter. Carter is obviously trying to impress her, no matter how many times we tell him he doesn't stand a chance, but she isn't fazed. I slot myself against her side.

"You know, you could give him a chance."

She laughs. "I'm hardly his type. It's the thrill of the chase. He'll get over it."

"Eh, he might surprise you." I rest my head on her shoulder. "But if he tries playing his normal games on you, I'll kick his ass."

It's clear she's considering it, but then her attention switches to something else. "Who's that talking to Grayson?"

I look across the room to find my boyfriend standing with none other than Knox Vaughn. The two of them together can never mean anything good, but damn is that a pretty sight. There's no denying Knox is hot, and his tattoos only increase his sex appeal. However, at least in my book, Grayson beats him by a mile.

"Knox? Don't pay any attention to him. He's nothing but trouble." I grab her hand. "Come on. Let's go dance."

GRAYSON

I watch Savannah as she and Delaney move to the beat. Even with a cast on her wrist, she's nothing but grace and beauty. The day I found out she had my father exonerated, I knew I'd never love anyone in the world more than her. I will spend the rest of my life making sure she knows just as incredible she is.

"She has no idea what you did for her, does she?" Knox asks. "How her father *really* died?"

Savi smiles at something Laney said and throws her head back, laughing. Happiness looks so damn good on her. I think of the letter I plan on giving her tomorrow morning, the one sitting in my desk—a notification of her acceptance and full scholarship to The Juilliard School. It arrived at the dance studio yesterday, and I picked it up from Brady. Her life is finally on the right track, and I'll do *anything* to protect that. To protect her.

"No, and she never will."

THE SAINT

HAVEN GRACE PREP, #2

DELANEY

Cruel.
Heartless.
A mistake waiting to happen.

Knox Vaughn is the epitome of a bad boy.
He's trouble in a sexy-as-sin package.
I know it.
They know it.
Even he knows it.

But, it's like a moth to the flame.
I can't stay away—even though I'm going to get burned.
You know what they say,
The sinners are much more fun.
And this saint is changing the game.

KNOX

Sweet.

Innocent.

Valedictorian.

Delaney Callahan is perfect,

Too perfect for me.

Hell, she's too perfect for anyone.

She's an angel,

But with me, she's playing with the devil.

I'm the last thing a woman like her needs.

And yet, I can't keep my hands—and mouth off of her.

We're from two different worlds,

Worlds that can't possibly work.

I'd do anything for her,

But I can't be the *SAINT* she deserves.

The Saint
Available Now

ACKNOWLEDGMENTS

There are so many people to thank for helping with this book. I'll probably end up forgetting some, but know I appreciate every single one of you so much!

A huge thank you to Christine Estevez at Wildfire Marketing Solutions. Your expertise is invaluable. Thank you for always being on top of things and keeping me on track, as well as helping me when my mind goes blank. I don't know what I would do without you.

To my editor, Kiezha Ferrell, thank you for making this book as perfect as possible and for all your insight in the process. You're a vital part in helping me improve my craft and I can't thank you enough for that.

Ashley Molina, the best friend I could ask for, thank you for always being there to listen and tell me whether something is a good idea or way over the top. I swear, you could add *Professional Sounding Board* to your resume. This book is so much better because of you. I love you.

To my beta readers, thank you for reading and giving me your honest opinions as I wrote this book baby. You're all so important to me and I appreciate each one of you.

And finally, to the readers. Without you, I wouldn't be

able to do what I love. So with my whole heart, THANK YOU. You're all fantastic and deserve all the happiness in the world.

If you've enjoyed this book, please consider reading a review.

xoxo,
Kels

P.S - Sign up for my newsletter and be the first to receive exclusive content, giveaways, and specials!

ABOUT THE AUTHOR

Kelsey Clayton is a 29-year-old mother from a small town in lower Delaware. Born and raised in New Jersey, she discovered her love for writing when she used it as a coping mechanism to get through hard times. Since then, she has been passionately writing novels that make people fall in love with the characters and the storylines. She writes from a mix of personal experience and imagination. As an avid beach lover, her dream is to write an entire book with her feet in the sand.

Books By KELSEY CLAYTON

The Sleepless November Saga:

Sleepless November

Endless December

Seamless Forever

Awakened in September

Standalones:

Returning to Rockport

Haven Grace Prep:

The Sinner

The Saint

The Rebel (June 2020)

The Enemy (July 2020)

Printed in Great Britain
by Amazon